/20

# NO BAD DEED

## A Novel

## Heather Chavez

wm

**WILLIAM MORROW**
*An Imprint of* HarperCollins*Publishers*

NO BAD DEED. Copyright © 2020 by Heather Chavez. All rights reserved. Printed in the United States of America. No part of this book may be used or reproduced in any manner whatsoever without written permission except in the case of brief quotations embodied in critical articles and reviews. For information, address HarperCollins Publishers, 195 Broadway, New York, NY 10007.

HarperCollins books may be purchased for educational, business, or sales promotional use. For information, please email the Special Markets Department at SPsales@harpercollins.com.

FIRST EDITION

Library of Congress Cataloging-in-Publication Data has been applied for.

ISBN 978-0-06-293617-2

20  21  22  23  24   LSC   10 9 8 7 6 5 4 3 2

For Alex

# NO BAD DEED

# 1

_____

If my kids had been with me, it wouldn't have happened. I would have stayed in the minivan, doors locked, windows rolled up. Just like the 911 operator instructed.

But my husband, Sam, had the flu. He had picked up Audrey hours before, and Leo was studying at a friend's house, so I was alone in the van.

Driving in full dark, I felt like I was alone in the world. Clouds thick with unshed rain drifted across a half-moon, drizzle seeping from them even as they threatened to split open completely. During commute, the two-lane road carried a steady stream of parents on their way to the elementary school up the road and nine-to-fivers headed to west Santa Rosa. Several hours post-commute, though, it was nearly deserted, owing equally to the time and the weather. I finally surrendered and switched on my wipers.

Only a couple of miles from home, my phone buzzed in my purse. A name popped onto the minivan's in-dash display: _Sam._ With the Bluetooth, it would've been easy enough to connect the call. Instead, I ignored it. After ending a twelve-hour shift fishing several dollars in coins out of a Labrador's stomach, I was too exhausted for another argument. Lately, all of our conversations seemed to start with the same four words: _I love you, but . . ._

Sam gave me only three rings to answer before ending the call.

In the sudden silence, my stomach grumbled. It was the third time that week I had missed dinner, and it was only Wednesday. Probably the reason Sam had called.

*I love you, but your patients see you more than me and our kids.*

That was a popular one.

I popped open the energy drink that had been sitting in the cup holder for days and took a sip. I grimaced. How did Leo drink this stuff? I was pretty sure a can of cat urine would've tasted better. I drained half of it anyway. Caffeine was caffeine.

On the north side of the road, from among the oaks and evergreens, the old hospital slipped into view. Paulin Creek bordered the campus on the south, open space and a flood control reservoir beyond that. Vacant for years, no one had reason to stop at the hospital. Still, I thought I saw movement between the buildings. A chill pricked the back of my neck. I wrote it off as the surge of caffeine.

Distracted, I almost missed the shape that streaked across the road.

I jumped in my seat. A deer? No, it ran on two legs. A person.

When I reached to return the energy drink to the cup holder, my hand shook, so the can caught the lip of the console. It bounced onto the passenger seat, liquid pooling around my purse.

The string of expletives I let loose would've gotten my teen son grounded.

I pulled onto the shoulder, threw the car into park, and peeled off my cardigan to sop up the puddle. As I used a wet wipe from the glove box to blot my sticky hands, I squinted at a spot near the hospital's entrance.

I strained to see what lay at the edge of my low beams. A sliver of moon softened the night, the headlights of my minivan slicing through the branches to the trail beyond.

*It's probably a jogger.*

*In the rain.*

*In the dark without reflective gear.*

The primitive part of my brain scoffed.

Raindrops pinged off my windshield. I switched on my brights and could see better now. I identified a second shape next to the first. Just off the road, they were about the size of the topper on a wedding cake.

I put the van in gear and pulled off the shoulder, driving slowly, trying to understand what I was seeing. With Halloween the next night, at first I thought it might be a couple of teenagers. What better place to stage a prank than a hospital that sat abandoned on a semiwooded hillside? But as I drew close, my focus sharpened. A man and a woman stood in the spotlight of my high beams. They were arguing. No, *fighting*. Sam and I argued, but this was not that. This was balled fists, shoving, rage, and because of that, the dark-haired woman in the yoga pants didn't stand a chance.

The woman curled in on herself, dropping her chin and tucking behind her crossed arms. Making herself smaller, even as the man, bald and more than a foot taller, did the opposite.

I stopped the car, but left the engine running. My fingers were clumsy on the keypad as I dialed 911. The woman glanced in my direction. But the man in the jeans and white T-shirt never turned my way. Less than twenty feet away, and he didn't so much as twitch.

"What's your emergency?" the dispatcher asked.

I startled at the voice, unable to answer. I trembled, double-checking that the doors were locked. I gave my location and then described the couple.

"They're fighting," I said.

"Is he armed?"

"I don't think so."

"What's he doing now?"

Before I could answer, the man picked up the woman and tossed her down the embankment toward the creek below. He showed no more strain than a Siamese tossing a lizard, and for a moment the woman was pinned to the sky by my headlights.

Then she fell, disappearing beyond the tangled brush at the trail's edge.

A sudden weight pressed against my chest. The dispatcher's voice, so loud a moment before, grew distant, warped. My lungs seized, and my vision darkened at the corners. An urge to hide overwhelmed me. I wanted to crawl into the gathering void and disappear. It felt like a memory, though it couldn't have been. I had no memory like this.

Suddenly, I felt as vulnerable in my locked car as the woman on that trail.

Was I having a stroke? Panic attack? My mouth was dry, my tongue a useless lump. I wasn't certain the dispatcher understood me.

*What the hell is happening?*

The man pulled something from his pocket. A cell phone? Something else? Then he was gone, maybe over the trail's edge.

Seeing him disappear was enough to snap me free of whatever had rendered me speechless.

"He has something," I said.

"What's he doing?" The dispatcher's voice remained neutral, but I was freaking the hell out.

"I don't know. They're not there."

"They've left the scene?"

"No. I just can't see them."

My hand dropped to the door handle, though I had no intention of leaving the van.

As if sensing the gesture, the dispatcher instructed, "Stay in the vehicle."

I formed a fist around the handle. Before the dispatcher could ask any additional questions, I slipped my phone in my pocket and opened the door.

I'M NOT ENTIRELY SURE why I got out of the van. It might have been because of that other girl. When I was finishing up my undergrad degree, there was this brunette in my microbiology class. I'm ashamed to admit I didn't remember her name. I remembered *his* name, though— Dirk. I remembered because it was one letter away from being entirely fitting. A certain kind of guy loved Dirk and, if I'm being honest, a certain kind of girl too. The kind who thought jealous rages and the bruises they left behind were romantic.

At an off-campus party celebrating the second-place finish of some sporting team, Dirk had openly berated for over an hour the girl whose name I didn't remember. He wasn't her boyfriend but wanted to be, and until that night, maybe she had wanted the same thing. Then he had started grabbing her. And pushing her. When finally, he had slapped her, only one guy grabbed Dirk's arm. But even that guy hadn't held on to Dirk's arm when he had followed the girl from the room.

Minutes later, she went over the balcony railing. She broke an arm and a couple of ribs and would have broken her skull if not for the hedge she bounced off before hitting the concrete. No one actually saw Dirk push her.

Maybe it was that girl who made me get out of the van now, or maybe it was just that anger always made me do stupid things.

My heart tumbled in my chest. About fifteen feet away, halfway between the trail's border and the rushing water, the man stood over the woman, his hand clenched on a switchblade. A knife. He had a knife.

Other than placing that 911 call, I could think of no way to be useful. It had been nearly twenty years since my last fistfight, and even back then, I hadn't been stupid enough to take on guys twice my size.

As the man's anger unspooled, his victim chose the defense often used by prey: she went limp, still. Her nose seeped blood.

I swallowed and shouted for him to stop, even as that stupid-making anger rose in me.

If the man was threatened by my sudden appearance, or even aware of it, he didn't show it. He reached for the woman, his hands tightening on her sweatshirt. He yanked her toward him, so close her chest butted against his, the knife dangerously near her cheek.

Still much closer to my van than the attacker, I risked a few steps forward. "The police are coming." I tried for threatening, but the tremor undermined me.

The man stared up at me, through me, rain tracing a slick line from scalp to stubbled chin. His muscles spasmed with rage, and there was a fuzzy disconnect in his eyes. At that moment, the man in front of me was hardly human. He was an animal, his body tensed, his breath ragged.

"You should go," he said.

"I don't think I should," I said, even as I flashed to thoughts of Audrey and Leo. While I didn't move closer, I couldn't leave her to him. My hand fell to my pants pocket and the outline my phone made there.

The man returned his attention to his victim, but his voice carried to where I stood. "Who do you love?" he asked. Though he looked at the woman, the way he raised his voice made me believe the question was for me. It startled me—not just his words, incongruous in the setting, but the voice itself, which lacked any of the emotion that corrupted his face.

The man dropped his victim to the ground, holding her there with one of his muddy boots. Then he twisted his head to stare up at me. "Your life is already fucked up. You just don't know it yet." He punctuated the commentary with a kick to the woman's torso. Then he dropped into a squat and repositioned his blade so it faced downward, toward his prone victim.

I tried to remember what I knew about how to handle aggressive animals. If nothing else worked, if a dog attacked, you were supposed to hit and kick it in the throat, nose, or back of the head. Look for a weapon. Break bones. I knew if it came to that, I would be the one broken and likely stabbed. I picked up a rock, felt its weight. I threw it, but in my effort to spare the woman further injury, the stone landed several feet from my target, swallowed by a flurry of soggy leaves.

I slid a few feet farther down the trail—still at a safe distance—and picked up another rock.

"Don't do it," I said.

He laughed at this, his full attention on the woman.

I threw the second rock, and it caught him on the cheek. With the back of his hand, he rubbed his skin there, once, but remained focused on his prey. His shoulder cocked. The woman struggled with renewed fervor, apparently recognizing, belatedly, that whatever emotional connection had once existed between them wouldn't save her. His anger wasn't going to blow over. He planned to use that knife.

Until that moment, each of my actions had been chosen: I had decided to pull over, to call 911, to get out of the van. To throw the rocks. But when the man raised the knife, the inexplicable terror that had seized me in the van returned, my lungs expanding in hot, rapid bursts. At the cusp of the darkness, I saw something that wasn't there—another woman, another time, imaginary but as real as the rain and the mud and the blood rushing in my ears.

I didn't intend to interfere more directly—not with the faces of my children so rooted in my thoughts—but I stumbled and found myself sliding down the embankment before my conscious mind recognized the immediacy of the threat. I was as surprised as the man when I stumbled into him, my trajectory a combination of clumsiness and luck, the blade intended for the brunette's torso instead grazing my arm. Barely a scratch, but I yelped, a sound I had heard many times from animals but that was unfamiliar in my own throat. He lost hold of the knife, and it tumbled into the water.

I fell backward onto the marshy creek bed. Perception became as slippery as the rain upon the rocks, my heart a thunderclap in my chest, the woman beside me still, the man's face warped with sick purpose.

Then, suddenly, he stopped. He dropped to a crouch beside me, grabbed my face between his hands. His eyebrows knotted together as he studied me. I had no doubt he could snap my neck with a single twitch. "Why the hell are you doing this?" he demanded. "Who are you?"

He was so close, his voice so thunderous, that my ears vibrated. It was then that I noticed a stain on his T-shirt that might have been blood.

I meant to tell him that I hadn't intended to interfere, that it was all a stupid accident, but the words wouldn't come. He reached out and grabbed a large handful of my hair, red and long and easily twisted around his fingers. He yanked it, pulling my face even closer.

Then—finally, thankfully—I heard sirens.

For only a second longer, he studied my face, and I his. Broad nose, a bump along its bridge. Left ear shriveled and folded in on itself. A white worm of scar tissue that prevented stubble from growing along one patch of jaw. A man who liked to fight, and not just with women half his size.

He seemed unconcerned that I would be able to identify him. Testify against him.

"Let her die, and I'll let you live," he said.

He nudged the woman with his toe. "Probably not much of a choice anyway. She's close enough to dead."

Then almost before I understood him, he loped away, up the hill and toward the road where I had so helpfully left my minivan and its key.

He would get to my car first. My registration. My purse. In moments, he would know my name, my address. And the names of my husband and children.

# 2

My trailside examination of the victim was brief, the moon providing the slightest of light. I had to get close to detect her breathing, barely a whisper on my cheek, and her pulse was weak. No moaning. No complaints of pain. Even when the paramedics moved her, she remained silent.

Half an hour after the ambulance took her away, I still waited for the police to release me. The rain had lightened to a mist that nevertheless glued my hair to my face and left my T-shirt sodden. I probably shouldn't have used my cardigan as a towel.

"You sure you don't want a jacket?" the officer asked again. I had to check his name tag to remember his name: Willis. That drew my attention to the body camera that had been recording for the past thirty minutes. That camera made me second-guess my answers and wonder if the pitch of my voice or slope of my shoulders might later be interpreted as guilt.

"I'm not cold," I said. And I wasn't. Soaked, sure, but not cold. My nerves numbed, my damp clothes felt as warm as bathwater. That probably wasn't normal.

A man approached from the street, stopping to talk to the female officer who'd interviewed me first. The new arrival wore gray dress pants that still held a crease despite the hour, a button-up shirt so white it reflected moonlight, and a tie with stripes of deep pink.

I turned my attention back to Officer Willis, clasping my hands to stop them from shaking. "How's my family?"

I ran through all the personal items stashed in my van and in my purse. Leo's football photos. A note from Audrey's first-grade teacher. Audrey's medication. And, again, the registration that bore my name and our address.

That man now had all of those things.

"Have you spoken with my husband?"

Officer Willis nodded, then gestured to my arm. "We should get you looked at."

My hand flew to the scratch from the man's knife. "I'm fine," I insisted. "What did you tell Sam?"

"We told him your van was stolen, but that you're okay."

"And they're fine? Sam? The kids? You still have a car there?"

"We still have a car there, and your family's okay."

I pushed. "You've checked recently?" Our home was a mile away. Less than two minutes at the posted speed limit.

"He's not going anywhere near your house." I turned to the man who had spoken: the detective with the carefully pressed pants and bleached shirt. Now that he was closer, I saw that what I'd taken for stripes on his tie were actually strips of bacon.

"Cassie Larkin? Detective Ray Rico." He stood only an inch taller than me, his brown face broad, his smile wide. His black hair was cut short, his dark eyes sharp above thick creases. I expected him to extend his hand with the greeting, but he didn't.

"These questions must seem repetitive," he said. Not quite an apology, but close. "I'm sure you're eager to get home. Willis, please bring Dr. Larkin a jacket."

There was no choice in it for either of us, so when the officer returned with a sweatshirt, I accepted it.

"At least the rain's let up, right?" Detective Rico said.

My jeans were soaked through, and I could feel my feet pruning in my sneakers. "Good thing."

He turned on a recorder and flipped open his notepad. He held a sheet of paper, too, though I couldn't see what was on it. "Walk me through what happened."

When I finished my story, Rico acknowledged its end with a curt nod. "That was really—*brave* of you, to get out of your car." I thought he may have been about to say stupid. I wouldn't have disagreed.

"Anyone would've done the same."

"I don't know about that." Rico consulted his notebook. "You didn't know him, though, right?"

"No."

"Not a patient, or the parent of one of your kids' friends?" When I shook my head, he asked, "You're sure?"

I remembered the man's face, twisted in anger, the casual way he had tossed the woman down the hill. "I've never seen him before."

"Would you be able to identify him?"

When I nodded, Rico held out the paper he was holding, facedown at first. "I'm going to show you some photographs."

He flipped the sheet over. On it were the photos of six men, all white, all bald or balding, all in their late forties to late fifties.

"The suspect might not be in this group," Rico said, his tone neutral. "So you're under no obligation to identify anyone."

I brushed a damp lock of hair away from my eyes, and my heart seized. It couldn't have been clearer if the photo had been ringed with fire. There, in the middle row, was the man with the ropy scar along his jaw and the once-broken nose.

"That's him." The finger I pointed shook nearly as much as my voice.

"You sure?"

"Completely."

Rico held out a pen and asked me to sign the photo I had identified. He left for a moment, and when he returned, he asked: "Recognize the name Natalie Robinson?"

I shook my head. "Is that the victim's name?"

The detective's eyes were twin chips of granite. "How about Anne Jackson?"

"No. Who's Anne Jackson?"

Rico didn't answer. He nodded and jotted something in his note-book, then gestured toward my arm. "Tell me again how you got cut."

At the mention of the wound, I became aware of its throbbing. "He tried to stab her, but he got me instead. It's just a scratch."

"Carver Sweet's a big guy."

My heart pummeled my ribs. "You know who he is?"

"Now that you've identified him, we do." His expression remained stony. "So, Carver's a big guy, and he had a knife. You have kids, and you'd already called 911. Why risk a confrontation?"

I remembered how my sneakers lost purchase on the hillside, the brush grabbing at my knees, rocks and sticks threatening to twist my ankles. How breakable I had felt when I had slammed against him. "I slipped."

"You slipped?"

"I'm clumsy, and the ground was wet."

Rico stared at me, letting the pause stretch. It reminded me of the times I had talked to clients who brought animals in with unexplained injuries or signs of malnourishment. It was the way you talked to someone you thought might be lying.

Rico consulted his notebook again, the creases under his eyes deep-ening. "You said Carver Sweet may have had blood on his shirt. At what point did you notice that?"

"Near the end."

"So when did you notice the victim was bleeding?"

The detective's question made me second-guess all I had done to save the woman. Had I waited thirty seconds too long to call 911? After her attacker fled, had I stanched her bleeding quickly enough? With the police, had I forgotten a detail that would lead to Carver Sweet's arrest? I forced these concerns aside, but when I saw Rico's face, a new one dawned: Would my delay in answering be misconstrued as calcu-lation?

"I noticed her bleeding after he threw her down the slope. Her nose." Had there been other injuries? I strained to remember.

"So when you first pulled over, she wasn't bleeding?"

"I don't think she was."

"You don't *think* she was?"

"She wasn't." Was she? My certainty ebbed the longer the questioning continued, and I wondered if Rico intended to throw me off balance.

"He hadn't taken out the knife yet? When they were standing on the trail?"

"No." But even as I answered, I was suddenly sure there was an injury I had missed, something that might cast doubt on the rest of my story. Rico's scribbling took several seconds, the scratch of pen on paper unnerving me.

"Will she be all right?" I asked.

The detective looked up, his brow wrinkled and eyes hooded. "The woman he attacked?"

"Of course." *Who else would I be asking about?*

"I don't know." He flipped to a new page in his notebook. "Did you notice any vehicles alongside the road?" When I shook my head, he explained, "We found two vehicles just off the road half a mile up. Crashed. If you'd driven a little farther, you would've seen them."

"If he forced her off the road, it wasn't random."

"What makes you say that?"

The attacker's question was fresh in my mind: *Who do you love?* And then, among his last words: *Let her die, and I'll let you live.*

"It seemed personal."

Rico considered this. "I arrested a guy for beating another motorist with a bat," he said. "Then he started in on the man's kid. All over a fender bender with less than a thousand dollars in damages. See, the guy with the bat lost his job the day before, and then some Lexus cuts him off at a stoplight. The boss who fired him had a Lexus."

"What are you saying?"

"Every crime is personal, even the random ones." Rico's mouth settled into a grim line. "You say you didn't know the man, but did you know his victim?"

"I've never seen either of them before." It was only after I answered that the first two words registered: *You say.* As if he doubted what I said was true.

"So you say you were coming from work?"

There it was again. "Yes."

"And you left at what time?"

"Just after ten."

"Anyone able to verify that?"

"I was alone for the last hour, but before that, certainly."

"Any surveillance cameras at your clinic?"

"No."

The rain that had soaked my clothes had wicked into the borrowed sweatshirt, the chill finally seeping into my skin. I shivered.

"The number three mean anything to you?" he asked.

I studied his face, but he hid his thoughts well. "No. Why?"

"Just something one of the officers found. Probably nothing."

Rico jotted something in his notebook, and he attempted a smile.

"Looks like someone may have spotted your vehicle in a grocery store parking lot, so we'll know more soon," he said. Then the smile disappeared and his eyes grew heavy. "Earlier, I said that Carver Sweet's not getting anywhere near your house, and I meant that. But you need to be careful. You're a threat to him."

The detective handed me his card, then called Officer Willis over to drive me home. When Rico walked away, he wiped his palms on his slacks, as if trying to rid them of something unpleasant.

# 3

---

We lived in a three-bedroom ranch-style house in Lomita Heights, a neighborhood that dated back to the early 1960s. Our family had moved in sixteen years before when I was pregnant with Leo. Back then, I would walk, stomach near bursting, along the gently sloping hill. Once, I had fallen on my backside on the sidewalk.

*Okay, maybe more than once.*

My legs didn't feel much steadier now, and as I walked toward the house, I realized I didn't have my keys.

After escorting me home, Officer Willis watched as I walked toward the door. Leo's face was already wedged between the slats of the blinds, hair disheveled, eyes bleary, mouth frozen in a scowl. Despite the fact that, at fifteen, he now had half a foot on me, he was still that bundle I had carried up and down that hill. Like then, the weight of being his mom threw me off balance.

He opened the front door. "What the heck, Mom?" A rumpled blanket on the couch suggested he had waited up for me. I knew he lingered more out of curiosity than concern, but I hugged him fiercely nonetheless. "The police came and talked to Dad, and now a cop brought you home? Where's the van?"

"Stolen."

"Really? Do they know who took it?"

"They do. I'll get it back soon." I trotted out my fail-safe distraction, "You hungry?"

Leo had eaten only an hour before, so of course he wanted a sandwich. I made two: turkey for him, veggie for me. Nerves roiled my stomach, but I forced down half the sandwich before grabbing a handful of batteries from the junk drawer and slipping them in my pocket. After Leo ate and returned to bed, and after I tested the lock on his window, I checked on a sleeping Audrey. Her bangs were plastered to her forehead. As usual, my first grader had insisted on falling asleep under a pile of blankets. I removed all but one and kissed her on her sweaty cheek, then felt her forehead. Damp, but not feverish. She hadn't yet caught her father's flu.

From Audrey's closet, I pulled out her old baby monitor, coated with several years' worth of dust, and switched out the batteries with the ones in my pocket. It still worked. I took the receiver with me.

Finally, in the hallway outside the master, I took a breath, bracing for an argument, and pushed open the door. Sam was waiting in his pajama bottoms on the end of the bed. My husband had the wiry build of an academic, and his nose was ruddy against pale skin. He was also beautiful. You weren't supposed to say that about a man, but he was: dimpled smirk, messed hair that invited fingers, thick lashes that, thankfully, our children had inherited. My own eyes were fringed with stubby lashes visible only through the magic of volumizing mascara.

"I would've come out, but it seemed like you needed some time with Leo," he said. I read judgment in his comment. He seemed to sense this, because he paused, then softened his voice when he continued. "Tell me what happened."

I placed the receiver on the dresser next to a bottle of cold medicine and told him everything—almost. I described coming upon the couple and about the casual way the man had tossed the woman over the embankment. I told him about my interview with the detective and how I sensed Rico was withholding some key piece of information. But I didn't tell Sam about my panic attack in the van, and omitted from my story the details that made me seem most reckless. I didn't want to hear those four words again: *I love you, but . . .*

*I love you, but you should've been more careful.*

As I talked, I removed my clothes, which were streaked with mud, and slipped on a sleeping shirt, one of Sam's. He watched me, and the nerves buzzed beneath my skin. I blamed it on the stress hormones.

When I stopped speaking, Sam sighed, his chest rattling with the effort. "Cassie." Part accusation, part concern.

He climbed off the bed, disappeared into the bathroom, and returned with the first aid kit. He switched on the light before sitting beside me on the bed.

"Give it here," he said, gesturing toward my arm. It was barely a scratch, but I extended my arm anyway. When he squinted to get a better look, I handed him his glasses from the nightstand.

"I'm a little irked with you right now," he said, the virus making his voice husky. He placed a pillow on my lap and gently rested my arm on it, then set to cleaning the wound with an antiseptic wipe.

"Irked, are you?"

He pulled a foil packet of antibiotic ointment from the kit. "Yes, irked. Why did you risk your life like that?" He gently dabbed the ointment on my arm. "The kids—"

I recoiled as if pushed. "I was thinking of the kids," I said. Every choice I made, every day, was viewed through the lens of motherhood. "What kind of mother would I be if I let someone else's daughter be victimized? Besides, you would have done the same."

When Sam looked up from his task, his blue eyes intense inside the black frames of his glasses, my breath caught in my throat. "It's not just the kids."

"I know."

He covered my cut with an adhesive bandage, then placed the first aid kit and his glasses on the nightstand. "The next time you see a man with a knife, don't get out of the car."

"You sound like the dispatcher."

"Promise me." His voice vibrated with more urgency than I had come to expect after seventeen years of marriage.

"I can't imagine it'll happen again." When he scowled, I hastily added, "But I promise."

Sam's lips parted as if he were about to speak, but instead, he stretched past me to switch off the light.

We climbed into bed. In the dark, his breathing rasped, and I mimicked his rhythms to steady my own. Reaching for him, my fingers grazed his back just as he turned away from me, toward the wall. The cold medicine dragged him into sleep within minutes.

*There will be other nights*, I thought, with the certainty of a long-married wife.

As I lay there, listening to the monitor with the blackness pressing in, the quiet that usually settled me instead seemed a presence, waiting, watching. Later, I would wonder if it was my intuition warning me of what was to come—of what, in fact, already had begun.

# 4

——

Having dreamed of large insects, even larger men, and bassinets filled with mud, I awoke groggy and with a headache. When I reached across the bed, the sheets on Sam's side were cold.

I fumbled for my phone on the nightstand and groaned when I saw the time. After a fitful night, it seemed I had nodded off just in time to oversleep. Setting an alarm hadn't been a priority the night before.

When I swung my feet onto the carpet, I caught the glint of copper on the edge of the bed frame. I reached down and picked up the object that had drawn my attention, not metal at all, but paper. I placed it in the center of my palm, studying it. It was an origami dog no bigger than a business card, which I guessed had fallen from the nightstand.

The paper dog, with its folded ears and tiny legs, made me smile. It reminded me of the early days of my relationship with Sam, when he would leave gifts like this in unexpected places. A mosaic tile on the back porch. A sketch on my dashboard. Once, he had created a remarkably detailed landscape from coffee grounds spilled on the counter.

It had been a while since Sam had created art for me, even something as simple as a dog of folded paper. Too busy, he said. We were both too busy—for art, for sex, for anything beyond the needs of our kids, his students, my patients.

My smile faded. I put the origami dog on my nightstand. Then I got up, put a fresh bandage on my scratch, and followed the sound of chaos to the kitchen. I stopped in the doorway, watching, but had only a second before I was spotted. Leo, wearing earbuds and a scowl, stood quickly. "Dad said we needed to let you sleep."

Before he could say more, his backpack caught the edge of the bowl Sam had been using to scramble eggs. The plastic bowl clattered to the floor, its contents splattering the cabinets. Our Chihuahua mix, Boo, skittered over to investigate the puddle of slime, sneezing when he inhaled egg, and Sam nudged the dog aside with his foot.

I grabbed a roll of paper towels off the counter and started sopping up the mess, while Sam retrieved a fresh bowl and eggs. I turned my attention to Audrey, seated on a stool at the counter. "Did you take your medicine, Peanut?"

Before she could answer, Leo took out one of his earbuds. "I need to go to school."

"Agreed. School's important."

Leo rolled his eyes. "I mean, like, now."

Audrey gasped, her eyes widening. "But you're not dressed."

"I'm dressed."

"Nooooooo." Audrey sighed as if her brother were the six-year-old. "You're normal dressed, not Halloween dressed."

She hopped down from the stool and twirled, showing off her black cat costume. Judging by the wrinkles, Audrey had worn the costume all night beneath her pajamas.

"See. I'm a princess cat, only not yet because my tiara's still in my bedroom. What are you going to be?"

"Late for my workout. Can't someone drop me off and then come back?"

"Yes, because that's reasonable," I said. "We'll rearrange our schedules because you've changed your plans at the last minute. Besides, we only have one car for the time being, remember?"

"So that's a no?"

I pointed at an empty stool. "That's a 'sit.' I'll take you after you eat."

Leo slumped back on a stool while I slid three slices of sourdough in the toaster.

Sam's eyebrows furrowed as he studied me. "How're you doing? Get any sleep?"

"Some."

"About the car, take mine. I'll grab a rental and a new booster seat for Audrey, after I call the locksmith."

"You're not going in?"

"Think I'll take another day." Sam hadn't missed work once the previous school year, but before I could think too hard on that, he said, "Audrey's medication is running low. I was going to stop by the pharmacy, unless you've already refilled it?"

I started to say that I had picked up the prescription the morning before, but then I remembered: my purse. Audrey's medication was one more thing I needed to replace.

"I can get it." After I canceled my credit card and stopped by the DMV. My headache intensified.

Sam slid scrambled eggs on three plates, and I added toast to each. He gestured—did I want eggs?—but I wrinkled my nose. I wasn't big on breakfast, and that morning, I felt even less like eating than usual.

As my family ate, I returned to the bedroom to get dressed. My hands trembled as I buttoned my shirt. Understandable, but still I sank to the edge of the bed. The night before, the man on the trail had been enraged. He hadn't so much asked for my identity as spit out the question as if it were sour on his tongue. Worse, he had followed it with a warning: *Let her die, and I'll let you live.* Had the woman survived? I didn't know, but I had made every effort to save her, which I guessed would void his offer of mercy. And this man—rabid and merciless— had my address. My keys.

The door swung open, and Sam walked in. He grabbed a small chunk of yellowed plastic from his dresser then sat beside me on the bed. "You're sure you're okay?"

"I'm fine," I lied. "You seemed distracted last night."

"You had just been attacked."

"You sure that's it?"

Someone who hadn't been married to Sam wouldn't have noticed the pause, brief as it was before the familiar smirk shifted into place. "Of course," he said. I wondered if he had read my lie a few seconds earlier as easily as I read his now.

Sam slipped into his mouth the piece of plastic he had been holding. "I wanted to give Audrey a preview of what I'll be wearing tonight."

"Wait. I thought Leo was taking her trick-or-treating?"

He fake-leered at me, exposing zombie teeth. When he went to kiss me, I pulled away.

"I thought the undead were sexy," he said. I suspected he was playing up the lisp, but I found my smile anyway.

"Vampires are sexy," I clarified. "Zombies are . . . zombies. So why isn't Leo taking Audrey trick-or-treating?"

"He made plans with Tyler."

"When did he make these plans? Did he tell Audrey? Please say you made him tell her himself."

"Yesss," Sam lisped. "He told Audrey. Now about this vampire favoritism . . . It's easy to be sexy with dress clothes and the ability to hypnotize the lasses—"

"Lasses?"

"—but think about the poor, dentally challenged zombie in his stained rags. How much harder he has to work to lure a woman to his bed."

I had to admit it: Sam, with his two-day stubble and his nose still red from the flu, was a damned sexy zombie.

"I never thought about that," I admitted. "I mean, I didn't even know zombies had beds."

"Zombies might not sleep, but they have needs," Sam said.

"Uh . . . gross."

"See. Exactly my point."

Before the demands of the clinic and Sam's job and the kids, it had often been like this. A small part of me resented that the old Sam had resurfaced on a morning I didn't have time for it.

"Another thing they have to overcome—the language barrier. You know—you want to tell a woman how bewitching she looks, but all that comes out is a grunt."

I found myself yielding to the insistency of his hands despite my distractions, and this time, I returned his kiss, flu be damned. "I'd say that's also true of some human males." I traced his mouth with my index finger. "But I see what you're saying. A vampire can tell a 'lass' he wants to drink her blood, and it sounds hot because of the accent."

"Exactly! Women love exotic men. Plus, some women find the smell of rotting flesh a turnoff."

"That does seem unfair. But I don't think you're making much of a case for the sexiness of zombies."

"Well—" Sam wrapped his arms around my waist and bent to kiss my neck. After seventeen years, he still got to me. "To overcome all these obstacles, a zombie has to be persuasive."

He kissed the other side of my neck. Plastic teeth scraped the skin.

"Attentive." His hands shifted to my lower back. "When a woman can so easily outrun you, you have to put so much more effort in the chase."

"Mmmm. I thought zombies were more the 'take by force' type?"

Sam pulled me closer, away from my distractions. I wished I hadn't promised Leo I would take him to school early.

Sam whispered in my ear, "Not the smart ones."

"I didn't know there were smart ones." It had been a while. A week? Ten days?

"See the prejudices they have to overcome."

"Mo-om." Leo added an extra syllable as he yelled through the door. "Can we go?"

I yelled back, "Pretty impatient for someone who canceled trick-or-treating plans on his six-year-old sister."

On the other side of the door, Leo grunted.

"I think Leo might be part zombie," I said.

Sam's phone trilled. His attention snapped from me to his screen, whatever had been happening between us suddenly as dead as any zombie.

"You have to go?" he asked, his tone pushing me toward the door.

I met his eyes—tried to read them—and crossed my arms. "I've got a few minutes."

The call rolled into voicemail, but the phone immediately started ringing again.

"I'm sorry," he said, "but I have to take this."

Sam opened the door for me, waiting for me to walk through it before he answered the call.

# 5

———

One of the oldest schools in the state, Santa Rosa High's brick exterior proclaimed its history. In an hour, the parking lots would be clogged, but I was able to drop Leo at the front steps.

After I left my son, I had my vet tech, Zoe, also my closest friend, reschedule my morning appointments so I could call the bank and stop by the pharmacy. Then there was the longest part of the morning: the DMV. A couple of times while waiting on those cheap plastic seats, I signed on to the local newspaper's website from my phone to check if there was anything about the attack, or the victim's condition. The incident likely happened too late to make that morning's print edition, but I thought there might be something online. Nothing. Probably still too early.

When I finally pulled into my clinic's parking lot toward the end of the lunch hour, my first thought was of Sam. I had met him here a month into my internship, when tragedy struck: Princess Jellybean had gotten sick. Sam, working as a substitute teacher in Mrs. Hawking's kindergarten class, had been frantic to get the guinea pig back on his pellets and greens before the kids noticed. (Yes, Princess Jellybean was a *male* guinea pig who had been named by a group of five-year-old girls.)

The vet I had been working with at the time had prescribed antibiotics and a special diet that required Sam to hand-feed Princess Jellybean. Even now, I smiled at the memory of him hunched over the rodent with a syringe.

A few weeks later, Sam and the guinea pig had returned. Princess Jellybean had seemed fine, a little chubby even, but Sam had claimed the rodent could benefit from some acupuncture. It took him another month, and several appointments, before he got up the nerve to ask me out.

I thought of Sam now because of the phone call. After seventeen years of marriage, we didn't have secrets. Or so I had believed, until he had rushed me out that morning to take that call.

When I entered the clinic, Zoe was stationed behind the front desk with Smooch, an orange tabby with one eye, nestled in the basket beside her. Smooch blinked in greeting before returning to her nap. *Cats.*

Zoe jumped up, and I braced myself. My lavender-haired friend was six feet of muscled curves and bleached-smile exuberance. She was also a hugger. That morning, though, her embrace was tentative, as if she were afraid anything stronger would break me.

"You okay?" she asked. No smile for me today.

"I'm okay."

"Promise?"

"Promise."

Zoe vibrated with curiosity but switched into business mode. "Daryl's on his way in with Lester."

Before I could ask why, the front door jerked open. Usually, Lester careened into a room, all crossed paws, blocky head, and thrashing tail. But that day, he stumbled in, dropping in a pile onto the floor. When I approached, the Labrador whimpered and peered at me from beneath the rim of his surgical collar, but, except for his eyebrows, he didn't move. I couldn't remember the last time I had seen slack in Lester's leash.

I knelt to scratch the Lab behind one floppy ear. "What's going on with our boy here?" I asked.

Though Daryl shared his dog's coloring and easy temperament, in motion they were normally opposites. With Lester splayed at his feet, though, Daryl seemed to absorb Lester's unspent energy. His shoulders jerked, unaccustomed to the lack of resistance on the tether.

"He's gotten worse since last night's surgery," Daryl said.

Concerned, I ushered Daryl and Lester into the exam room. We lifted the Labrador onto the stainless-steel table, and I checked the dressing on the wound. There were no signs of swelling or discharge.

"When was the last time he ate?" I asked.

"Breakfast. He was fine last night, then this morning, he started acting like he'd scarfed down a whole plate of pot brownies."

"There's no chance he did?" I asked. "Eat any pot brownies?" This was Lester. I had to ask.

"Nah," Daryl said. "At first, I thought it might be the drugs."

"The anesthesia?" Again, it was Lester. Better to verify.

"Yeah."

"So he was groggy, but he ate. Was his appetite normal?" When Daryl nodded, I asked, "He's been drinking water?"

It was cool in the exam room, but Lester began panting, drool dripping from his tongue onto the exam table. "Yeah, he's had water. What's wrong with him, Doc?"

Two sets of forlorn eyes pinned me. I wanted to tell Daryl it was normal post-surgery behavior, or, barring that, reassure him that the problem could be easily fixed. I could do neither.

"I'm not sure," I said. I pulled back Lester's lips, checking his gums and the inside of his cheek. Both were pale. Since he'd just had surgery, I worried his pale gums indicated a hemorrhage. He needed blood work immediately, and I silently ran through the tests I should order.

Then there was the ophthalmic exam to check for pupil reactivity, which could also be useful in determining a toxicosis diagnosis.

"You kept him in his crate last night?" I asked.

"You know how he is, Doc. It's hard to keep him out of trouble," he said. "But I've done my best. Crated him last night. Took him into the bathroom when I showered. The only time he was out of my sight was when some guy selling salvation knocked on my door, but even then, it was less than a minute. Thirty seconds."

"Not in the market for salvation, huh?" I placed my stethoscope to the dog's chest. One hundred and sixty beats per minute.

"Always. Something's wrong, isn't it?"

I got that familiar shiver in my gut, equal parts intuition and experience.

"His heart's beating faster than normal, and his respiration's labored too." Daryl stroked Lester's fur, attempting to calm them both, but the dog's whimpering grew louder. "Has he vomited, or had diarrhea?"

"No."

"Excessive urination?"

"No."

I wondered at Lester's stumbling entrance earlier. "Tremors?"

"Nothing like that." But then Daryl's face clouded. "He *has* been a little shaky."

Lester cooperated when I took his temperature. Usually, he wiggled with enough vigor to require a second set of hands. When I palpated his stomach, he whined. Some pain there.

"His temperature's on the high end of normal," I said. "In that unsupervised minute, or at any other time, did Lester have access to any toxins?"

"You think Lester ate something he shouldn't have." It wasn't a question. We both knew the Lab's proclivity for eating unusual items, like the coins I had surgically removed less than twenty-four hours before.

"It could be anything—moldy food from the garbage, antifreeze, medication, some plants, chocolate. Snail or gopher bait. Nicotine. Anything like that?"

I hadn't noticed any burns in Lester's mouth that would suggest the ingestion of chemicals, but such effects might not show for hours.

"I watched him," Daryl said, his voice tight, as he rubbed his dog's ears. Lester remained still, head resting between outstretched paws. "I would've noticed."

The Lab shifted on the table, suddenly restless, his quiet whimper becoming an insistent keening.

"I know you take great care of him, Daryl." As I continued the exam, I weighed my options. Should I induce vomiting? That would only be useful if he had ingested the poison within the past hour. I worried it might be too late for that, that whatever had poisoned Lester might have already started to irreparably damage his organs, and I feared the Lab's recent surgery would leave him ill-equipped to fight the toxin's effects.

Just then Lester heaved, the vomit thick and a brown that was nearly black. In my practice, I had treated several dogs for chocolate toxicity, and all had survived. But something about this case disturbed me. Some detail was different. I stared at the discharge, but saw nothing.

"Looks like chocolate," Daryl said. I detected relief and understood why. With the many things Lester had swallowed over the years, and the scary-sounding toxins I had named a few minutes earlier, chocolate must have seemed the least of the potential dangers.

But I knew what Daryl didn't: there was no antidote to theobromine, the chemical sickening Lester now. I could only treat the Lab's symptoms. I could give him diazepam for his tremors, or propranolol for any arrhythmia. I could, and would, administer activated charcoal for the chocolate that lingered in his stomach and intravenous liquids to prevent dehydration. I could make him comfortable.

There was a lot I could do—except guarantee I could save him. And, of course, that was the only promise Daryl wanted.

As if reading my mind, Daryl asked, "Is he going to be okay?"

I started to give the only possible answer, that I would do everything I could, but then Lester vomited again, and I realized what had disturbed me a minute earlier. In the pan was a thick, dark liquid. Only that. No scraps of silver or plastic. In the other cases of chocolate toxicity I had treated, there had always been bits of wrapper.

It could have been a fluke. The evidence could still be in Lester's stomach, awaiting later discovery. Still, I suspected I would never find a wrapper, and even someone who hadn't gone to veterinary school knew enough about canine anatomy to know this: dogs don't unwrap their food.

# 6

---

I stabilized Lester, then transferred him to a facility with twenty-four-hour care. I tried not to dwell on the missing wrapper. Daryl baked his special brownies at least a couple of times a week, and it was conceivable the Labrador had stolen unwrapped chocolate from Daryl's pantry.

Though the explanation didn't fully satisfy me, I was distracted by a more immediate concern: Why wasn't my key unlocking the front door to my house? The key slid in, but there it stuck. No amount of twisting freed the bolt.

Foggy-headed as I was, for a second, I wondered if this was how my marriage to Sam ended: with a key stuck in a lock, preventing entry to the home we had shared for sixteen years. Exhaustion opened the way to doubt. No matter how strong our marriage was, Sam had always been a better person than me. For the first few years, I had expected him to realize this, to pull away after getting a full look at who I truly was: a wild teenager who had morphed into a reckless and adrift young woman.

But somehow the opposite happened. With him, I found mooring. I know—you aren't supposed to try to change the person you love, but we got married young, so we weren't fully formed. Change was inevitable, and because of Sam, I changed for the better. At least that's what I told myself. My father might have had a different opinion.

Still, there I was, standing on my front porch and doubting Sam because he had been too preoccupied to make love for a couple of weeks and had that morning preferred to take a phone call in private. In my place, Sam wouldn't have doubted me. Like I said, a better person.

I tried the key again. Still stuck. Then I remembered the envelope Sam had dropped off to Zoe while I had been treating Lester, at the same time he had swapped his car for the rental I'd just driven home. The envelope contained my new house key, to fit the new locks. It should have made me feel safe.

I retrieved the new key, opening the door to darkness and a tiny dog bouncing at my feet. Other than Boo, the house was empty. Leo had texted to ask if he could spend the night at Tyler's, but where were Sam and Audrey?

Sam's blue Toyota Camry was still in the driveway, parked next to my rental sedan. He must have taken Audrey trick-or-treating in the neighborhood. Without me.

I had no reason to blame him. We had agreed to leave at six, and it was now after seven. I was late getting home, again, and I knew how impatient six-year-olds could be. It was my fault, entirely my fault, but it nevertheless bothered me that I had missed another family ritual.

I leaned down to scratch Boo behind his ears, locked the door behind me, and went into the kitchen. A pot of spaghetti sat on the stove, two jars of pasta sauce on the counter beside it. I touched the side of the pot. Warm, so they hadn't been gone long. I struggled to remember the last time I had cooked dinner.

I called Sam. It took a few rings for him to answer.

"Cassie." He said my name in that way only he did, his voice made huskier with the flu.

"I'm home."

I waited for an invitation, but got none. "We shouldn't be out much longer. Audrey's already starting to drag."

"I can meet up with you guys. I wouldn't want to disappoint Audrey."

To his credit, Sam didn't point out I already had by being more than an hour late. "Like I said, we'll be home soon. We made spaghetti."

"I found it."

"Audrey insisted on making the sauce."

"I'm surprised she could open the jars."

"I helped with that and pouring it into the pan. But she's a heck of a stirrer."

In the background, I heard a chorus of "trick or treat." I closed my eyes and pictured Audrey's face in a throng of children. With my eyes shut, I could more clearly hear Sam's breathing, quick but even. Probably a result of his mouth being pressed against his cell phone. His voice was low when he next spoke, though his words were unmistakable. "We need to talk."

With that brief statement, the doubt sauntered back, like a cocky friend I was expecting but wasn't particularly happy to see. "About what?"

"We'll be home in half an hour, maybe sooner," he said. "Love you, Cassie."

Sam hung up before I could say that I loved him too.


I ATE THE SPAGHETTI standing up, not bothering to rinse my plate. The doorbell began ringing then. After passing out tiny chocolate bars and packets of sour gummy worms to the first wave of trick-or-treaters, I put the bowl of candy on the porch with a "take two" sign, turned off the lamp in the living room, and settled on the couch. Boo jumped up beside me. For the dog's sake, I covered myself with a fleece throw and sank back into the pillows, intending only a short rest. Just until Sam and Audrey got back.

My eyes burned and, unlike the night before, sleep came quickly.


MY VIBRATING PHONE WOKE ME. That and the tickling on my foot. I answered, expecting Sam. It was Daryl.

"Sorry it's so late, Doc," he said. "Lester's still on an IV, and they gave him some medicine to slow his heart rate. But he's not vomiting anymore."

"I'm glad he's doing better."

"Thank you, Doc."

"You don't need to—"

Daryl interrupted me. "Yes," he said. "I do. That first time I came into your office, the incident with the sliding glass door . . ."

"Wasn't your fault."

"I know that, but I was high, and I was sure you would notice and make judgments. But you didn't."

That day five years before, he couldn't have smelled more of skunk if he'd been sporting a white stripe down his back. "I noticed."

Daryl chuckled, though it was more muted than usual. "Oh, yeah, I know that. My eyes were red as shit. What I meant is, you didn't judge."

Boo's fur brushed my toes, so I jiggled my foot. "That's not my place."

"It's nobody's place, but that doesn't stop people from doing it," he said. "So thanks. Not just for today."

The catch in his voice humbled me, and for a moment, neither of us spoke. Finally, I asked, "Still no idea where Lester got the chocolate?"

"I've been thinking about it, a lot, but I have no idea."

Boo continued to graze my foot. Maybe it wasn't his fur. A paw? "I appreciate the update, Daryl."

"Yeah, well, sorry again it's so late, but I figured with kids, you'd still be up, since it's Halloween."

It wasn't until Daryl hung up that the full meaning of his apology registered: *Sorry again it's so late.*

I checked my phone. 9:07 p.m. It had been nearly two hours since I had talked to Sam. I punched in his number, but it went straight to voicemail.

My mind picked over possible explanations, my heart beating faster with each I discarded.

Sam could have taken Audrey for a hamburger—except they had already eaten spaghetti.

Ice cream, then. But Sam wouldn't allow our daughter ice cream when she already had a bucketful of candy. Because of the liver transplant, we were both watchful of how much sugar she ate.

Would Sam have taken Audrey to the grocery store to pick up some milk? Leo used mixing bowls for his cereal, so we went through a gallon every few days.

Concern became panic when I realized Sam couldn't have gone for a burger, or ice cream, or groceries. His car was still at the house. *Wasn't it?*

I jolted from the couch, earning a yelp from Boo, who was tucked into the couch next to my hip. I pulled open the curtains even as my subconscious tingled: *Tucked into my hip?*

I didn't know which I had been hoping to see—the car, or an empty driveway. Without a car, Sam would likely be in the neighborhood. If the car had been gone, it allowed the possibility that he had taken Audrey to a friend's house, or stopped by work to pick up some paperwork, or gone to the pharmacy for more cold medicine.

Sam's blue Toyota Camry was still parked in the driveway.

Suddenly, the absence of options felt like a tangible void.

I flicked on the light, and my subconscious drew my attention to the foot of the couch and to the tickling that couldn't have been Boo.

I screamed when I saw it. Black eyes were pinpricks in its large, round head. Stripes crossed its plump body, nearly two inches long. Mandibles jutted from its alien face, and it hopped on spiny legs. Toward me. I jumped back, grateful no one was there to witness my reaction.

Just a stupid Jerusalem cricket. Still, I shuddered to think that thing had been on my foot.

I grabbed an empty glass from the coffee table and trapped the bug beneath it, the insect's antennae testing the walls of its new prison. *Ping, ping.* Only a stupid insect, but in light of the events of the past twenty-four hours, it felt like something else. An ugliness that had breached our threshold. A reminder of how vulnerable we were. *Ping, ping, ping.*

My hand trembled as I texted Leo: *Heard from dad?*

The response: *No. Why?*

*He wanted to know what time your football game is tomorrow.*

I could hear the eye roll in his reply, no emoji needed: *Dad doesn't know the time?*

Even Leo saw through my lie. Understandably. Sam hadn't missed a game. I was the one who sometimes ducked in at halftime.

I checked the time again: 9:10 p.m. Not so late. Maybe Audrey had gotten a second wind.

My subconscious sneered at the attempt at self-deception. After another unsuccessful call to Sam, I grabbed my keys, stepped around the tiny monster encased in glass, and headed out to find my husband and daughter.

# 7

With its mature trees, older homes, and sidewalks sloping toward the sky, Lomita Heights had always felt like a monument. It might've been the iconic stone sign at the base of the hill or that some of the families had been living in their homes longer than I had been alive. It felt solid, entrenched. Safe.

But tonight, I felt none of the usual security. There were shadows in the trees, and the sidewalk felt as if it could slide down the hill with only a minor jolt, crushing homes and trick-or-treaters alike in a tide of crumbling concrete.

That image certainly didn't help my state of mind.

Shortly past nine, the streets were nearly empty. Even the older kids had started packing away their candy bags and halfhearted costumes.

This lack of pedestrian traffic made the house a few blocks over stand out. With its over-the-top decorations, the two-story home could have passed for a commercial enterprise. Ghoulish heads streaked with stage blood impaled on fence posts. A headless scarecrow with a leering jack-o'-lantern tucked under its arm. A reaper cast in the greenish glow of carefully aimed spotlights, skulls at its feet, bony hands protruding from freshly dug plots. Then there were the usual foam headstones, warning signs, and rubber rats, all shrouded in dry-ice fog and the soundtrack of ghostly moaning and rattling chains.

It was the only house that still had traffic. Among the stragglers was a black cat wearing a tiara.

*Audrey.*

I couldn't get to her fast enough, and when I reached her, I fell to my knees beside her. I pulled her into a hug, so tight she might have melted into my ribs, but then immediately worried my violent affection might frighten her. I pushed her back, just far enough to get a look at her face, and realized my daughter was already frightened. And why not? Sam was nowhere in sight.

"I take it you're the mom?" I looked up and found myself staring into the face of a witch I didn't know.

"Mm-hmm," was all I managed before embracing Audrey again. "Where's your dad, Peanut?"

My daughter's small shoulders lifted in a shrug. Her mouth was smeared with chocolate, her cheeks with tears. "I think he lost me," she said. "I saw Savannah from school. Sometimes she's nice. Tonight she was a cat, too, but she didn't have a tiara, and she was brown.

"I said hi to Savannah, and then Daddy was gone."

Audrey's voice broke several times in the telling of her story. Expectation lit her face, only inches from mine, and I read every unspoken thought: *Mom's here. Mom will find Dad. Mom will fix it.*

Her confusion was a gut punch. Sam was the reliable one. He was the parent who kept track of the kids' overbooked schedules. Remembered to reorder Audrey's medication, or buy Leo's cleats. Made sure the kids were fed, even if it was only pasta and jarred sauce.

Sam would know what to do. My fingers twitched, muscle memory wanting to tap out his number on a keypad. But Sam wasn't answering his phone.

"Good of you to finally show up." A second female voice. I turned and saw that a short-skirted pirate in fishnets had joined the witch. I ignored the judgment, nearly as thick as the smell of wine on the pirate's breath.

"Where do you remember seeing Dad last?"

"Before I saw Savannah." She grabbed some candy from her bucket and held out her hand, palm up, for inspection. "She gave me all her sour candies, and I gave her one of my chocolates and all the purple ones that taste like cough syrup." Her voice was hollow, and the candies plunked against the plastic as Audrey dropped them back into her bucket.

I glanced up at the women. "How long has she been alone?"

The pirate pursed her lips. "She's not alone. *We're* with her. But *we're* not her parents."

The witch added, "Her dad's been gone for fifteen minutes. At least. We would've called, but your daughter doesn't know your number, and she doesn't have a cell phone."

The witch said the last part the way she might've lamented Audrey being shoeless. I stood, pulling Audrey so she rested against my hip. "She's six. Of course she doesn't have a phone."

"I got my Clementine a phone for her fourth birthday," the witch said.

The pirate's turn now. "Not that it's okay to dump a child on people you barely know."

"Sam asked you to watch her? Why?"

Both women ignored me. By the witch's curt nod of agreement, I could tell that this topic of discussion had preceded my arrival and wouldn't end until all bullet points were addressed. "We're busy watching our own children."

"Besides," the pirate continued. "Nice neighborhoods like this, kids come in from other areas."

I read her meaning clearly: these "other" children brought trouble with them.

Against my side, Audrey trembled. I stripped off my sweatshirt and wrapped it around her.

"Are you from around here?" the witch asked.

I frowned. "Why? Thinking of throwing a block garage sale?"

The witch picked up on the sarcasm, but the pirate didn't.

"That's a good idea, but that's not why I was asking." The witch shot her friend a "don't be stupid" look.

I gave both of them one of my own. If I thought a six-year-old had been abandoned by her parents, I would've pounded on doors until I found someone who knew the child. But maybe that was just me. I also hadn't thought to get my daughter a phone for her fourth birthday.

I took a breath, swallowing my irritation. It wasn't really these two women who had me upset.

Well, okay, it was a little bit them.

"You said Sam left Audrey with you?"

The pirate pointed to the witch. "With her. I was at my house getting a bottle of water."

Yeah, *water.*

The witch nodded. "Sam recognized me from carpool. We usually drop off around the same time."

"Then where did he go?"

"No clue. He said he wouldn't be gone long, but that was *fifteen minutes* ago."

"And neither of you have seen him since?"

The witch shook her head, but the pirate shrugged. "I've never met him," she said.

I scrolled through the pictures on my phone, selected one of Sam, then held out the phone for the pirate to see. "Him."

Her brow furrowed as she studied the screen, then she smiled in that way my husband often made women smile. "Yeah, I saw him, but it was earlier. Before he dumped your daughter on my friend here. He looked like he was waiting for someone."

When Audrey burrowed closer to my hip, I wrapped my arm more tightly around her shoulders. "Why do you think he was waiting for someone?"

"He kept checking his phone, looking around," the pirate said. "He was texting too. Then he must've connected with whoever, because he put his phone in his pocket."

"How long ago was that?"

They shrugged in unison. "Longer than fifteen minutes," the pirate said.

We were going in circles, and I needed to get Audrey home. I tried one last question, "Where did you last see him?"

"Over by the ghosts." The witch pointed to the far side of the yard, toward a palm tree.

I went for my wallet, intending to give them a business card, then realized I hadn't thought to grab it. "Let me give you my number. In case you see him again."

I recited my number, which the pirate punched into her phone.

"Thanks for looking out for my daughter," I said. "I don't want to take you away from your kids any longer."

I took some pleasure in the women's sudden panic as they looked around and realized they had no idea where their children were. I would've probably taken more satisfaction if the same couldn't also be said of my husband.

# 8

———

I dropped off Audrey and Boo at Zoe's. It didn't take my daughter long to fall asleep, still in her cat costume. A minute after she did, I was back in the rental car.

I wanted to stay with her, to be at her bedside if she should awake, but Audrey didn't need my comfort. She needed me to find her dad.

So I drove. Santa Rosa is about forty square miles, and I searched each one of them. Some twice. Moving, I had purpose, and with purpose, I didn't have to stare too closely at the problem. My husband hadn't come home, and one of the last things he had said to me had been: *We need to talk.*

Never good words to hear, even less so under the circumstances.

As I drove, I called Sam's closest friend, Ozzy, several times. Straight to voicemail each time. I kept checking my call log and texts, just to make sure I hadn't missed any notifications from him or Sam. I hadn't.

I pulled into a grocery store parking lot and rested my forehead between my hands on the steering wheel. When I stripped away all the hope, all the doubts, it came down to this: Sam had either left voluntarily, or something—someone—had made the choice for him.

Midnight approached and, alone in the car, the explanations that had been playing as background noise in my head no longer made sense.

Originally, I had considered that Sam had left to visit a friend. But that meant he had made the choice to leave our six-year-old daughter with a woman he only recognized from carpool. Besides, Sam wasn't the type to grab an Uber, so unless he was visiting someone within walking distance, he would have needed his car, and his car still sat in our driveway.

But what if he hadn't needed his car? He might have left in someone else's—either coaxed into it or carried. My mind churned like one of those farming combines—reaping, threshing, winnowing possibilities, each more terrible than the last. A car could have clipped him as he crossed the street. He could have tripped. We lived in an older neighborhood, and tree roots pushed up concrete in some spots, throwing up blockades waiting to stub toes and twist ankles. A falling man could crack his head and lose his memory—or his life.

Sam could have been shot, stabbed, or beaten to death—for his wallet and phone, or for no reason at all. If his wallet and phone had been taken, how would the hospital know who to call? If his wedding ring had been stolen, too, how would paramedics even know he had someone back home worrying about him?

My hand trembled as I Googled hospital phone numbers. Each time I connected with the emergency department, I held my breath, but each time I got the same response: no one matching Sam's description had been admitted.

That left the police and the morgue. I wasn't ready to make either call.

Of course, there was another option. Sam's disappearance might be connected to the attack the night before. We had changed our locks, but we hadn't changed our address. Carver Sweet would know we had kids if he had opened my wallet, and what felon would leave a wallet unopened? So we had kids, it was Halloween . . . he could guess we would be trick-or-treating in our neighborhood. Out from behind our locked doors. Easy prey.

Even as I cast aside a thousand explanations, one returned again and again: Sam might be having an affair. He might've left Audrey with a woman he barely knew because the alternative was to bring her to meet his lover.

But if that was true, why hadn't he called me to pick up our daughter?

An answer came as quickly as the question: maybe he had seen me searching for them. Despite what the costumed moms had said, fifteen minutes wasn't long. I had been in that neighborhood at least half that time. Sam could've seen me, known Audrey was safe, and left to consider how to tell me he was leaving. Or, rather, had already left.

His words hit me again: *We need to talk.*

Another possibility: Sam had instead intended to break it off with his lover, and she had reacted badly. That brought back the images of Sam unconscious, waiting to be discovered in a bush, a ditch, or in someone's trunk.

I gripped my cell phone tightly, resisting the urge to toss it on the floorboards. The sleek chunk of circuitry gave only the illusion of connection. I scanned my contacts, but there were few people I could call at that hour. Sam had no family except for cousins, aunts, and uncles, all out of state. I didn't have the numbers of his coworkers, and I wouldn't have called them if I did.

I put the car in gear and headed to Ozzy's.

My husband's friend lived in Healdsburg, a small town twenty minutes north of Santa Rosa. Known for its wine and the nineteenth-century plaza at its core, Healdsburg was surrounded by brewpubs and boutiques and restaurants with tiny patios where patrons could sip cold brew coffee, or sample locally sourced vegan or upscale Guatemalan fare. The plaza had one of those large gazebos, draped with garlands and lights at Christmas, stars and stripes around patriotic holidays. It had no doubt been filled with the town's children earlier but sat empty now. Tourists and locals alike were tucked in for the night.

A short walk from downtown, Ozzy rented the upstairs granny unit of a century-old bungalow. Peeling blue paint. Broken brick leading up the walkway. Single-paned windows, one of which was covered with plywood. Healdsburg property values being what they were, such a home wasn't labeled run-down, but *historic*.

I knocked on his door. Despite the hour, Ozzy answered quickly. If I awakened him, he gave no indication. His greeting was alert, if guarded.

"Hey, Ozzy." I tried to smile but had no stomach for it. "I was wondering if you've heard from Sam."

Ozzy Delgado had grown up in Austin, and the drawl crept into his voice when he was tired.

"I got your message earlier, Cassie, but I haven't seen him." He brushed a curl away from his face and opened the door just enough to show the left half of his body. He was wearing cargo pants and a floral-print, button-up shirt, his cold-weather attire. His summer look was the same, except cargo shorts instead of pants. So Ozzy hadn't yet been to bed. I waited to see which way he would go with the door: open it so I could enter or keep me on his doorstep. It was late, but it was also chilly.

He didn't invite me in.

"Seeing him and hearing from him aren't the same thing," I said, staring past him into the living room. I couldn't make out anything in the darkness. The only illumination came from the back of the house, which I knew from past visits with Sam was Ozzy's bedroom.

Ozzy closed the door a little, only a third of him showing now, his lips pinched. "Haven't heard from him either."

"No calls? No texts?"

"I'm aware what 'heard from him' means."

I pushed. "So, no contact?"

He swatted away another curl, his scowl and drawl deepening. "I'm sure Sam will be in touch."

"And I'm sure you're being evasive."

A few seconds passed, and my steady glare brought only a sigh.

"Sam took Audrey trick-or-treating," I said. "When they didn't come home, I went looking for them. I found her. Didn't find him."

His eyes widened slightly. "He left Audrey alone?" Good. He was concerned now.

"She was a few streets from our house, with two women I've never met."

His face relaxed. "Did Sam know them?"

"He recognized one of them from carpool," I admitted. I didn't like the way Ozzy looked at me when I said that. Like he felt sorry for me. Like he knew something I didn't.

"Well, there you go."

"It's odd timing, don't you think? For Sam to walk away from our daughter on Halloween."

"Would there have been a good time for him to leave?" Ozzy exhaled deeply. "It's late, Cassie," he said, rubbing an eye for emphasis. "I'll let you know if Sam gets in touch. Anyway, I hope you guys work it out."

He shut the door, leaving me stunned. What the hell had he meant by that last part?

On my walk back to the car, I considered Ozzy's final comment. I replayed my marriage to Sam and Sam's role in it. I remembered the way he had tended my cut after the attack on the trail and the intensity in his expression when he had learned I had been reckless. He was playful, stubborn, affectionate, and sometimes he would retreat into himself if things didn't go his way. He often thrust me into the role of disciplinarian with the kids, and he despised confrontation—so much that he would avoid talking about his desire to divorce?

I rejected the thought as soon as it popped into my head. True, Sam had been secretive with his phone call that morning, but he was also the man who had paid for acupuncture for the classroom guinea pig. In high school, he had once stepped in when a group of guys was bullying a smaller, curly-haired teammate, ending up with a bloodied nose and Ozzy's friendship. Sam was an optimist, but he was also a fiercely protective husband and father, the kind of guy who dressed up like a zombie to take his six-year-old daughter trick-or-treating.

After considering everything, I couldn't believe Sam wasn't happy.

The thought pricked at my consciousness before I could shoo it away: maybe it wasn't that he wasn't happy with me, but that he was happier with someone else.

I started the car. Twenty-two minutes later, I turned onto Terra Linda Drive. In those twenty-two minutes, I had reassured myself that Sam loved me, he loved our children, and he wouldn't have left without an explanation.

When the explanation came a minute later, it wasn't what I had been expecting: a text from Sam just as I was pulling up to our home. Two words. *I'm sorry.*

I parked in the middle of the driveway. There was no need to park on the right, the side usually reserved for me, because sometime in the past hour, Sam's car had disappeared.

# 9

---

I entered the house and stood in the dark, the empty spot reminding me of all that might be lost. Closing my eyes, I saw Sam and me as we had been in those first months in this house. I saw Sam lifting an infant Leo in the air, standing in front of the living room window, both of them haloed in midafternoon sun. Then Leo vomited all over both of them. Sam laughed—because what else was there to do?—and then he looked at me, eyebrow arched, and asked for a "very large" towel. When I opened my eyes, the memory was near enough that I squinted in imagined sunlight and caught the scent of soured milk.

I loved Sam then, loved him now, would probably love him always. Even if he had stopped loving me.

When I flipped on the light, the first thing I noticed was the glass on its side in the middle of the living room floor. I puzzled over it a moment before I remembered: the Jerusalem cricket I had trapped before leaving the house. While I had been looking for Sam, he had entered our home, knocking over the glass, then had driven away.

Now freed, the insect had likely found a dark corner to hide in, under a bed or inside a shoe. I could picture it out there, only inches away: its alien eyes watching me, mandibles twitching, and its prickly feet—used to burrow into things moist and decaying—preparing to scuttle across my path.

I hated those little bastards.

Zoe insisted that insects like crickets and lady bugs, even spiders, were good luck. But Jerusalem crickets weren't true crickets, so its hidden presence felt like the opposite. Though I knew it was irrational, that the insect's escape coincided with Sam's disappearance felt like an omen.

I grabbed a change of clothes for both kids before going into the master bedroom to pack my own bag.

I was still thinking of that insect and of Sam when I saw it: on the nightstand, the dog made of folded paper. It might have been the dread still curdling my stomach, or my bone-deep exhaustion, but the origami creature seemed less innocent in near darkness than it had in that morning's light. I walked to the nightstand, but hesitated before reaching out. When I touched the paper, I almost expected it to bite.

Again, I blamed stress, but with its ears folded downward and its broad paper skull, it reminded me of a Labrador. I lifted it to my nose and sniffed. I thought I caught a hint of chocolate. My hands jittered as I unfolded the origami figure, spreading it into a sheet of foil-lined paper. Stamped on the coppery exterior was the brand name of the baking chocolate we sometimes bought.

On the other side, a number had been etched in pencil.

2.

I remembered what Rico had asked me after the attack: Did the number three mean anything to me?

Sometimes, we step across life's thresholds without noticing. We say goodbye to a high school friend in June, not realizing she'll move away over the summer. We sign up for the microbiology class that will change the direction of our careers, or, on a random Tuesday, meet the person we'll marry.

But this threshold came with blinking arrows and exclamation points.

2.

I didn't know what the number meant, but I knew it meant something. Staring down at the square of paper, a question occurred to me: If Sam hadn't been the one to leave the folded dog on my nightstand, how had the person who *had* left it gained access to our bedroom?

I hastily folded the paper in quarters and slipped it into my pocket.

# 10

———

Zoe lived in a Mediterranean townhome with a tile roof and Juliet balcony. Along the path leading to her door, succulents bloomed in bottle-brushed spikes and pink-tipped rosettes, and wispy grass and purple flowers bowed to the wind.

When I got to Zoe's, Audrey was sleeping. Zoe wasn't.

Zoe had unlocked the door when I had texted I was on my way. When I entered, my lavender-haired friend was on the couch, long legs tucked beneath her, the one-eyed Smooch draped around her shoulders like the world's creepiest scarf. Earlier, I had been able to avoid Zoe's questions. The stony set of her face told me avoidance wasn't an option this time.

"How's Audrey been?" I asked.

"Didn't wake up once. Any word on Sam?"

I sank in the overstuffed chair facing her, hugging a throw pillow to my chest. "He texted that he's sorry."

"And . . . ?"

"That's it. He's sorry. Oh, and his car's gone now." I shifted in my seat and released my grip on the pillow. I suddenly had no more energy to hold it, and it slipped to the floor. "When I talked to Ozzy, he said he hoped we could work it out."

Zoe's face was a canvas, her emotions vivid brushstrokes impossible to misread. Currently, the color of choice was red. "What the hell did he mean by that?"

"He didn't say."

"You guys are solid."

But was that true? I thought hard on this. When Audrey was a baby and needed a liver transplant, I hadn't handled it well. I had let myself slide back into patterns abandoned years before—I drank a little more than was healthy, I worked longer hours at the clinic, so I could feel like I was actually of use to someone—because, as a mom and medical professional, I had failed my daughter. It had taken jaundice setting in for me to recognize the symptoms, and by then she was sick. Really sick. And I was angry. Really angry.

Sam, though—he took in my anger, and he took in our daughter's pain, and he carried our family through the crisis. I could always count on him, even when he couldn't count on me. But lately, I had been working longer hours again, and this time, Sam had pulled away. Just a little. Just enough for me to notice.

Part of me had been waiting for him to say: *I love you, but I can't do this anymore.*

I filled Zoe in on Sam's behavior that day and told her more about the assault I had witnessed the night before.

When I finished, she said, "You've always had a savior complex."

Her comment surprised me, but then I remembered: she hadn't known me before. She hadn't known the Cassie who had watched while college psychopath Dirk abused his almost-girlfriend. I'd thought about that attack twice in as many days. Why?

I answered my own question, "There are a lot of things in my life I could've done differently."

"Like what?"

That night in college, I'd been the one to call 911 when that girl had gone over the balcony. But I had watched from above when the police came. Everyone had watched, at least those who hadn't fled the party, focused more on hiding their inebriation than the fate of the girl on the ground.

We were in shock, I had justified. Now I recognized that immobilizing emotion as guilt. If that girl had died in those minutes before the police came, she would've died alone.

I ignored Zoe's question. "I'm just grateful I was on the trail that night." I changed the subject. "I think Sam was in the house. When I went inside to grab our things, the glass I'd used to trap a Jerusalem cricket had been knocked over. So unless it had injected steroids . . ."

"I can't believe you take the temperatures of bull mastiffs but are afraid of a bug barely bigger than your thumb."

"Yeah, I know, and spiders are good luck. There's something else."

I took the chocolate wrapper from my pocket and showed it to Zoe.

"What's this?"

"I found it on my nightstand this morning. It was folded in the shape of a dog."

"Like origami?"

"Yeah. At first I thought it might be from Sam, but now . . ."

I let her sit with that a few seconds, waiting to see if she would come to the same conclusion I had. I recognized the moment she did. As I had done, she sniffed the wrapper.

"It smells like chocolate." Her eyes and mouth widened, her voice breathless as she asked, "Lester?"

"I thought so, but I have no idea what the number two would mean."

"Hmm."

"Hmm?"

"Nothing. So it's a two."

"After I witnessed that attack, the detective asked if the number three meant anything to me."

"Does it?"

"Other than being the number between two and four, I haven't a clue. But it feels like a threat, especially after what happened with Lester."

She paused, her face scrunching. "I thought you found it *before* Lester was poisoned?"

"I did."

"Hmm."

"I should call Detective Rico . . . What?"

"I know you're upset."

"Of course I'm upset. My husband might've just ended our marriage with a two-word text."

"Remember when Bobby and I broke up, and I wanted to go see him?"

"You wanted to put sardines in his gas tank."

"He cheated on me with my cousin. It wouldn't have worked anyway. I would've had to pry open his gas tank, so he would've noticed that before the sardines could do any real damage."

"Because *that* was the flaw in your plan."

"Anyway, you stopped me. You knew I was upset, that I wasn't thinking clearly, and you told me not to put sardines in Bobby's tank."

"You really think me calling Rico about Sam and that wrapper is the equivalent of vandalizing your ex's car?"

"Not at all. It's just . . . I'm sorry, Cassie, but you aren't thinking straight. And you shouldn't be, not with what you've been through recently, but as your friend, it's my job to be the logical one here."

"The logical one, huh? Weren't we just talking about your plan to slip fish into your ex's gas tank?"

Her expressive face split into a grin, but there was sadness at its edges. "Okay, so I'm not usually the logical one, but let me give it a shot here. First, the wrapper. When you showed it to me, I didn't see a number."

"What then?"

She turned it over and traced a section of raised foil, where the pencil mark on the other side had left it embossed with its mirror image. "The letter S. I guess it could be a two, or at least I can see where you'd think that. Power of suggestion. You were thinking of that detective's question, so you saw a two, whereas I was thinking leaving an origami dog seemed like something Sam would do. So I saw an S."

"But you agree it smells like chocolate."

"I've been to your house. It's a brand you use."

"You think it's a coincidence?"

"How would someone get into your house? Into your bedroom?"

"Carver took my van, which had my keys. We didn't get the locks changed until late yesterday morning." I thought of the bug freed from its jar. "If it's related to that night and he's done something with Sam— he'd have the new house key too."

"It just seems a little—much. Isn't it more likely that Sam left it for you as some romantic gesture that only seems sinister now that he's gone?"

I took the wrapper back but said nothing.

"And isn't it more likely that, given that text you received, Sam left because . . ."

"Because?" But I knew where the sentence had been headed.

Zoe flushed and reached out to rest her hand on my knee. "Because he wanted to."

"Then it would seem an inappropriate time for romantic gestures."

"So what I'm saying doesn't make sense to you?"

I twisted my wedding ring. "I think Sam's been trying to tell me something for weeks, and I've missed it. Still, if there's even a chance that his absence isn't his choice . . ."

Zoe finished my sentence. "You need to do whatever you can to find him."

Smooch slid from Zoe's neck onto her lap. Zoe's petting grew more aggressive as she considered her next words. Thanks to her remarkably expressive face, I could read what was coming. Finally, she said, "I hope Sam's having an affair." Having settled on an explanation that was both logical and meant Sam was safe, her voice grew more animated. "Sam's been acting shady, he says you guys need to talk. Those women mention it looked like he was waiting for someone at that house where you found Audrey. That text he sent. And Ozzy's obviously covering for him." She paused to catch her breath. "I hope Sam hooked up with some bimbo and he's just taking some time to figure everything out, because if that's what happened, he'll be back."

Even as the idea broke my heart, I thought: *I hope so too.*

# 11

———

I fell asleep with my hand on my phone and woke up the same way. I checked the screen. No more texts from Sam.

From the kitchen, I could hear Audrey making breakfast with Zoe. Laughing. The morning before, that had been the four of us, in our own kitchen, Sam scrambling eggs and none of us realizing it might be our last breakfast as a family.

I wasn't yet ready for Audrey's questions, so I pulled the blanket around me and called my son.

"Hey." Leo's voice held the usual hint of teen impatience. "What's up, Mom?"

"Just checking in." I forced a lilt in my voice. *Everything fine here.* "Did you and Tyler have fun last night?"

"Yeah, I guess. Why'd you call?"

"Just to say I love you."

"Love you too. You and Dad coming to the game?"

It took a moment for my throat to clear. "I'm not sure if Dad's going to be able to make this one."

"But you're coming, right?"

"I was thinking you shouldn't go either."

"What?" If I'd told Leo we were moving to the Congo to live with the bonobos, he would've reacted with less incredulity. "You're kidding, right?"

"I was thinking that instead, you, Audrey, and I can go to dinner."

"Why would we do that?"

"Eating dinner is actually quite common."

He sighed, unimpressed with my attempt at levity. "But it's Monty." Montgomery High, Santa Rosa's rival. "I'm not missing Monty. No way. Coach would kill me."

I considered forcing Leo to miss the game. I was the mom. I could do that. But then I thought: just as our family might've already eaten our final breakfast together, tonight might be Leo's last game. If Sam never returned, missing Monty would no longer top Leo's list of worst things.

"I just worry about you."

Leo caught the slight break in my voice. "Everything okay, Mom?" A pause. "Why isn't Dad coming to the game?"

The lie came quickly. "Dad's at a conference, and I'm fine. I think I'm still shaken up from the other night."

"Yeah, well, if everything's okay, I really gotta go." The impatience returning. "Tyler and I are gonna hit the weights before school."

"Text me later."

"Why?"

"Because I'm your mom."

"Yeah, and you worry about me, I know. Whatever. Tyler's mom's leaving so . . ."

"Go."

"See you at the game?"

"Audrey and I will be there."

In the kitchen, Audrey laughed again, a rumble out of place in such a small child. Her spirit had always been outsized like that. Now, it was her and Leo that steadied my legs enough to stand and provided the focus I needed to face what was likely destined to be another hellish day.

ON THE RIDE TO SCHOOL, Audrey's layers had her puffed up like a campfire marshmallow. I risked a glance in the mirror to the back seat, where she wriggled to get comfortable in her booster seat.

"Mommy, next year, can we have one of those pumpkins that looks like it's throwing up?" she asked. "You know, with the seeds and stringy parts coming out of its mouth?"

At last, a question I could answer honestly. Earlier, when Audrey had asked where her dad was, the lie had been bitter in my mouth: I told her that her dad had apologized for leaving her alone and that he had left early that morning for a teachers' conference. The same lie I had told Leo. It had made it so much worse that they both believed it without question.

I pulled alongside the curb near Hidden Valley Elementary.

"Sure. We can have a pumpkin like that next year."

My breath snagged on the last two words. *Next year.* What would that look like for our family?

"Savannah says her dad carved a pumpkin that looks like a bat, but I think a puking pumpkin would be way cooler."

With that, Audrey grabbed her tiara and backpack, gave me a quick hug, then bounded toward a group of girls who squealed in greeting. My heart constricted. Forget next year. I didn't even know what the next *day* would look like.

Earlier, I had canceled all but my most urgent appointments, referring those to another vet. With no patients or kids to tend to, I considered my next step.

A dozen calls to Sam had gone unanswered, the most recent less than thirty minutes before. For the first time in months, I almost called my father, but it had been years since we had spoken. Six years. Our last conversation had been a stilted call a month after Audrey was born. He barely knew Leo, and he didn't know Audrey at all, so what help could he be now?

The brick facade of the high school appeared in front of me before I fully realized where I was headed. I pulled into the staff lot and looked for Sam's blue Camry. When I didn't find it, I parked. Audrey's elementary started fifteen minutes after the high school, so classes were already in session. I supposed I could call the office, inquire as to whether Sam had shown up for class, but I knew the answer: he hadn't.

I sat in my car for twenty-five minutes, until the bell signaled the end of first period. I gripped the steering wheel as I scanned the crowd, not for Sam, but for Leo. In the flood, it took me a moment to figure out which awkward, beautiful teen was mine. Then I saw him, and, as it did every time, my heart swelled. Leo walked with Tyler and another boy I recognized but couldn't name. My son smiled, in that way he did when he was around his friends and didn't know Mom was watching. Leo balanced on the cusp of adulthood, but he was still very much a boy who needed a father who acted responsibly.

On my phone, I typed another text to Sam, hitting send before I could second-guess myself.

As I waited for his response, I re-read the message: *Give me a reason not to file a missing person report. You've got five minutes.*

Sam needed only three: *I need time.*

*Well, our kids need a dad.*

*I know.*

*Call me.*

Several minutes passed before another text popped onto the screen: *I can't. Not yet.*

*Why not?*

*It's complicated.* And then: *I'm not alone.*

Despite my thought the night before that Sam might be cheating on me, what I pictured now was Sam hiding in a closet, or in the trunk of some stranger's car. In both scenarios, he was bruised and bleeding.

Once my mind went dark, another possibility slipped in: Sam might not be the one texting me.

*Who's with you? Are you hurt?*

He answered only the second question: *I'll recover.*

*Then call me.*

When no response came, I dialed his number. It rolled into voicemail without ringing.

His text came a second later: *I'm sorry.*

*I see you're getting real use out of that Big Book of Clichés.*

*What do you want me to say?*

*I want you to tell me what the hell is going on.*

I sat with that for a moment before summoning the courage to ask the question I didn't really want answered. *Are you having an affair?*

The bubbles signifying Sam was typing lasted several minutes, but the text that came was just four words: *Give me until tonight.*

I pushed: *You didn't answer me.*

I waited for the bubbles to appear again. Thirty seconds passed. A minute. Finally, I typed: *How do I know this is really you?*

The reply came quickly this time. *Who else would it be?*

Another nonanswer.

When Audrey and Leo were babies, Sam had slept with the monitor on his side of the bed. Even when they had started sleeping for longer stretches, Sam would check on them at least once each night. "Just in case the monitor's not working," he would say.

*Why did you leave Audrey with that woman?*

*Tonight. I promise.*

*I don't know if I can give you until tonight.*

The bubbles again, then: *The first time we met. Princess Jellybean.*

I inhaled sharply. *What?*

*You asked if this was really me.*

My hands trembled when I asked the question he still hadn't answered: *Are you having an affair?*

In the cold rental sedan, thick with the scent of canned pine, I waited for Sam's response, and when the bubbles popped on the screen, my heart's thundering grew so loud I half expected the windshield to flex. Then, for a moment, my heart stopped. My whole world stopped, because the last text I received from Sam was a single word: *Yes.*

# 12

____

Clouds of pulled cotton hung above the skylight in the Santa Rosa Police Department's main lobby, midmorning sun filtering in through a stand of anemic maples. I entered the station and asked for Detective Ray Rico. He wasn't in, but the police technician at the counter, a reedy man with a sharp nose, said he would get someone else to help me, leaving me to wait. I hadn't been good at that even before Sam went missing.

The woman who came out five minutes later—five minutes that felt like an hour—was my height with a tight bun and heavily contoured cheeks. She introduced herself as Marisol Torres and ushered me into a room off the lobby. Despite the severity of her hairstyle, the officer's manner was sympathetic, and her slight smile seemed genuine.

Then again, my marriage had seemed genuine too.

Torres gathered contact information, social media passwords, and a description of my husband. When she asked for a photo, I scrolled through half a dozen photos before I found one that worked. It was from a few years back when we had gone hiking in Annadel State Park, in an area since scorched by wildfire. The green trees and Sam's crooked smile were both relics from another time.

"This must be difficult for you," Torres said. "When's the last time you saw your husband?"

"Yesterday morning, shortly before seven."

"Six-thirty? Six-forty-five?"

"Six-forty-five."

"Any other contact yesterday?"

"We spoke on the phone at 7:14 p.m." This I knew exactly because I had checked my call log. Repeatedly. "When I got home just after seven, he had already left to take our daughter trick-or-treating."

"What did your husband say the last time you spoke?"

I didn't need to think about that. I had replayed our last conversation on a loop since Sam had disappeared. "He said he and Audrey would be home in about half an hour and that we needed to talk."

"About what?"

"He didn't elaborate."

She studied me intently. Though she tried to soften her eyes, I was no longer sure Officer Torres was on my side.

"What did you do then?" she asked.

"Waited for them to come home." I kept the fact I had fallen asleep to myself. Partially out of guilt, but mainly because of the questions it might raise: *You took a nap? With your husband and child missing? What kind of person are you?*

She would have phrased the questions differently, but that would be what she would be thinking. Torres didn't need more reasons to doubt me.

I continued, "I got a call regarding a patient a few minutes after nine, and it hit me that Sam and Audrey hadn't come home yet."

"It didn't hit you that they hadn't returned until . . . what? . . . nearly two hours after talking to your husband?"

In hindsight, it may have been stupid to omit mention of the nap. Too late now. I kept my face as dispassionate as the officer's.

"That's right."

"What did you do when you realized your husband hadn't come home?"

"I went looking for him." I told Torres about my search of the neighborhood and about finding Audrey with the two women.

"No other contact from Sam since?"

I hesitated. "There have been some texts," I said. "But I'm not sure they're from Sam."

I showed them to her anyway.

Torres shifted in her seat, her pen poised above the clipboard she balanced, with practiced nonchalance, on her knee.

"Why do you doubt these texts are from your husband?" she asked.

On the drive to the station, I had considered that question at length, so my response came easily. "Have you been in a relationship, Officer Torres?"

"Everyone's been in love."

I shivered at the similarity to Carver Sweet's comment two nights before. "Why do you say that?"

Torres looked at me as if I were an alien who had just asked to make earrings of her eyeballs. "Hey, it was your question."

"Sorry. Anyway, once you're in a relationship, people always ask how you met, right? At first, the Princess Jellybean reference threw me, but then I thought about all the times we've told that story. And everything else . . . it didn't sound like him."

"How so?"

"For one thing, he didn't ask about the kids."

Torres's jaw clenched. "You don't think there's a chance your husband left voluntarily?"

I shook my head on reflex, but of course there was a chance. Though she kept her expression neutral, I sensed she wasn't convinced. I couldn't blame her. I hadn't completely convinced myself.

"Even if the texts are from Sam, he mentions right here that he's injured." I tapped the screen where I had asked Sam if he had been hurt, and he had responded he would recover. "If he's injured, you should follow up on that. And if the texts aren't from Sam . . ." I let my voice trail away. We both knew what might have happened if Sam hadn't sent those texts.

Torres stared for several seconds before saying, "Does Sam have any history of mental illness or substance abuse?"

"No."

"Financial problems?"

I started to say of course not, but I hadn't thought to check our bank balance or credit card receipts. I took care of the clinic's finances, and

Sam handled the home accounts. It had seemed a fair division, but now I realized I didn't even know how much we paid for cable or car insurance. "I don't think so."

Torres paused, tapped her pen, then said, "Mrs. Larkin, I know this may be hard to hear, but you can't discount this: two women with no apparent agenda told you they saw Sam right before he disappeared and that he looked like he was waiting for someone. That he willingly left your daughter in their care. We'll stay open to all possibilities, but you should too."

I didn't like the way Torres's perfectly tweezed brows drew together over narrowed eyes. The slight smile now seemed more pity than sympathy.

Still, my husband's disappearance kept coming back to a single fact: "Sam wouldn't have left Audrey alone."

Torres's expression remained neutral. "She wasn't alone. Even if you didn't know that woman, your husband did."

Though her comment hadn't aimed to wound, it did. Sam knew the mom in the witch costume because he was the one who dropped Audrey off at school every day. He was the one who was there. Until now, when he suddenly wasn't.

"Why would he leave Audrey with someone else with our home only a few blocks away?" I asked. "Besides, you didn't see Audrey last night. She was upset. Crying. If Sam had planned to be gone more than a few minutes, our daughter certainly wasn't aware of it."

"Do you have the numbers of these women?"

I shook my head. Another failure on my part.

Torres nodded, as if my oversight was understandable, but I sensed her judgment. Or maybe I was judging myself.

From my purse, I pulled the chocolate wrapper I had stashed there earlier. I handed it to Torres. I told her about Lester being poisoned and about finding the wrapper folded into the shape of a dog on my nightstand.

She took the wrapper from me and set it on her clipboard. "We'll look into this, and we'll enter the information about your husband into a national database." I braced myself for the "but" I could hear coming. "We'll look into this, *but* unless we find something to indicate your husband is at risk, there's little we can do. Unfortunately, adults are allowed to come and go as they please."

Torres put down her pen and leaned forward, a gesture probably meant to draw me in. Establish a connection between us.

"Most missing adults return within a few days," she said. "Adults are more likely to have left voluntarily than to have been victims of a crime. It may not seem like it now, but that's a good thing. Odds are Sam's safe."

Though the words were what I wanted to hear, I found no reassurance in them.

"We'll look into this, but there are things you can do too: check with friends, hospitals, homeless shelters. And again, if there's any evidence that Sam left involuntarily, we'll investigate it as we would any other crime. Just because the odds are that isn't what happened doesn't mean we won't consider it."

I nodded, signaling my acceptance that the interview was over. But apparently, it wasn't.

"One other thing. By filing this report, you're entitled to know if we find your husband safe."

"Meaning?"

"That's all you have a right to know. If we find your husband, and he doesn't want you to know where he is, we can't share his location."

She adjusted the clipboard in her lap and shifted gears again. "You were involved in an assault case a couple of days ago, right?"

"It's been a hell of a week."

She straightened, her posture suddenly as guarded as her eyes. "Cops look for patterns. The assault by itself could be bad luck, bad timing. Or good luck, if you consider it from the point of view of the woman whose life you saved. But add to that a husband who disappears almost exactly twenty-four hours later and the murder—"

When she didn't immediately finish her sentence, I pushed, "The woman he attacked died?"

"Wednesday was a busy day for Mr. Sweet. Before he assaulted that woman, he poisoned his wife," she said. "You're sure you don't know him?"

Since the attack, I couldn't escape the memory of Carver's face. Most of all, I remembered the scar—puckered flesh trailing his jaw like an albino snake. The mark of a predator. I wouldn't have forgotten seeing that scar, even under ordinary circumstances.

"Never met him. But the woman he beat up—she survived?"

Torres's gaze sharpened, and I felt color bloom in my usually pale cheeks. "Ms. Breneman was released from the hospital yesterday."

I was usually good at reading people, and I read anticipation in the slight pause in the officer's breathing, the way her hands clenched the clipboard.

"I'm glad to hear it," I said.

Torres nodded, finally standing. "We'll let you know if we hear anything. We'll also let you know when you can pick up your van."

I'd forgotten about that, and I nodded in thanks. "Your purse, though . . . It wasn't in the van when we found it. He either took it with him or threw it away." Neither option provided comfort.

Officer Marisol Torres walked away, all her original warmth replaced with an efficient brusqueness.

I thought of Sam, watched the officer depart, and considered that maybe I wasn't as good at reading people as I believed.

# 13

---

When I left the police station, the autumn sun had finally won its battle with the cloud cover, but the fight left it weak and unable to offer warmth.

I paused outside the station. I should go home, check the computer, sift through phone records and credit card statements. But when I thought of home, I thought of Sam making tamales, setting off the fire alarm when a batch of cornhusks caught fire, or Sam tending to scrapes on Audrey's knees and elbows, insignificant injuries made instantly better with Dad's attention and a superhero Band-Aid. I thought of the last time Leo had the flu, when he had allowed us to sit next to him on the couch. We had spent an entire Saturday afternoon there, sharing a blanket and watching *South Park* reruns and Miyazaki films.

I couldn't go home.

Even though I hadn't yet decided on my next step, I walked with purpose toward the car. Keep moving, I told myself, just as I had the night before. Reflection could wait until tonight, when I spent another night on Zoe's sofa, or my first night alone in the bed I usually shared with Sam. I wasn't sure I was brave enough for that yet.

Still struggling to come up with a plan, I drove past the station— and saw it. A little metal box, its black lens pointed at the street. I turned around at the next block and headed toward home after all.

―――――

I TURNED A FEW blocks before I reached our house. The cold sun stole the magic from the neighborhood where Sam had disappeared, ghosts now recognized as bedsheets, skeletons clearly plastic instead of bone. A witch, robbed of its shadows and glowing orbs, listed to one side on a fence post. Someone had splattered its tattered dress with egg.

Not yet 11 a.m. on a Friday, the street was deserted, but I wasn't looking for people. I was looking for cameras. Women like the ones I had met a night earlier—the pirate and the witch who had groused about kids who came in from "other areas"—were exactly the type who might want to surveil outsiders.

I walked down one side of the street—past ranch, traditional, and midcentury modern homes—and down the other, yards accented with live oak and flowering pear trees, boxwood hedges and drought-resistant plants. I scanned doorways, second-floor balconies, and roof-tops for surveillance cameras.

I saw none. I supposed they could be stashed under eaves or camou-flaged in shrubbery, but wasn't the whole point of surveillance to deter crime? And what about doorbell cameras? Someone could be watch-ing me using an app on their phone, and I might never know.

I felt a familiar itch of frustration. As a high school freshman in Phoenix, I had joined the cross-country team but had realized quickly I hated running. There were blisters and leg cramps, and my lungs often felt on the verge of bursting. No endorphins, just a painful slog and the fear that, yes, this time I might actually vomit, and wouldn't that be embarrassing?

But I finished the season. That's what I did: I finished. So, standing on the block where Sam was last seen, I retraced my steps, looking more closely at doorbells now.

I almost missed it, as focused as I was on the high points. But it wasn't a camera that drew my attention; it was a pumpkin. Pushed as it was to the side of the porch, I hadn't seen it on my first pass. Soft spots had started to form on the squat squash, its color begin-ning to fade. The jack-o'-lantern, though, was expertly carved. Its eyes drooped, forlorn, its eyebrows arched slits of dismay, its mouth down-turned. Out of that mouth, between carefully carved fangs, spilled a generous mound of stringy and seed-specked pumpkin guts.

*As if it were throwing up.*

This was exactly the kind of pumpkin Audrey had mentioned earlier, and it sat on the brick steps of the two-story home two doors down from the haunted house where I had found her.

Free newspapers were scattered on the doorstep next to the pumpkin, a few more on the front lawn. A side window was cracked, covered with cardboard.

Even though I expected no answer, I knocked.

"You selling something, or looking for the Gardners?" I turned toward the voice, which belonged to an older woman in leopard-print glasses, a floral blouse, and periwinkle slacks. "Because if you're looking for the Gardners, they moved out the middle of this month."

But if the house had been vacant for a couple of weeks, the porch light shouldn't have been on the night before. And if the light hadn't been on, how had Audrey seen this pumpkin? I myself had nearly missed it in daylight.

The woman in the periwinkle slacks, hair just a shade lighter, took my pause as a sign I wanted to know more. "Stan, he's the husband, used to manage a car lot. Lost his job a few months back. The wife, Christina, she's an adjunct professor, but they couldn't support a family of five on that. Not in Sonoma County. They moved to Ohio." She held out her hand and I shook it. "I'm Helen, by the way."

"Pleased to meet you. I'm Cassie." I pulled out my phone and displayed a photo of Sam. "Have you seen this man? Maybe last night?"

The older woman adjusted her glasses and leaned in. "Is that your husband?"

When I nodded, Helen smiled. "He's a handsome young man. I've always been a sucker for dimples. My Bob had dimples."

"Do you remember seeing him?"

"Of course. Mainly because of the little girl. She sparkled and was so polite. Some of them don't say thank you, but she did."

My heart skipped. "You saw Audrey?"

"The little girl? She was adorable and the only cat wearing a crown I saw last night."

"What time was that?"

"I ran out of candy around eight, and they were one of the last. A quarter till?" She thought about it a second, then nodded. "Yes, that sounds about right."

That was shortly after Sam had called me. Thirty-one minutes, to be precise. Sam had promised to be home in thirty. "Was there anyone with them?"

The woman tilted her head, curiosity edging toward suspicion. "Are you two having trouble, is that what this is about? Because I don't really like to get involved."

I imagined the Gardners would disagree.

"My husband's missing." Saying it aloud, for the second time in an hour, made the stone I carried in my stomach heavier. I tried a slight smile to soften the words, but I feared it came across as rotten as the pumpkin on the stoop.

"And you think he might have gone off with someone? A woman?"

"He might have."

She considered this, running her fingers through her periwinkle hair. "I thought my Bob was cheating once, after we first got married. I found a box of condoms. Doused them with that ink that only shows up under UV light."

I couldn't help myself. "What happened?"

"The first time I noticed a few missing, I waited until he was asleep and got out my special light. Checked his hands. Checked everything. He was clean. Turns out the condoms belonged to a friend, and Bob was keeping them for this guy so his wife didn't find them. I gave the wife the box and the light."

So much for Helen's policy about not getting involved. Or maybe that was how that policy had started. I couldn't imagine the gift was well received.

"As to your question, it was just him and the girl."

"If you don't mind me asking, which house is yours?"

"The yellow ranch." Helen pointed to a house across from where we stood.

I handed the older woman one of my cards. "If you hear anything . . ."

Helen took the card and slipped it in the pocket of her slacks. "You're sure you don't know the Gardners?"

When I shook my head, the older woman continued, "The two younger Gardner kids aren't in school yet, but the oldest is in eighth grade. Poor kid. Must feel like his life has been turned upside down."

I pulled my hands up into the sleeves of my sweatshirt, suddenly cold again. What would my own children do if their father never came home? "That would be terrible," I agreed.

"But Ohio's nice. I have a cousin who lives there," the older woman said. She studied my face and then winked. "I hope you find your husband."

She patted me on the arm and walked away.

# 14

———

I had been so fixated on the neighborhood where Sam had disappeared, at first, I overlooked my own. Then I drove past Gino Baldovino's house.

Though he had been married three times, Mr. Baldovino currently lived alone. It was always the wife who left. I had learned this when, shortly after we had moved in, Mr. Baldovino had crossed the street to tell me I was overwatering my strawflowers.

Mr. Baldovino had talked to us only once since, the previous autumn when a rake had disappeared from his front yard on the same day Leo had a couple of friends over. I could not convince my neighbor the boys weren't involved—rakes, as I had pointed out, weren't high on the wish list of most teens—and he had left muttering in Italian.

The next day, Mr. Baldovino had installed a surveillance camera. Every day since, it had been pointed at our house.

My breath quickened in concert with my step as I crossed the street to the Baldovino home. My knock was only slightly louder than my heartbeat.

When Mr. Baldovino didn't answer, I rang the doorbell. The curtains parted, then fell back together again.

Five minutes passed, but I continued standing, resolute, on his porch. I knocked again and, when that didn't stir him, I rang the doorbell.

Between the knocking and the ringing, I had gotten a nice rhythm going when the door finally opened. The crack offered a glimpse of only one eye and half a nose.

"What do you want?" he snapped.

Small talk would be wasted on my neighbor, so I opted for brevity: "Your surveillance from last night and early this morning. Please."

The single eye narrowed. I guessed he was torn between his natural urge to shut the door and his desire to learn more about a possible crime in his neighborhood. Curiosity won out over ill manners. "Why?"

Reluctant to share my story with him, I sought a lie. "A hanging planter on my side gate went missing."

"I don't remember a planter."

I cursed that I hadn't thought to say Audrey's bike or Leo's cleats. He wouldn't have cared about those items. Actually, I had doubts he would care if the kids themselves went missing.

"I just hung it last night," I said.

"Were your sons' friends visiting?"

I sighed, refocusing my patience. "No."

"What was in the planter?" he asked, his eye still a slit in his face.

"I don't know. Some tiny yellow flowers."

He snorted at this. "'Tiny yellow flowers.' Because that narrows it down."

But my ignorance convinced him, and he opened the door wide enough so I could see both eyes. "Go buy another one."

"The flowers were new, but the planter was my mother's," I lied. Again. I had nothing of my mother's.

Mr. Baldovino considered this. "They're *my* DVDs."

*Why else would I be here?* I thought. "I can pay you."

His frown deepened. "I don't need your money. You can return that rake your son stole."

How had this man attracted three wives?

"My son didn't steal your rake, Mr. Baldovino, but I can certainly buy you a new one."

"You wouldn't get the right kind."

I choked back another sigh. "Is there anything you want, Mr. Baldovino? I can run some errands for you."

He didn't have a car and was in his eighties, but he immediately puffed up his chest at the offer. "What? You think I'm some kind of invalid?"

"Of course not. How about some clippings from our garden?"

This interested him. "I want a tree," he said. "The Japanese maple."

"Of course."

I expected him to leave so he could retrieve the recording. Instead, he closed the door without a word and, a few minutes later, still hadn't returned.

I started knocking again.

"What?" he bellowed through the door.

"Can I get the DVD?"

"I'll bring it to you after my nap."

I considered pushing Mr. Baldovino on this but thought any disagreements might result in further demands of trees.

I hadn't wanted to return home but, forced to wait for the recording, I now had no choice. Still, I stood rooted to Mr. Baldovino's walkway like the Japanese maple soon to be ripped from my front yard.


NONE OF THE LATE morning light penetrated the room-darkening curtains in our living room. The curtains had been installed shortly after Audrey was born, at the same time we had purchased the sleeper sofa. Audrey had been colicky and slept in spurts, so I had lived in this room for the first eight weeks of her life.

Standing in the dark, with no distractions, I remembered that time with new clarity. I had felt overwhelmed and utterly alone. It had gotten worse when Audrey was diagnosed. That's when I had started pulling away. At the time, I had believed Sam was having an affair.

The suspicion had been fleeting, banished the night Sam had taken to sleeping in the living room beside me, but now I wondered if I dismissed my suspicions too quickly. Had he been cheating as far back as then?

I didn't embrace the theory, but neither did I turn away from it. Since finding Audrey alone the night before, I had been seesawing between faith and mistrust, each piece of evidence viewed as either proof Sam had left voluntarily or a contradiction to what I knew to be true.

If I doubted Sam so easily, did it matter which was right?

Our home didn't have a dedicated office, so we had created a work space on one side of the dining room. Years earlier, Sam had found an old desk dumped curbside, then had spent a weekend scraping, sanding, sealing, and painting it a deep green. The family computer was positioned at its center, clutter shoving against it. On the right, Leo's history book, piles of notebook paper, and a glass half-full of water. On the left, Audrey's artwork and bottles of glitter glue. And, perched on a shelf above the chaos, the picture: the one of Sam and the kids at Sugarloaf Ridge State Park, taken when Leo was still small enough to tuck beneath his father's chin. As usual, I wasn't in the photo.

I settled in the chair and signed on to our bank's website, scanning the transactions for the past month. There were debits for groceries, gas, utilities, and restaurants, mostly the kind where meals were served in a bag. We had smogged and registered my van that month. There were several other online charges I didn't recognize, but when I cross-referenced those, the items were expected: a new phone case and sneakers for Leo, a couple of books for Audrey.

I went back another month, and still saw nothing suspicious. There were no large cash withdrawals, nor a series of small ones. Over the past two months, only three hundred and twenty dollars had been taken out of the ATM. As far as I could tell, no flowers, romantic dinners, or lingerie had been purchased. But if Sam was having an affair, he was certainly smart enough to pay cash.

I found only one surprise, but it wasn't any of the charges. It was the absence of one. After combing through two months of transactions, I could find no mortgage payment listed.

I navigated to the mortgagor's website. There, the transactions confirmed what I already suspected: the house payment was forty-five days late.

I tried to think of a reason for such an oversight, because that was what it had to be: an oversight. Sam had been distracted lately. We both had been. If we had fallen behind on our bills, Sam would have told me. He wouldn't have risked the roof over our children's heads. We didn't have secrets like that.

I caught myself: there was that lie I'd been telling myself. Of course we had secrets. I just hadn't thought they were important ones. The week before, I had told Sam I was coming right home but instead spent an hour browsing the bookstore. Last month when I bought Leo the sneakers, to avoid an argument, I had lied that they were on sale. Better that Sam find out when he balanced the checkbook than at the end of a long workday.

*I love you, but you spend too much money on the kids.*

Until Sam had disappeared, I thought those were the kinds of secrets we had. Covert errands and overpriced sneakers. But maybe that was how it started. Small secrets become larger ones until your husband goes missing and you discover your house payment is past due.

What else didn't I know about my husband?

I returned to the list of banking transactions and switched my focus to the credits. Using the calculator on my phone, I added up Sam's paychecks for the past two months. I didn't know what he made down to the dollar, but the total was lower than I expected. I went back six months and compared those totals to the current ones. The current deposits were significantly lower. Two weeks before, there had been no deposit at all.

I struggled to decipher what it all meant. Had Sam been getting cash back from his paychecks, squirreling it away until he could escape? Had he gotten a cut in pay he hadn't told me about? He certainly hadn't told me about the missed house payment, so what else could he be hiding?

Fury surged, bitter and sharp. *What the hell, Sam?*

I swept the framed picture of Sam and the kids from the shelf so that it fell facedown on the desk, that stupid desk, painted that shade of green because Sam said it matched my eyes. I expected the glass to shatter, but it remained intact, which felt like a betrayal. I yanked open a drawer and lobbed the photo inside. This time, the glass spiderwebbed.

Perversely satisfied, I slammed the drawer. Then I opened it and slammed it again, harder. The second impact loosened the brushed-nickel knob, so that it bobbled when I slammed the drawer a third time.

*Where are you, Sam? Why aren't you here?*

Angry tears threatened, but I gritted my teeth against them. It wasn't just Sam. It was all of it. The attack on the trail. My patient's near-fatal poisoning. Finding Audrey with women I didn't know. My father. Myself.

Then there was Carver Sweet, a man who had killed his wife and knew where we lived.

I waited until my hands stopped shaking before turning my attention back to the computer. My fingers awkward on the keyboard now, it took a couple of tries to correctly type Sam's password. He used the same password for all of his social media accounts, for everything really, so it was easy enough to check all the sites he frequented. Or at least the ones I knew about. Then I pulled his laptop from the messenger bag he kept stashed beneath the desk and checked that. I found no surprises. Sam had always been concerned about setting a good example for his students, and he was careful about what he posted.

With Sam gone less than a day, I felt like a voyeur. A stalker. I considered posting a plea for information on my own social media accounts. *Have you seen my husband?* But such a plea felt premature.

Should I call Sam's out-of-state relatives? The media? Should I hire a private investigator?

Every option I considered seemed more pointless than the last, primarily because I avoided the more difficult ones.

Sam could be in jail.

He could be in the hospital.

He could be . . .

I shook that last thought off and navigated to a database of local inmates. When that got no hits, I called hospitals, again. Finally, reluctantly, I called the coroner. Waited five minutes while records were checked. But they had not accepted the bodies of any unidentified males.

I moved on to our family's mobile phone records. I clicked on Sam's number, looking first at his calls, then his texts. I scrutinized most carefully the calls that were made when I wasn't home.

I inhaled sharply. Two numbers stood out: One I recognized, one I didn't.

The number I knew stood out because of the timing. Sam had texted only two numbers since his disappearance: mine and, apparently, Ozzy's. Sam's friend had lied to me.

The second number, the one I didn't recognize, appeared three times on the day of Sam's disappearance. None of the calls lasted longer than five minutes. One of those came in the morning before, when Sam had excused himself to take that call. Another came only minutes before we spoke that final time.

Someone knocked, loudly, and I tensed. On the doorstep stood Mr. Baldovino, a shovel in one hand and a DVD tucked under his arm. He pulled it out and thrust it at me. "Here," he said.

When he saw me noticing the shovel, he added, "It's best to dig it out now since it's dormant."

It took me a second to realize he was talking about the Japanese maple I had promised him. I killed any plant I touched, but Sam loved to garden. Out of habit, I almost offered Sam's help. Then I remembered. I leaned in to the door frame for support.

"Thank you," I said as I took the DVD.

He grunted. "I don't like being lied to," he said. I was about to ask what he meant when he added, "There's no hanging basket."

*Of course he had watched it.*

"So," he asked, motioning to the DVD. "Who's the man taking your husband's car?"


WHEN I CLOSED THE DOOR, Mr. Baldovino still stood there, but I didn't have the energy to answer his question. Alone again, the need for pretense gone, I slipped to the floor before my buckling knees could give way. Sunlight puddled in front of me, but I sat in shadow, the DVD in my hand. I felt as if I had been hollowed then refilled with an oily, sour blackness.

It had been easier to believe in an affair, and that Sam had left voluntarily, and I realized now that was why I hadn't entirely discounted that theory. Rather, I had clung to it, the idea a raft in a vast and merciless ocean.

I stared at the DVD I held and told myself Mr. Baldovino was elderly, his perpetual squint proof of failing eyesight he was too proud to admit. Surveillance footage could be grainy, or so I had heard. I had never had the need to review any myself. The man my neighbor thought was someone else could indeed be Sam, caught at an angle that made him appear taller or shorter, thicker or thinner, or in some other way unfamiliar.

Even as I placated myself with this, I knew I couldn't afford to. I needed to let go of the raft and see where this ocean carried me, even if I doubted my capacity to survive it.

The DVD clutched in one white-knuckled hand, I crossed the room to the DVD player. I brushed off the layer of dust—other than home movies, we never used the machine anymore—and slid in the DVD. I sat cross-legged in front of the TV, less than two feet from the screen, the remote cradled in my lap. The player started automatically.

The footage was sharper than I had imagined it would be. Dread carved out a space between my shoulders. The picture was crisp enough that the slim hope I had harbored that Mr. Baldovino hadn't recognized Sam, even from across the street, disintegrated instantly.

I fast-forwarded the footage to the moments before I had returned home from the clinic. I told myself there might exist a clue visible as Sam and Audrey left the house—perhaps he was carrying a bag, or the mystery woman followed. But in truth, I just needed to see him again.

When I did, my heart broke. The way he moved—hoisting Audrey over his shoulder, his long legs skipping a step on the front porch, placing our daughter on the sidewalk with an exaggerated twirl—was distinctly Sam. Lean, athletic, relaxed. Even now, under these circumstances, my heart raced for reasons other than worry.

I imagined I could hear Audrey giggling and see Sam's smirk. But I couldn't. They were shapes and shadows and light and life, and then they were gone.

I skipped backward on the DVD and watched it again. By the third viewing, the pair blurred, fusing into a single entity joined by my unshed tears.

I focused on my breathing as I fast-forwarded past my own arrival home, then my hurried departure later. I had been frantic, but also oblivious, my world still intact.

The images on the DVD continued to buzz by. As I saw myself pull away from the house on the screen, I slowed the playback and leaned in, my eyes intent on the blue Toyota Camry parked on the left side of our driveway.

It happened at 12:36 a.m. The shape popped out of the right side of the TV screen—if another vehicle had transported the interloper, it happened off screen—and moved toward the car. Less than five minutes earlier, I had focused on regulating my breathing, but now it seemed a complicated puzzle to get my lungs to process oxygen at all.

Mr. Baldovino was right. The man on the screen was not Sam. But my suspicions that a stranger could have taken the car were unfounded. Although I had only met him once, the man on the screen was instantly recognizable: huge, still wearing the same clothes he had been the night before, the attacker from the trail slipped into Sam's car and drove away.

The thief hadn't needed to break a window or force the lock. All he'd had to do was pull Sam's keys from his pants pocket.

# 15

I made a copy of the DVD and put it in my desk drawer. I slipped the original in my purse.

I also printed a still from the recording of the man who had taken Sam's car. The man I believed to be Carver Sweet. The clearest image was a profile, and robbed of his movement, he could have been anyone—if not for the stubbled chin, dark except where the scar would've been.

I folded the paper into a tidy square and slipped it into my purse next to the DVD.

At the police station, the same thin, sharp-nosed officer was stationed at the desk. I asked for Detective Ray Rico.

Like the night we had met, Rico wore a crisp white shirt, but this time instead of bacon, his tie was embellished with tiny hot dogs.

"Back to cured meats, I see." I handed Rico the DVD.

"This is the closest I get to them these days. Watching my sodium." He looked down at the DVD. "What's this?"

"You heard about Sam?"

"I got a copy of the report."

"Hear anything yet?"

"It's only been a few hours." Though true, I caught the hint of frustration in his voice. Even I knew how crucial these early hours were. "You okay?"

The question surprised me, and it required a longer answer than I had time to give. "That's footage from a neighbor's camera. I'm pretty sure Carver Sweet took my husband's car."

Rico motioned toward the back of the station, where I guessed his office was, but I shook my head. "I have somewhere to be, but I wanted you to have that."

Rico's eyes remained sharp, but they were less forbidding than they had been in that first interview. "You didn't answer my question."

*What question?* My mind stumbled back across our brief conversation, and I fell to it the second he asked again, "You okay?"

I wanted to trust Rico, but I knew the first person the police looked at when a husband went missing was the wife. The air in the station was dry and too warm.

"Only thing that will make me okay is finding Sam and Carver Sweet being arrested."

"We'll find them both, Dr. Larkin," he said. "Torres mentioned you found a wrapper folded into the shape of a dog. The number two written inside."

"A friend thought it might be an S."

"Looked like a two to me." A simple statement, but I could again breathe fully. It was if I had been carrying a heavy piece of furniture, up a staircase, and Rico had suddenly taken hold of one end.

"That night on the trail, you asked if the number three meant anything to me. Did you find something like that?"

Rico stroked his tie, as if his hot dog craving could be satisfied that way. "Not origami, no." The detective stared in that way he had, his eyes scraping my skin. If I'd had secrets, I would've confessed them all. "It was a rock. Painted with the number three."

"Painted?"

"Acrylic, we think. White paint, gray rock. It's being analyzed."

"Where'd you find it?"

"In Carver's car."

I bit my tongue with enough force to draw blood.

*Carver.*

Though irrational, I imagined him here, watching us. Taking pleasure from my frustration. But perhaps he was no longer in Santa Rosa, instead in a moldering basement hundreds of miles away, inflicting horrors on my captive husband.

Unless Sam had left voluntarily. I kept coming back to that.

Either way, without Sam, I felt unmoored, adrift, and swept toward long-ago discarded habits. The old me was the kind of girl you'd love to take to a party. She mixed a killer mojito, knew the answer to every trivia question, and had your back if you picked a fight with your ex's new girlfriend, even if you were in the wrong.

But Old Cassie could be a bitch to live with. She was surly and held a grudge, and she didn't always think clearly, especially after too many of those mojitos. I didn't like having Old Cassie in my head again.

"No news on where Carver might be?" I asked.

"Nothing yet, but we're looking."

The silence stretched, and I sensed I'd be getting no more information from Rico. Besides, I needed to get to the grocery store. Just thinking about my next stop stirred my irritation and thus my impatience.

"You'll reach out if you hear anything?" I asked.

Detective Rico gave a curt nod, then smoothed his hot-dog tie. "Of course," he said. I was 25 percent sure I believed him.

TEN MINUTES LATER, I pulled into the grocery store parking lot. Counting to ten wasn't cutting it, so before I got out of the car, I counted to one hundred. Even so, my breath was jagged, my cheeks flushed when I closed my car door.

Inside the store, I approached the customer service desk and a blonde whose tag gave her name as Beth R. I asked for the manager.

Beth R. pushed her glasses up the bridge of her nose with her middle finger then blushed when she realized how the gesture might be interpreted. She overcompensated with a smile that strained her cheeks. "Is there something I can help you with?"

"Not unless my husband is texting you too."

The smile slipped into a frown, and her eyebrows shot together. "I'm sorry?"

"The manager, please." As an afterthought, I forced a smile of my own. She scurried away as if I'd kicked her.

Beth R. returned a moment later with the store manager, whose attempt at a grin faltered when he saw me. Apparently, all three of us were terrible at faking it.

"Hey, Ozzy," I said, my voice full of false cheer. "I figured you'd be working today."

Ozzy reached for my elbow, likely intending to steer me to a more private spot, but dropped his hand before he made contact.

He looked uncomfortable in his button-up shirt and tie, his usual curls restrained by hair gel. One lock had exerted its independence, corkscrewing onto his left cheek.

"It's . . . uh . . . great to see you again, Cassie." His Austin drawl betrayed his nerves.

"I don't think you mean that, but that's fine. Right now, I'm not really glad to see you either."

Beth R. had returned to her spot behind the customer service desk a few feet away. She pretended to straighten something below the counter even as she leaned in to better hear our conversation.

Ozzy noticed and gestured toward an office behind the counter. "Do you want to talk somewhere quiet?"

"Oh, I'm good. So, I was going over Sam's phone records, and I noticed you guys have been texting."

"Come on, Cassie." His drawl grew more pronounced as he glanced again toward the office.

"Which is weird, because when I came over last night, you said you hadn't heard from him. That was before you said if you did hear from him, you'd let me know."

Beth R. dropped the pretense, staring openly now. Another worker who had been passing stopped in his tracks, listening too.

Ozzy brushed aside an errant curl, his dark eyes pleading. I sighed and headed toward the office.

He closed the door behind us. "Thanks for that. The employees sometimes—"

I cut him off. "Why did you lie to me?"

"Sam's my friend, Cassie."

"I'm your friend."

"You know it's not the same."

"You didn't have to tell me everything, but you should have told me something. If not for me, then for the kids."

He stuffed his hands in his pockets and looked away.

"After we spoke, Sam texted me too." I held out my phone, the same way I had with Officer Torres. "But here's the thing—I don't think it was Sam. And if it wasn't, then Sam probably wasn't the person texting you either."

"You can't be sure."

"True." I took the picture of Carver Sweet from my purse and placed it faceup on his desk. "But there's this. Two nights ago, I witnessed this man assaulting a woman. Last night, while I was on your doorstep, the same man took Sam's car from our driveway. He had Sam's keys. Why wouldn't he have his phone too?"

Ozzy still couldn't meet my eyes. "Sam texted you he wasn't alone. Maybe he knows this guy. Besides, it's not a very good picture."

"Look, Ozzy, I don't care if Sam's having an affair." My voice was tight. Of course I cared if my husband was sleeping with someone else. It just wasn't my main concern at that moment. "I need to know that my husband, the father of my children, isn't lying unidentified in a ditch on some rural road."

Ozzy sank into a chair behind the small, laminate-topped desk. When he spoke, his accent was thick. "He's having an affair."

My chest hitched, but I forced myself to say: "Tell me."

"I don't think—"

"Tell me."

He pulled a water bottle from one of the drawers and took a long drink, probably wishing it were a beer. If it had been, I might have asked for a drink myself.

"When did it start?"

Ozzy shifted in his seat and took another swallow before responding. When he did, he avoided eye contact, staring instead at the bottle he cupped in his hands. Curls fell in his face, a curtain to hide behind.

"I'm not sure."

"A month? Longer?"

He shrugged as he picked at the bottle's label, flicking the pasty flakes that stuck to his fingertips. "I don't know."

"What did he say in the texts?"

"Nothing much." He twirled the bottle so the water sloshed in circles.

"Has he ever mentioned that he planned to leave?"

When Ozzy didn't answer, heat flared in my cheeks, and I couldn't stop my hand from snaking out and grabbing the bottle. I threw it across the room. What water remained splashed on the wall against which it landed.

Ozzy jerked in the chair, and he stared. "Sam didn't tell me he was cheating on you, not right away," he said. He loosened his tie and unbuttoned his shirt at the neck. "I went to the high school about a month ago to see if Sam wanted to grab coffee during his free period, and I saw them walking together. He told me she was a parent of one of his kids, and of course, I believed him. I mean, come on, this is Sam, right? He's always been crazy about you. And as crazy as he is about you, he's doubly that for those kids. He's the kind of guy who shows the rest of us that marriage doesn't have to suck."

"Not sucking. That's always been our goal."

Ozzy took a second water bottle from the drawer. He took a drink and grinned at me as he replaced the cap. He tilted his head toward where the first now empty bottle rested on the floor. "Didn't know you have a temper."

He hadn't known me back then. "No one's threatened my family before."

"Right." He pushed the bottle to the side and folded his hands in his lap. No distractions. "I saw her again last week in his car."

"What were they doing?"

"Nothing like that. It just looked . . . suspicious. Then when he was at my house a few days ago, he left the room to take a call. He's my friend, I'm not going to judge, but like you said, you two have kids together. I didn't want to see him throwing everything away, you know?

So I called him on it. He denied it, told me he was trying to help a student of his. Hannah."

Ozzy looked embarrassed. "I believed him. But then he texted me later that day and admitted everything."

"What did he say?"

"He asked me not to say anything to you, said you guys were just working through some crap."

"When was that?"

"A week ago."

Before I met Carver Sweet. Before he had access to Sam's phone.

"It was just those texts? You never again spoke about the affair in person?"

He smiled. I recognized the expression. It was the same one I had seen on Torres's face earlier and on Ozzy's the night before. Pity.

"We spoke briefly. I told him whatever was going on with Hannah's mom needed to stop. He said, 'It's already gone too far.' That was it. I didn't push. He knew he'd screwed up."

"What's her name?" When Ozzy shook his head, I asked, "You don't know, or you won't tell me?"

"I don't know."

"Then what did she look like?"

"She had brown hair, or dark blond. She was short. Then again, Sam's tall. Most women look small next to him." He hesitated, trying to think of more details but failing. "That's all I really noticed. Sorry. But I think they met at a coffee shop downtown."

*A coffee shop downtown. Yeah, that narrowed the options.*

"Last night, what did Sam say in his texts?"

Ozzy looked down at his desk and scratched at his scalp.

"He said he was sorry."

My chest tightened. "For what?"

"For putting me in the middle, I guess."

When the silence stretched, I prodded, "What else?"

"I don't know. He didn't say much."

"Important things don't always take long to say." Like *I love you.* Or *goodbye.*

"Sam told me not to worry and that if I talked to you, I should tell you the same."

His eyes caught mine for an instant before he dropped them again. "I was going to tell you, but . . . I didn't know how to mention the part about Sam being okay without telling you the rest of it. Honestly, I thought he'd be back by now." Ozzy looked up, his expression suddenly hopeful. "It's been less than a day. He'll be back."

I pointed at the picture of the man taking Sam's car. "If he's just taking time to work through his issues, how do you explain this?"

As Ozzy realized he had no explanation, the optimism drained from his face. My expression remained unchanged. I had started to lose hope the moment I had first seen Carver Sweet on the TV screen.

# 16

There were no recent charges for coffee shops in our bank records—
either Hannah's mom had paid, or Sam paid cash—so finding the right
one became a game of how well I knew my husband. A few days ago, I
would've been confident I could meet the challenge. Now, not so much.

The muscles in my right hand twitched, as they had before I had
thrown that water bottle across Ozzy's office. The question nagged:
*How well did I know my husband?* After talking to his best friend, it
seemed more likely the reason for Sam's absence was an affair. My
skin felt hot, bruised.

Picturing Sam with another woman, *touching* another woman, I
staggered on a memory: me as a teenager, punching a girl in the nose.
Breaking it. Because she ridiculed me for not having a mother.

Another time, a boy, a knee to the groin. I hadn't wanted him to
touch me.

*You need to stop,* my father had told me.

*I can't stop,* I'd said, even as I had realized how badly I wanted to. So
Red had paid for kickboxing lessons. With the pads, I could hit harder,
and my opponent didn't get hurt. It became my therapy.

I wished I had kept up the sport, because I very much wanted to
kick someone.

The closest coffee shop was a drive-thru with a walk-up window.
Because it was across the street from the school, it was popular with
students. Sam wouldn't have gone there. Not enough privacy.

Throw an empty coffee cup in any direction and you could hit a Starbucks. But Sam would've preferred something local.

The four spots most likely, then, were all either a long walk or a short drive away. The gourmet place that also served beer was probably out. Great reviews, but not Sam's style. So that narrowed it to three places. Unless I also counted diners that served coffee. I rubbed my temples.

I started with the one across from the bookstore. No one recognized Sam.

I got lucky at my second stop. A blue-aproned barista with a plug that stretched his earlobe nodded when I showed him Sam's photo.

"That's that teacher dude," he said. "Nice guy. Always tips. Orders medium roast, sometimes tea. Both black."

The shop smelled of coffee and cinnamon rolls, and my stomach grumbled. I hadn't eaten since—I strained to remember. Then it came to me: the spaghetti Sam and Audrey had made together the night before. Not hungry but knowing I should eat, I grabbed a banana from a basket on the counter and a wrapped pesto-mozzarella sandwich from the rack.

As I paid, I glanced at the young man's name tag. Josh. "When's the last time you saw him?" I asked.

"He used to come in most days, first thing, but I haven't seen him for a couple of weeks," Josh said. "But I've been starting later, so he could be coming in before my shift."

I asked Josh what time he usually started, and he said he didn't come in until noon. But, he added, the manager, Linda, worked most mornings.

When I asked to speak with Linda, the young barista tugged on his apron. "She had to run out—sick kid—but she'll be back later."

*Damn.*

I gave Josh my contact information, then asked the question I'd purposely saved for last. "Did Sam ever meet anyone here?"

The chatty barista's eyes went flat. "He usually came in alone."

I had a teenage son. I was pretty good at recognizing the lies of young men. It was the older ones I apparently couldn't read.

"So who'd he meet when he did have company?"

Josh gnawed on his lip. "I said he was alone."

"You said *usually*. Which implies sometimes he wasn't."

The barista realized his slip. His knuckles went white as he clenched the straps of his apron. "He came in by himself," the young man insisted.

Though I was sympathetic to Josh's situation, that didn't mean I wouldn't push. "I get it. I wouldn't want to tell a wife that her husband routinely had coffee with another woman either. But I already know Sam met someone here. Hannah's mom?"

"I don't know her name." The young barista's cheeks reddened. Another slip. I felt sorry for him. He actually squirmed. I'd seen Leo do the same when I asked about homework he hadn't completed.

"What did she look like?"

Josh fiddled with his earring. "I don't remember."

"Blonde? Brunette? Redhead?"

He looked to his right, hoping for customers, but the place was empty. He tried the excuse anyway. "I can't really talk. I've kinda got a lot to do."

When I lifted an eyebrow at that, he added, "I've gotta prep stuff. Wipe off the counters. Refill the creamer. Take out the trash."

His face lit up at that last task. He called over a coworker, a short woman with a crew cut, and asked if she could watch the counter.

"Why?" she asked.

"So I can take out the trash."

"Already did," she said before returning to her own "prep" work, which evidently involved heavy use of her cell phone.

"Seems like you have a minute after all, Josh."

The young barista's chest deflated. Finally, he said, "She wasn't a redhead. Brunette maybe?"

I was going to ask about the woman's height, but before I could, Josh added, "They always sat on the patio, so they're probably on video."

My heart sped up. He hadn't thought to lead with this? "You have video?"

Josh nodded. "The owner put in cameras a few months back, after someone spray painted a penis on the window."

The door opened, letting in a gust of wind and an older couple. Josh stood straighter and smiled. "I'm not sure if we can let you see it, but I'll check with my manager as soon as she gets back," he said.

He started to walk away, but on impulse, I reached out. "What do you get paid a week?"

He raised an eyebrow. "I don't know. A couple hundred. Why?"

"You convince your manager to send me that video, and I'll return with a week's pay."

For the first time since I'd started talking with him, Josh looked happy that I'd come in. He grinned. "Probably should've said five hundred, huh?"

Then he tightened the strings on his apron and hurried away to take the couple's order.

# 17

---

Time seemed to pull the sun through the sky at an alarming speed. When I checked my phone, it was already time to pick up Audrey.

Waiting alongside the curb, I had three minutes to inhale half of the sandwich before Audrey climbed into the car. I offered her the banana and the rest of the sandwich. She stuffed a third of the banana in her mouth. Though a tiny thing, my daughter had the appetite and eating habits of a piranha.

"Slow down, Peanut."

Around a mouthful of banana, Audrey mumbled, "What's a peed-o-pill?"

I used a familiar trick. "Can you use it in a sentence?"

"Your dad is a peed-o-pill. P-E-D-O-P-H-I-L-E."

My shoulders tensed. She must have really studied the word to spell it so perfectly. "Did someone say that to you?"

The bleat of a horn intruded, and I pulled into the heavy after-school traffic.

"I know I'm not supposed to talk to strangers." She sounded offended.

"Then why do you ask that?"

"'Cause of the note."

When I pulled to the side of the road abruptly, the car behind me honked again. I blamed exhaustion and stress for what I did next. As the driver passed, my middle finger shot up in salute.

I immediately chastised myself: *That's the old me. Pre-Sam, pre-kids.*

In the past thirty-six hours, I'd been spending more time than usual with the old me.

The motorist looked only slightly less shocked than Audrey, my daughter's eyes wide, food-filled mouth agape.

"Don't ever do what I just did," I said. "Where's the note?"

"Mommy," Audrey gasped, still reacting to my transgression. "That's like a bad word with your finger."

She wasn't so shocked that it affected her appetite. She finished off the banana and started on the sandwich.

"You mentioned a note?" I prodded again.

"The note the man left in my backpack," she said between bites of sandwich.

"What man?"

"A man with a funny-looking shirt. It had a bear on it, but the bear was smoking something. Bears can't smoke. Plus smoking causes cancer." Audrey smiled, bread crumbs at the corners of her mouth, proud that she had remembered something her dad sometimes told her. "Nana Beatrice died of cancer before I was born."

"Yes, she did." I tried to keep my voice calm. "Did this man say anything to you?"

Audrey shook her head. "I don't think he wanted me to see him, because he left the note when my backpack was still in the cubby. But I saw him because it was my day to water the plant."

I grabbed my daughter's backpack and reached inside, where I found a crinkled Post-it that read: *Your dad is a pedophile.*

"I showed Ms. Dickerson the note, but I don't think she knew what the word meant. She had a funny look on her face when she read it, though, kind of like that driver just now when you pointed your finger in the bad way."

I expected I would be getting a call from Audrey's teacher.

"Ms. Dickerson tried to keep it, but I wanted to show it to you so I took it back. That's why it's wrinkled."

Sandwich finished, Audrey fished a gummy worm from her pocket, picked off the lint, and popped it into her mouth. "So then I asked

Bonnie, she's in third grade, and she said it means someone who likes little kids."

So I could probably expect a call from Bonnie's parents too.

She reached for another gummy worm, but I stopped her. "Watch the sugar, remember. Anything else?"

"Well, I thought maybe Bonnie didn't really know, so I asked my friend Jackson—"

I groaned.

"—but then I saw your car, so I decided to just ask you."

*Thank goodness for that.*

"Did you see where the man went?" I scanned the crowd for a man wearing a T-shirt like my daughter had described. When Audrey shook her head, I asked, "Do you remember anything else about him? Like, what color his hair was?"

Audrey's faced scrunched in thought. I hoped I was wrong about what was coming. "I don't think he had any."

My grip on the steering wheel tightened.

"I don't understand what Bonnie meant," Audrey said. "Of course Daddy likes little kids. I'm a little kid, and Leo's not but he used to be, and he loves us."

"Yes, he does." I reached across the console to the back seat to squeeze Audrey's hand. "A pedophile isn't someone like Daddy. It's someone who says they like kids but who hurts them."

"Oh! Like a molester?"

Now it was my turn to look shocked. "Yes, like that."

Audrey nodded in sudden understanding. "Addison said that Kendra's uncle went to prison for being a molester. But I told her to mind her own business because it's not nice to gossip."

"After you asked what it meant?"

Audrey nibbled on the edge of her thumbnail. "I might've maybe asked. Oh, and he gave me an envelope."

"An envelope?"

"I know I'm not supposed to take anything from strangers, but he put it in my backpack, so that's different, right?"

"That's different. You didn't open it?" I had no idea what was in-

side, but I didn't imagine it would be anything I would want Audrey
to see.

"No. Is Daddy home yet?"

I took the envelope from Audrey's backpack and stowed it in the
glove box. For the second time that day, I considered calling my father.
This time, the idea lingered a little longer. I decided the momentary
lapse was because my children were missing their own father. I knew
I had to tell them that Sam was gone, but I wanted to break the news
when they were together. Tonight, after Leo's game. So I told Audrey
the lie I had been practicing, "Your dad has to be away at his conference a little longer than expected."

"Okay," she said, bouncing her legs as she stared out her window.
"Can we get ice cream?"

"I have to drop you at Zoe's so I can run an errand."

"After?"

Because of her transplant, I had always been careful about my daughter's diet, but even after her pocket gummy worm, I found myself unable to deny her this.

"If there's time before Leo's game."

Audrey continued to bounce in her booster seat, humming off-key.
Despite the interaction with the stranger, Audrey's world remained a
place of mint chocolate chip, a night watching a game at the big-kids
school, and both parents at home to love her. I dreaded the evening
ahead, when I would have to break my daughter's heart, and open the
envelope, which might break my own.

AS I CIRCLED THE BLOCK, Audrey recounted her day, lingering over
the details of a lunchtime game of freeze tag and the successful trade of
an orange for a bag of pretzels. By Audrey's telling, the negotiations had
been as intense as any UN peace talk.

I drove around the block for a second time but still saw no sign of
the man in the smoking bear T-shirt.

"Are you lost? Because you're supposed to turn there." Audrey
pointed to the main street that led toward Zoe's house.

"Thanks." I headed in the direction of Audrey's outstretched finger. As I did, I realized there was one possible witness to Sam's disappearance who had received only a passing interrogation: our daughter. In those early hours, I had been fairly certain of Sam's return and worried about upsetting Audrey if I probed too deeply. Such concerns had evaporated in the time since.

I turned down the radio and waited for Audrey to wrap up another story, this one about a half-finished drawing that might turn out to be either a dragon or a dog. Then I asked, "Did you and Daddy have fun trick-or-treating last night?"

"Mm-hmm. But where did Daddy go?"

I hated lying to my children. Even when Audrey had asked the Christmas before if Santa Claus was real, I had answered with a version of the truth—some people believed, some didn't. To which Audrey had replied, with surprising indifference, "I knew he was fake. But unicorns are real." I had been glad she hadn't pressed on that last part.

"Daddy went to a conference, remember?"

From the back seat, Audrey sighed dramatically, as was her habit. "I know that." Her voice was suddenly serious. "I meant where did Daddy go last night?"

Struggling for words that contained some honesty, I pulled in front of Zoe's house and parked. I turned in my seat to face Audrey. "I'm not sure. I thought we could try to figure it out together."

I kept my tone light, as if I were suggesting a game that promised great fun. "I saw that pumpkin you mentioned," I prompted. "It was cool."

"The puking one?" She smiled, but it was soft at its edges. Talking about the night before bothered her. "Do you think it would be hard to make? Daddy's good at art, so I bet he could do it."

Her smile disintegrated, and a hand closed around my heart. "I bet he could. Did he see it too?"

Audrey's small shoulders rose, then fell. "He was talking to the lady."

The hand holding my heart squeezed. "What lady?"

"The one in the house."

I thought of the neighbor, Helen. I described her to Audrey and asked, "That lady?"

Audrey shook her head. "The lady in the house with the broken windows."

I tried to uncoil the tension in my shoulders, forcing my words out slowly to hide my surging anxiety. "Was she on the steps with you guys? Or inside the house?"

"Like I said, in the house."

"Was the porch light on?" Realizing it was starting to sound like an interrogation, not wanting to upset Audrey, I added, "Just tell me what you remember."

"I don't think the light was on. She didn't have candy. The house before gave out regular candy bars, not the small ones. If we're getting ice cream, can I still have my Halloween candy when I get home?"

Because we both knew the answer would be no, I ignored the question. "What else do you remember?"

"I don't know." Audrey started to fidget. "What time are we going to get ice cream?"

I tried to read whether this was the typical impatience of a six-year-old or something else. But too much rested on her answers to stop asking my questions. "Do you remember what the woman looked like?"

At first, though I could tell Audrey remembered, she didn't answer. *Why?*

Then she said, "Her hair was gray."

*Gray? Not what I was expecting.*

"Was the woman's hair short or long?"

"Long. And her face was gray too. Except for the black marks on her forehead. I think it was supposed to look like she was broken."

So she was in costume. A sudden thought chilled me, *If she was even a she.*

"Was the woman big?"

Audrey looked confused, and I realized to her, all adults were big. So I rephrased the question, "Was she as tall as Daddy?"

"I don't think so. Daddy's tall."

"Did she go to the haunted house with you and Daddy?"

Audrey squirmed in her seat, turning away from me and toward the window. "I don't remember. That's when I saw Savannah." She looked at me again. "Did I tell you she was a cat too?"

"Yes, you did. She was brown and didn't have a tiara, I think you said."

"She *was* brown." Audrey began reciting other details about Savannah's costume—her whiskers were apparently drawn on with her mom's eyeliner—before expanding her description to other costumes she had seen the night before.

Suddenly, I was certain: my questions were making Audrey uncomfortable. Did she sense what might have happened even as I tried to hide it from her? Or had she seen something she couldn't quite remember but also couldn't fully forget?

"Did something happen you don't want to tell me?"

"I'm okay."

"You don't seem okay. You seem sad."

*Of course* she was sad.

Audrey's voice was small when she answered, "I don't like that Daddy left me."

My heart broke, and I leaned into the back seat to kiss the top of my daughter's head. "I don't like it either."

My daughter's face filled with the light of sudden clarity. "I know! Why don't we just call Daddy and ask him where he was after I saw Savannah?"

I squeezed her hand, and then told her another truth that nevertheless felt like a lie. "I don't think Daddy's available right now."

"Can we call him later then?"

"We can try."

"It doesn't matter," Audrey said. "Daddy will call us. He always does when he goes away."

I thought, *Not this time.* But I said, "I bet you're right. Daddy loves you very much." The last part, at least, wasn't a lie.

# 18

Parked outside the high school, I opened the glove box and pulled out the envelope—large, tan, and unsealed. I propped it on my lap so it rested against the steering wheel.

Every choice I had made since Sam's disappearance I had immediately doubted.

If I had spent more time questioning those moms, they might have remembered more. They might have offered the phone numbers I'd forgotten to request.

If I had been home instead of confronting Ozzy that first night, I would have been there when Carver took Sam's car. The police could have arrested him then.

Then there were the other choices I had made before Sam went missing. The late nights. The missed connections.

But this latest choice—whether to open the envelope—seemed straightforward. Of course I should open it. Knowledge was always better than ignorance. Wasn't it?

I tossed the envelope on the passenger seat, took out my phone, and dialed. My father answered on the first ring.

"Cassie?" The excitement in his voice chipped at my heart a little.

"Hi, Red." It had been a long time since I had called him Dad.

"How've you been, sweetheart?"

How to summarize six years of life in less than thirty seconds? "The clinic's doing well, and the kids are pretty amazing."

"They would be." Neither of us pointed out how long it had been since our last conversation. We both knew how long it had been, and we both remembered how that last call had ended. "Leo must be huge by now. And Audrey—she's okay?"

"She's okay," I confirmed. "Leo just got his permit."

He chuckled, a familiar rumbling. "Teaching you to drive . . . scariest months of my life."

My father wasn't exaggerating. In my teens, I had been a reckless driver. Back then, I had been reckless in most things.

"I got better once I had kids."

He sighed at that. "I'm sure you're a great mom."

"There's nothing I wouldn't do for them."

It wasn't meant as a judgment, but an uncomfortable silence followed. Then: "I should've been tested." It was the closest my father had ever come to an apology. "But you know how I hate needles." Apology ruined.

Audrey had been born without bile ducts in her liver, a condition known as biliary atresia. Not that we knew anything was wrong for the first few weeks. She had seemed to have that singular attribute every parent wishes for a child: perfect health. All toes and fingers had been accounted for, and even the flakes of cradle cap disappeared quickly, leaving behind pink skin and, except for the occasional robust demand for a bottle, a sunny personality.

Then her pink skin had started to yellow, and she had gotten crankier. At the doctor's appointment, I had known what I would hear: our daughter needed a transplant. Audrey now carried a piece of Sam's liver inside her.

"There was no need," I said. "Sam was a match, and Audrey's fine."

"Still, I should've been there for you, and for my granddaughter." Since he had never met Audrey, it was strange hearing him call her that. Not bad strange. Just strange. "Is everything okay, Cassie?"

I stared at the envelope. "I've had better weeks."

"Is there anything I can do?"

When Audrey had been a newborn, my father had asked this same question. When I had said yes, there was, he had changed his mind about the offer. After all these years, I should have been able to forgive him, but I had never been much good at that. Anger was easier and felt less like weakness. A throwback to my brawling days, I guessed.

When I didn't respond, he asked, "What's wrong?"

In the quiet car, speaking to a man who had become almost a stranger to me, it was safe to say the words aloud. "I think Sam's left me."

"I'll get a flight."

"It's okay."

"I can be there tonight, tomorrow at the latest."

"No," I said, more firmly this time.

"Why'd you call, sweetheart?"

"I told you. Sam's gone."

His voice was gentle as he prodded, "But why me? We haven't talked since Audrey was a baby."

There it was. I closed my eyes and drew a deep breath. "When I was a child, did I have panic attacks?"

"Are you having them now?"

"I'm not sure."

I briefly described the sensations I'd experienced when Carver had thrown that woman over the embankment. The darkening vision and arrhythmia. The nightmares that had followed. The way the air around me even now felt as if it had weight, grinding me into the ground and making each breath a chore.

Little things like that.

A few seconds passed, no longer, before he answered, "Never." But the hesitation, however slight, made me wonder if he was keeping something from me.

"It felt—*familiar.*"

No hesitation this time. "You were a colicky baby, a stubborn toddler, and living through your teen years nearly killed me," he said. "But you also had—*have*—the most generous heart of anyone I've met and a smile that knocks me back every time I see it." He paused. "I miss that smile."

I didn't know what to say to that, but, fortunately, my father let me off the hook. "As a baby, you were prone to earaches," he continued.

"You had bronchitis when you were about Audrey's age, and you've broken both your right arm and your left ankle. That doesn't include the sprains. Several of those too." The chuckle again, warm and deep. "Oh—and a preschool classmate stabbed you near the eye with a pencil.

"But no, no panic attacks. Still, it's understandable why they'd be starting now."

"Thanks, Red," I said. "I—it was good talking to you."

I had already moved to disconnect, my finger hovering above the icon, when I heard his voice again.

"Wait."

I lifted the phone back to my ear.

"Earlier, you mentioned you'd do anything for your children. So you know."

"Know what?"

"That I'll be there on the first flight that has an open seat."

Then he was gone.

I sat there for a couple of minutes, clutching my phone and eyeing the envelope that rested on the passenger seat. Nope, still not ready to open it. But there was something else equally as uncomfortable that I could do.

I hadn't written down the number, but that didn't matter. I had memorized it the moment I had seen it in Sam's phone records.

Uncertain what I would say, I dialed anyway. Part of me hoped for voicemail, a greeting that included an identification. That's all I really needed. I could wait to find out the rest. If someone actually answered, I might be forced to share a sliver of truth. I wasn't sure I could do that, or if I could handle a stranger sharing her truth with me. Because, ever since talking to Ozzy, I feared it *was* a *her*.

On the third ring, the call connected, and my fear was confirmed. A woman answered.

"Hello." She was out of breath. I tried not to ponder why.

I introduced myself and awaited her response. Would she recognize my name? And if she did, would she pretend not to?

She replied with a single word, "Yes." The woman recognized my name but didn't offer hers in return.

I wasn't sure what to say next. What was the protocol when speaking with a woman you suspected was sleeping with your husband? I settled on, "Do you have a daughter named Hannah?"

"I don't have kids, but I mentor a girl named Hannah."

Sunlight flooded the car's interior, but it was an illusion. The air was frigid. "Can we meet?" I asked.

In my head, I had a list of what I expected her to say. *Yes. No. Go to hell.* What she actually said wasn't on that list. Not even close.

The woman with the unfamiliar number and unrecognizable voice sighed, deeply, then said, "We've already met."

# 19

---

*We've already met.*

When I asked the woman to explain, she gave me her address and said she would be home in half an hour. When I pushed, she said, "Later." Then she hung up.

That wasn't at all how I'd expected that call to go.

I stared at the envelope for two minutes, then, with twenty-eight more minutes to kill, I got out of the car.

Santa Rosa High's hallways were nearly empty at that hour. Though this was Sam and Leo's domain, it wasn't a place I had visited more than a couple of times, and I paused as the leg of the T-shaped hall ended at a wall. A "Go, Panthers!" banner was hanging there, one of its corners curling inward, having pulled free of its tape. I tried to fix it, but the tape would no longer hold, and my hands came away spotted with orange glitter.

I forced myself forward, turning right. My sneakers squeaked as they led me to the door marked Administration. Before I entered, I adjusted the envelope tucked under my left arm. I hadn't been able to open it, but neither had I been able to leave it behind. It felt like an unnecessary weight now.

Behind the counter sat a blonde wearing a green sweater and an expression of annoyance. It was directed at her computer screen, but she swiveled to share it with me.

I hadn't thought about what I might say, beyond asking for Sam.

When I mentioned his name, the woman's expression shifted. I couldn't quite read all it contained, but the edge of hostility was unmistakable.

"Are you one of the parents?" she asked.

I felt suddenly reluctant to introduce myself, so instead I repeated, "One of the parents?"

Cranky Blonde didn't clarify but motioned toward the envelope I held. "Is that for Mr. Diggs?"

I moved the envelope from underneath my arm and clasped it to my chest. Some of the glitter had transferred from my hands to the paper. She waited for me to speak, but I pressed my lips shut. Cranky Blonde seemed the type who liked to fill silences.

True to my opinion of her, only a few seconds ticked by before she said, "If you're one of the parents, you really should talk to Mr. Diggs. He's handling the situation."

She wrinkled her nose as she spit out the last word.

Before I could ask what she meant by "situation," a man with a long neck and an Adam's apple the size of a golf ball emerged from one of the offices. He was in the middle of shrugging into his coat when he stopped in front of me.

He smiled, his eyes dropping to the ring finger of my left hand before landing on my face. "Did I hear you needed to speak with me?" he asked, extending his hand. His palm was slick, but I suspected my own was too. "I'm Charles Diggs, the principal here, but you can call me Chuck."

"Cassie Larkin."

His smile slipped, for no longer than a heartbeat, before he replaced it. The office attendant's reaction was less subtle. Behind me, she snorted.

"My husband is a teacher here, though I suspect you've already made that connection." I gestured toward the blonde behind the counter. "Your office attendant mentioned there's a *situation* involving Sam?"

"Hmm." Chuck Diggs nibbled on his fingernail and screwed up his eyebrows, as if trying to remember something I knew he already had. He shot a less-than-friendly look at the office attendant. "I can't discuss personnel matters, but it was a pleasure meeting you, Mrs. Larkin."

He moved to leave, but I blocked his path. "Have you seen Sam today?"

"No, I'm sorry. But we have so many on staff, I can't keep track of all of their schedules. Have a great weekend, Mrs. Larkin."

He bid a quick goodbye to the woman—apparently, her name was Pam and not Cranky Blonde—before he stepped around me and out the door.

"So you're his wife and you don't know."

I turned toward the office attendant, the taint of hostility I had noticed earlier still there, but now mingled with something else. Pity? What did it mean that I kept getting that reaction?

"Know what?"

"I can tell you Sam didn't come in today. I just can't tell you why."

"He's been sick, I know that."

She snorted again. "He hasn't been to work in weeks."

My mind stumbled on that. *Weeks?* So it wasn't the flu that had kept Sam from his classroom the past couple of days. My first thought, *Why hadn't Sam told me?* My second, *Why hadn't Leo?*

I flashed to what she had said a few minutes earlier. "Is this the thing with the students?"

My question was vague, but the woman behind the desk grasped at the excuse to tell me more, and to destroy illusions she believed I held.

"Wives don't always know," she said.

I guessed then that a relationship had ended badly for this woman, and rather than find kinship with me over shared grief, she hated me for what she perceived as my ignorance.

But I couldn't argue with her preconception. I *didn't* know. If she hated me for blindly standing by Sam, I would play to that. "The students are lying."

I expected outrage but got confusion. "You've talked to his students? I wasn't aware any of them had officially come forward."

I swore to myself before changing stories. "Of course I haven't spoken directly with any students. I only meant the rumors aren't true."

"It's more than rumor, Mrs. Larkin." She stood and hooked the strap of her purse over her shoulder. "People sometimes do stupid stuff, even teachers as respected as your husband." The word *respected* sounded like an insult.

"You've wanted to tell me something ever since you heard my name. So tell me."

Spots of red blossomed on her cheeks. "I don't want to get involved," she said, though she remained rooted to her spot behind her desk.

"Yes, you do."

She wielded her next words as if she hoped they would do damage. "Sam has . . . a reputation."

"Define *reputation*."

"He's a bit of a flirt."

Sam had always been friendly, and on occasion, the dimpled smile had been misconstrued as something more. In my experience, this had always been a mistake in perception, not intent. But maybe this woman was right, and I had misread earlier warnings.

"You're claiming he's friendlier than he should be with colleagues."

The blonde's mouth settled into a grim line. "Not with staff. With his students."

When it came to Sam, my faith had been shaken lately, but cold certainty filled me now. "You're lying."

She hadn't expected that. The twin stains of red on her cheeks darkened. "In the past, I wouldn't have thought such a thing was possible either, but a couple of weeks ago in the parking lot, I heard two parents talking. They said he has favorites, and they're usually pretty girls." Pam puffed up her chest, her voice raising to emphasize her point. "They said one girl who's got a one-point-something GPA got an A in his class."

"That's damning evidence. I trust you contacted the licensing board?"

She scowled at the sarcasm. "I checked, Mrs. Larkin, and it's true what they said, that some of his female students are getting A's in his class while failing others."

As her voice rose, mine quieted. "I assume you checked to see if the same is true of his male students?"

She quirked an eyebrow, her lips thinning even more. "Why would I do that?"

"Being a champion of the truth, I would expect you'd check that out."

"No." She was indignant, though not yet certain why.

"Well, did you check to see if the reverse is true—girls failing in his class but excelling in, say, history or math?"

"That's really not the issue here."

"I disagree. You're making the argument that all great artists should be equally talented in other academic areas, so I think considering all the data is *exactly* the issue."

Pam crossed her arms, her lips puckering at my challenge. "Regardless, when I learned about Sam's . . . *issue* . . . I felt compelled to call it to Mr. Diggs's attention."

"I'm sure that was a difficult decision for you."

She stood taller, trying to intimidate with the three extra inches of height she had on me. "Awfully judgmental for someone who doesn't know what her own husband is up to."

Pam was nearly shouting now, my own voice little more than a whisper, but I could tell by her puckered lips that she heard each word when I said, "I'd advise you to stop spreading rumors about my husband."

Allegations like this could ruin careers, true or not.

She winced. "Or what? You'll sue me? Try to get me fired? With who as a witness?"

Heat settled into my balled fists, and my cheeks flamed. Still, I kept my voice low. "Witnesses aren't always a positive."

She glared but took a step back. "Are you threatening me?"

"Did I threaten you? With what I just said, I had hoped you'd learned how dangerous assumptions can be."

To steady my breathing, I forced my eyes away, and they landed on her desk. A file, closed, rested on the otherwise uncluttered surface. On the tab of the file, a student's last name was obscured by a sheet of paper, the type on the paper too tiny to read. But I read the first name on the file's tab clearly enough.

*Hannah.*

———

I LEFT PAM THERE, glowering after me, my knees unsteady as I walked back to my car. I climbed inside, leaving the door open, and before I could lose my nerve, I ripped open the tan envelope some creep had given my six-year-old daughter.

The envelope contained a single photo. It had been printed on copy paper rather than glossy photo stock, and faint lines marred the image. Nevertheless, there was no misconstruing the activity depicted, or the identity of at least one of the participants.

Two tangled bodies, one of them my husband's.

The picture showed Sam having sex with another woman.

If she was a woman at all. The female was thin and faced away from the camera. She easily could have been in her teens.

If I'd eaten more than half a sandwich since Sam disappeared, I might have vomited on the asphalt.

I closed my eyes, hard, but the inside of my lids proved an ideal screen. Images unspooled in flashes: two bodies in movement, slow at first, growing more insistent, finally falling away in exhaustion.

My eyes snapped open, but I couldn't again look at the photo. I turned my head, focusing instead on the fabric of the passenger's seat. A seam had started to fray, thin worms of thread tangled where the seat butted against the center console. There was also a small chip in the cup holder. I hadn't noticed these imperfections before. Not that they mattered. The car wasn't mine.

I turned my attention back to the photo. I pictured Sam and me in similar moments. I remembered the first time, when he had tried so hard to be a gentleman but the tequila had insisted. Then the next morning, when daylight should've sobered us, but instead had intoxicated us further. There was that morning we celebrated the close of escrow. The night we popped the air mattress while camping. The afternoon we decided, hey, why not go to Tahoe and get hitched. Then there were the two random workdays we had conceived our children, special only in hindsight.

There were countless such memories, each with a jagged edge designed to wound.

But none of these was recent, and maybe it was this distance that gave the mental images their glow. The closest we had come to creating a new memory was the morning before, when Sam had modeled those ridiculous zombie teeth, and it had almost been like before. But as always, life distracted. Though just a day earlier, I hadn't realized then how close we were to being broken.

I tried to study the photo, searching for signs that it had been created with photo-editing software. That was Sam's face, but was that his back? Was that his arm?

After a few seconds, I had to look away. Hands shaking, I folded the envelope and stuffed it into my purse.

I understood why this envelope had been given to Audrey rather than me. Whoever was behind the photo wanted me to know how vulnerable I was, how easily my children could be hurt. The monster had gotten to Audrey. What if, next time, the intent wasn't just to deliver a threat?

Because that's clearly what this was. A threat against my family.

What wasn't as clear was who was in the photo with Sam. Was it this mysterious Hannah? Someone else?

I flipped the photo over. On the back, written in black marker, was a number: *1*.

# 20

The address Sam's maybe-mistress had given me was a Craftsman downtown with peeling white paint and a meticulously maintained yard.

A brunette with the wide eyes of an anime character answered the door. She wore yoga pants and a sweatshirt, baby blue this time, with her dark hair secured in a ponytail. I would have recognized her even if she hadn't been dressed almost identically to the way she had been that night on the trail. The bruises, for one thing. The worst of them the purple-black of a ripe avocado, they took up nearly half of her face.

She greeted me by name then introduced herself as Brooklyn Breneman. "I'd shake your hand, but pretty much every part of my right arm is broken or sprained," she said.

What did I say to that—*Sorry? Glad you're healing? Kinda feel weird about saving the woman who may have been sleeping with my husband?* Everything I considered sounded inane, so I settled on a silent nod.

She stepped aside so I could enter. As I passed, I sized her up. Her hair color was right for the photo I'd been given, but I wasn't yet sure about her build. One thing of which I was certain: the faint smell of hard alcohol.

"I assume you got my number from Sam's phone?" she asked.

Great conversationalist that I was, I nodded a second time.

She gestured to a chair for me, patches of the beige microfiber worn nearly to white, while she took the couch. She winced as she settled into the cushions, cradling her arm.

"Tea?" she offered. On the table sat a teapot and two cups, one empty. The second was filled with an amber liquid that definitely wasn't tea.

I declined her offer. She took the filled cup and sipped. "This is my friend's place," she said. "I can't go back to my place until they arrest Carver."

"He knows where you live?"

"He knows a lot about me. Probably about you too."

Of course it was true. He had stolen my wallet and van. Still, the way she said it made my flesh crawl.

"What do you mean by that?"

She settled back into the couch and shrugged with one shoulder. "We have a lot to talk about."

Brooklyn placed a throw pillow on her lap, then her injured arm on top of the pillow. She pulled up the edge of a bandage, and the gesture was so close to Sam's tending of my scrape the night of the attack that I couldn't breathe.

While I figured out how my lungs worked, she said, "I guess I should start by thanking you. If you hadn't been there, I'd be dead."

I meant to tell her that anyone would've done the same, but I was having trouble finding my voice. I had so many questions—how she knew Sam, how Hannah fit into all of this, what she had meant by her comment that Carver probably knew a lot about me. But one question was more urgent than all the others.

"Do you know what happened to Sam?"

When she nodded, her impossibly large eyes widened further. I could see my husband being taken in by those eyes. "I know part of it, at least. But it's complicated."

"I can handle complicated."

Her expression was one of doubt as she again picked up her mug of fake tea. She didn't drink. I suspected she only wanted to occupy her hands.

When she didn't immediately start talking, I prodded: "How do you know Sam?"

She stirred the tea with her index finger, then absentmindedly wiped it on her yoga pants. "He was helping me with Hannah."

There was that name again: *Hannah.*

"Helping how?"

"Hannah's—troubled," she said. "You know, of course, that Sam was suspended a couple of weeks ago?"

Though I did now, thanks to chatty office attendant Pam, it bothered me that this woman had known longer.

When I nodded, she continued, "I'm Hannah's mentor, through one of those youth programs. Her foster mom is cool, but her biological mom—she's not a nice person."

"I don't need backstory. I need to find my husband." I might've emphasized the last two words more than necessary.

"I don't know where Sam is. But I know where he *was.*" She sighed, then drained her mug. "Like I said, it's complicated."

"And like *I* said, I can handle that."

Brooklyn set her empty mug in her lap. "I could tell you a thousand stories about Hannah, but I'll just tell you one," she said.

"I don't—"

She held up her hand to silence me. I bristled, but I let her talk. "Hannah's about four years old, and she doesn't come when her mom calls her for lunch. According to Hannah, her mom hated it when she or her sister hid. So, of course, Hannah expects to be punished, but instead, her mom tells her she's going to teach her to garden. She hands Hannah a pair of work gloves and a shovel. In their yard, there's this huge oak tree, more than a hundred feet high, and her mom makes her start digging in a spot underneath. The ground is hard. It would be a challenge for an adult, and Hannah's a child.

"As she digs, her mom asks her what she wants to grow—peppers? Roses? Snap peas? Goading her. The poor girl's feet are bloody by this time, because, see, she's wearing these ballet slippers. Every time Hannah puts weight on the shovel, it slices the bottom of her foot.

"When Hannah finally manages to dig a small hole, and it takes hours, her mom drops this sack on the ground next to her and says something like, 'I know. How about we plant this?' That's how Hannah finds out her dog got hit by a car. It's also her first real memory."

The story is horrible, but I've come for answers, not stories. Still, I feel a pang of guilt when I ask, "Why is this relevant?"

"Because you should understand what Hannah comes from before making judgments on what she might've done to Sam."

My guilt burned to ash and scattered. "And what was that?"

"Hannah was having problems in Sam's class. He reached out to me. He was trying to help her, and it worked. Her grades and attitude improved. Then Sam and I—" She didn't finish the sentence.

"You're claiming you're sleeping with my husband." My voice cold.

"He never hid the fact he was married."

"*Is* married," I corrected.

Her eyes dropped to her lap and the empty cup there.

"He's attractive, of course, but it was his sense of humor that got me, and his empathy. He's a great guy." I bit back a retort about how I knew my husband, thank you, and how "great guys" didn't cheat.

"Glad you think so."

Her blue eyes flashed, and at first I thought it was with shame and that an apology would follow. But when she spoke, it was in my husband's defense, not her own.

"Hannah's eighteen now, so even if she and Sam slept together, she was an adult at the time," Brooklyn said. "I think it's more likely, though, that Hannah knew what was going on between Sam and me and that she was jealous. Two people she cared about were involved in a relationship that didn't include her. She started spreading rumors that Sam had pressed her for sex in exchange for an A. Those rumors came to the attention of the administration. You know the rest."

Was that why Sam had kept his suspension from me—because he couldn't separate that news from an admission that he was having an affair?

"You said you know what happened last night."

Her face clouded, and she gave a slight nod. "We met a few blocks from your house."

I instantly thought of our sixteen years in that house, the bedroom we shared, our kids, and felt sick. "You've been to our home?"

Brooklyn opened a drawer on the end table and pulled out a small bottle of tequila. She refilled her teacup before placing the bottle on the table. No pretense now.

"The night you and I met, I was leaving your house," she said. "I had dropped off a bottle of cold medicine. That's all."

That may have been all that happened that night, but had there been others? And if I had arrived home earlier, would I have met Brooklyn there instead of on the trail?

As if I had asked the question aloud, she said, "I knew you were working late."

She didn't add that Sam had called to tell her this, but I knew. I had memorized the log of calls and texts to Brooklyn's number. They had spoken twice the night of the attack.

The police's suspicions of me suddenly didn't seem so unfounded: the wife is there when her husband's mistress is attacked, and twenty-four hours later, the husband disappears. In Detective Rico's place, I would have questions too.

I prodded, "So you arranged to meet Sam in this neighborhood . . ."

"Near this abandoned house," she said, and my skin prickled. I easily pictured the rotting pumpkin on the stoop and the shattered window. "We were only supposed to be a few minutes."

"Romantic."

"It wasn't like that," she objected. "We met to talk about Hannah, the allegations she'd made against him, and to come up with a plan. Find a way to salvage Sam's reputation, while also protecting Hannah. Audrey was with a friend, and Sam and I didn't want to leave her for too long."

Each detail was a blow: the clandestine nature of their meeting; Brooklyn's casual use of "Sam and I" as if they were a couple; her show of concern over my daughter. Audrey was not hers to worry about.

Though I doubted she would answer, I asked anyway, "What's Hannah's last name?"

She shook her head firmly. "I'm only telling you as much as I am because you saved my life, and because I want to find Sam as much as you do. But you know I can't give you her last name."

"I'll find out."

"Maybe, but not from me." A sad smile played at the corners of her mouth. "You hate me, don't you?"

"I don't know you."

"I'm sleeping with your husband. You know that."

Brooklyn nursed her tequila and waited for my response. Finally, I said, "Not really."

"Not really, you don't hate me? Or you don't really know that Sam and I are sleeping together?"

"The affair part, but I suppose both are true." I had spent a lot of time hating as a teen, and I had no more energy for it. What energy I had was focused on a single task: finding my husband. "You said you and Sam met on Halloween. When did you last see him?"

"I'm not sure of the time, but we weren't together more than a few minutes when I saw Carver. He must've been tracking my car."

There was another possibility, one I had considered earlier but that nevertheless shook me now: Carver had been watching Sam.

Brooklyn paused, and maintaining eye contact seemed a great effort. Her voice wavered as she said, "I ran."

"Did you call the police?"

"As soon as I was a safe distance, of course I did."

"You didn't warn Sam?" There was no hiding the edge to my voice.

"Why would I? Carver was after me, not him." Her tone became dismissive. "I'm still not sure Carver's the reason Sam disappeared. Sam's obviously dealing with his own problems."

The anger swelled suddenly, hot in my chest. It still wasn't hatred, but it was closer. Before this happened, I would never have left Sam behind, especially without warning him. I would have gone to my death protecting him. If I were being honest, I was pretty sure the same was true now.

"You should've warned him."

Brooklyn refreshed her drink. When she spoke again, she slurred.

"I slept with him too. Carver." Her face flushed, I guessed more from the alcohol than embarrassment. "Just once. It's not like with—" she choked back my husband's name. "Anyway, I guess I have a type. Unattainable men. Just didn't think I'd also pick a homicidal one."

Then Brooklyn stood, which was a production. When she left the room, the alcohol and her injuries made her steps slow and wobbly. She returned a few minutes later with a small stack of photos. I thought they might be pictures of her with Sam, but then I noticed that two of the photos were starting to yellow around the edges.

"I took these from him." She offered the photos to me. When I didn't accept them, she pressed them into my hand. "I knew he'd been in prison for killing a girl, but the way he told it, he was innocent. Plus he was only eighteen or nineteen when it happened, so I let myself believe him.

"Then I saw those."

The first picture—yellowed, the paper flaking—was of a girl in her teens, head tilted and smile wide. I flipped to the back. A rough hand had scribbled a name on it: *Natalie*.

The second photo, of a woman in her forties, was newer. The subject wore a blue dress and had been captured in profile. On the back of the photo was written another name: *Anne*.

While questioning me, Detective Rico had mentioned both those names: *Natalie* Robinson and *Anne* Jackson.

There was no name on the back of the third photo. Only a question mark, written in pencil. But I didn't need a name. It was a photo of me.

I traced the question mark, wondering if the same pencil had etched the number two on the chocolate wrapper.

Though Natalie, Anne, and I weren't related, we could have been. We were all redheads with light eyes, though it was hard to tell if Anne's and Natalie's were the same green as mine.

There was one more photo, which Brooklyn had placed in the stack facedown.

As I flipped it over, she said, "I'm sorry. But you had to know."

I had assumed the last photo would be of Brooklyn. It wasn't. Faded, obviously decades old, it was another of Natalie. No smile in this one.

Her eyes were swollen slits, and though her lips were parted only slightly, I could see gaps where teeth should have been. She had been wedged in a box, then lowered in the ground, a mound of dirt at the edge of the frame. Obviously dead, and abused beforehand.

I dropped the stack on the table, hands shaking. I was so *over* being confronted with horrifying images.

"That's a copy of the original, which I turned over to the police. There's no picture of it, but Anne's dead now too. So that just leaves me, who Carver tried to kill—and you."

My fingers burned where I had touched the photo of the dead girl. "I don't know him."

"That doesn't mean he doesn't know you," she said. "And in case you're thinking I'm not his type . . ." She slipped the case off her phone and pulled out her driver's license, which had been tucked inside. "This is how I looked when I met him."

She handed me her license. The photo showed the same blue eyes, the same pale skin, but the hair was a shade lighter than mine. At one time, Brooklyn had been a redhead.


"I KNOW THIS IS a lot to take in," she said.

I wasn't convinced of my part in any of this. "That night on the trail, he didn't seem to know me."

"You're sure?"

I considered this. "He seemed surprised."

She let out a small laugh. "Let's say a man comes home to find his wife and best friend having sex. He's going to be mighty surprised, but that doesn't mean he doesn't know them." She winced. "Sorry. Bad analogy. But that night, did he ever ask your name?"

He had asked who I was, but it had sounded less like an inquiry, more like an accusation: *Who* are *you?* Was that the same thing as asking for my name? "The situation on the trail didn't exactly lend itself to introductions."

"So what do you remember Carver saying that night?"

I remembered the threat about letting Brooklyn die, of course, and Carver asking whom I loved.

But what else?

Mouth suddenly dry, I poured myself a cup of cold tea. I drained the cup.

Carver had said my life was fucked up, but I didn't know it yet. As if he had known it because he knew *me*. But maybe I was just letting Brooklyn get into my head.

When I didn't answer, she said, "What I remember from that night is he could've killed you, easily, but he didn't. He seemed shaken that you were there."

I was skeptical. "You say Carver killed Natalie. He killed Anne. He tried to kill you. So, if that pattern holds, and he has a photo of me, why wouldn't he kill me?"

"I only know what I believe."

"Which is?"

She hugged a pillow to her chest with her good arm. "Before he killed Natalie and Anne, he loved them. I think that's his pattern. He identifies a woman who interests him, stalks her, gets to know her from a distance, woos her. Loves her. Then he gets bored, or angry, and he fixates on someone new."

I studied her eyes, wide and blue and framed with a fringe of dark lashes. Innocent, or the illusion of it anyway. I looked for tells that she was lying, but I could find none.

She continued, "I think he fixated on you while he was following me, because of my relationship with your husband."

If I believed her, there was a question I needed answered. I braced myself and asked, "Was Sam planning to leave us?" Because it was *us*—me, Leo, and Audrey—that he had abandoned.

"If he was, it wasn't for me."

Since I had arrived, I had been uncertain whether to believe her, but this was the first statement I was sure was a lie.

"Early on, I had illusions it might be something," she said. Too quickly. "But it was never that way for him."

I pulled the envelope from my purse and unfolded it. "There's a photo I'd like to share with you too." I slid it across the table. "Is this you?"

Her face blanched, but she recovered quickly. "No."

On this, I believed her. The young woman in the picture was thin like Brooklyn, but taller, with longer arms and a narrower torso.

"Is it Hannah?"

Brooklyn remained silent, her eyes cemented to the photo in front of her.

"Is Hannah a brunette?"

She looked up then, and her nostrils flared. She exhaled and faked a wince, trying to pass off as pain the anger I recognized in her eyes.

I asked the same question she had refused to answer earlier, "What's Hannah's last name?"

Her eyes shuttered, her lips thinned. "I'm tired," she said. "Call me if I can be of more help."

She tried to sound sincere, but we both knew if I did call again, she wouldn't answer. Regardless of what she had professed moments before, Brooklyn had indeed believed her affair with Sam wasn't just about sex. She had brought him cold medicine and worried over his children. She had just had a conversation with his wife about his disappearance. It was all very civil and adult. Brooklyn had likely believed that when Sam returned, he would make his choice, and there was a better than 50 percent chance he would choose her. She had probably already considered how we would share custody.

*Like hell we would.*

But now, seeing a photograph of someone else having sex with the man she loved confirmed a truth Brooklyn hadn't wanted to face: she wasn't special.

I understood, because I knew exactly how that felt.

# 21

I went straight from the home of my husband's mistress to my son's football game at Santa Rosa High. It was dusk when I arrived, the junior varsity game not yet started, but I still chose a spot at the top of the bleachers. No one to look over my shoulder that way. I held the envelope with the photograph in my lap, the cold aluminum leaching through the seat of my jeans. The empty bench reminded me of Sam's absence.

Soon, dusk succumbed to full dark, and I huddled in my fleece-lined sweatshirt, alone, until Zoe and Audrey joined me midway through the JV game. They arrived late because they had stopped for ice cream.

"Thanks for watching Audrey."

"I'd pay to watch her." Zoe's fingernails were painted with messy polka dots, the same lavender as her hair. "Even got a free manicure out of it."

Audrey looked up at me, a smear of ice cream still on her cheek. She squirmed when I wiped it away with my sleeve. "I tried to paint Smooch's nails, too, but she wouldn't let me."

"Smooch is independent like that," Zoe said.

"So I had to put a bow on her tail instead." Smooch was even more of a saint than Zoe. "I was gentle, like you say. And I gave her a treat after."

"She might've given her several."

"I love Smooch." Audrey beamed, then wrinkled her brow. "I put a bow on Boo's tail, too, but he didn't like it as much, so I took it off."

With more than an hour to go until the varsity game started, the bleachers were just starting to fill, but the parents and students already there supported the JV team with full enthusiasm. Except for Audrey. She fidgeted more than usual. It was a relief when, midway through the third quarter, she noticed a classmate a few rows down.

Once Audrey left to sit with her friend, I filled Zoe in on my conversation with Brooklyn. Then I handed her the envelope.

"At school today, a man slipped this in Audrey's backpack." I couldn't bring myself to mention the Post-it that had accompanied it.

Zoe scrunched her nose and raised an eyebrow. She pulled out the photo, then angled it to get better light. She quickly swallowed a gasp and worked hard to keep the shock from her face. I loved her a little more for that.

"Sam?" she asked. She had no reason to recognize him. Unlike me, she'd never seen him naked.

"Yes."

"You're sure?"

I had studied the photo enough that I didn't need to look at it now. In truth, I wasn't sure I *could* look at it again. "Yes."

I watched Leo, standing, arms crossed, on the sidelines, and glanced at the scoreboard. The Santa Rosa Panthers led by twelve. The rival quarterback threw too high, the ball bobbling off the fingertips of the intended receiver, allowing one of the Panthers' safeties to intercept it. He ran ten yards before he was taken down. The crowd's cheering sounded shrill in my ears.

"That's horrible." I wasn't sure whether Zoe referred to the man slipping the picture into Audrey's backpack or the actual act photographed. Both were pretty horrible. "She looks—"

Zoe stopped, so I finished her thought. "Young."

She turned the photo facedown on her lap and pulled me into a hug that nearly crushed me. "I'm so sorry, Cassie." Her mouth, her eyes, her shoulders all fell on her exhale. "This sucks."

Audrey and her friend had wandered about twenty feet away, to the side of the bleachers. "Audrey, not too far," I called. I turned back to

Zoe. "It does indeed suck," I agreed. My hand shook as I turned the photo faceup again. "But is it real?"

That was the main reason I had decided to share the photo with Zoe. My social media–obsessed friend had a gift: even in the age of Photoshop, she could find the flaw in any picture.

Zoe took a deep breath and returned her attention to the photo. "Lighting seems consistent," she said, aiming for neutral even as her voice broke. "No shadows or highlights where they shouldn't be."

She tucked a lock of lavender hair behind her ear and furrowed her brow. "If it's edited, there aren't any obvious artifacts left behind, and perspective's spot-on."

My heart plummeted. "So it's real?"

"I'm not sure." She moved the photo closer. "Overall quality isn't great. That doesn't necessarily mean anything, but sometimes editors will disguise tweaks by making the whole photo look crappy."

She looked up. When her eyes settled on mine, I knew she believed the photo to be authentic. Still, she asked, "Do you mind if I take this? I'd be able to tell more easily with better lighting and a magnifier."

I held up my hands, which felt dirty just from touching the envelope. "Take it," I said. "And Zoe—thank you."

She tucked it inside her jacket. "So you showed this to Brooklyn?"

"I did."

"No chance it could be her in the photo?"

"Depends if it's been edited," I said. "There's a number on the back. Just like with the wrapper."

I intended no recrimination, but Zoe winced. "Sorry, Cassie, I really thought it was an S."

I waved off the apology. "So . . . 3, 2, 1. Counting down?"

"To what?"

I shrugged and handed her Leo's yearbook. "On the way here, I picked this up too. I thought maybe we could research all the older girls named Hannah."

"Let me do it," she said. Zoe tensed for another hug, but she stopped short and instead grabbed my arm, nearly crushing it. She bounced on the bleachers, coming down with such enthusiasm, I got a little air too. She pointed to the field. "He's going in."

My eyes had been on Audrey, but when I shifted my focus toward the field, I could see Leo had indeed strapped on his helmet and taken his place behind the defensive line. I felt my lungs seize, at once proud and wary.

On the field, the center botched the snap, but the quarterback fell on the ball, losing yards but not possession. On the second play, the quarterback passed off the ball to a running back, for a gain of five yards. On both plays, Leo was minimally involved in the action. Both times, he sprinted forward but stopped short when a teammate got there first.

The third down was different.

The wind blew weakly, but with an icy edge. As the Panthers lined up on their thirty-five-yard line, I forced myself to breathe, the action followed immediately by superstition. I had held my breath for the first two plays, and Leo had remained standing. Ignoring superstition suddenly seemed a wrong, even dangerous, choice. I tried recalling the oxygen to my lungs, feeling it like a weight inside my chest.

But it was too late.

The ball spiraled high in the air, too high. A bad throw, it was anybody's to take. Black jerseys and white converged, bodies crashing against one another, receivers and linemen alike fighting to be first to snatch the ball from the sky.

Leo won the battle, catching the ball before, a fraction of a second later, he was tackled. A pile of white jerseys pinned down my entirely breakable son.

The referee's whistle trilled, the pile cleared, and Leo emerged, unbroken.

I let the oxygen back into my lungs.

Zoe grinned at me as she clapped. "Worried for a second?"

"As a mom, always."

As the Panthers defense switched with offense, I was surprised to see Leo stay in the game.

Riding a wave of euphoria, I was momentarily unconcerned that the rival defenders towered over the Panthers line. Though nearly the same height as my son, the largest of the defenders outweighed Leo by, I guessed, fifty pounds.

The quarterback threw the ball downfield, on the side opposite of Leo's, and the white jerseys swarmed the receiver.

Leo ran, too, but he was the farthest Panther from the ball. Only one player was farther: the mountainous defender who, for some reason I couldn't fathom, raced at an angle away from the ball. Then I saw, and I understood, though because it didn't make sense, my lungs continued pumping as if they, too, were oblivious to the danger.

Leo didn't see it either, turned away as he was, toward the ball and away from the unknown threat. Because he didn't see it coming, Leo didn't brace himself as he might have. When the hit came, helmet to helmet, Leo was knocked in the air, crashing to the turf as the defender pounced, coming down hard, with every pound of his extra fifty.

The referee blew his whistle, nearly as apoplectic as the Panthers coach, and Leo's teammates started shoving their opponents at the obvious foul. This brought a new wave of whistle-blows, coaching staff and players gesturing and shouting from the sidelines.

This time, Leo didn't get up.

# 22

My phone buzzed once in my pocket, but for the first time since Sam disappeared, I didn't immediately reach for it. My eyes were fixed on the midfield, where my son lay unmoving.

For a moment, I was as frozen as Leo was. Then I raced down the bleachers, grabbing Audrey's elbow as I passed. The metal stands vibrated beneath our feet. From the bleachers, we stepped onto concrete, which we followed to the short fence that circled the track. At the edge, I hesitated, pulling Audrey hard against my chest, as if such a gesture could protect her from the harm that had befallen her brother, and perhaps her father before him.

Why had I let him play? I should've pushed harder to keep him out of the game. I should've done more to keep him safe.

Leo was still prone on the field, but now he was circled by a contingent of medical and coaching staff. So still, like a bird swatted from its nest. I zeroed in on his chest. I thought I saw the rise and fall of his breathing

"Mom, too tight," Audrey complained, wriggling in my grasp.

I loosened my grip, but only slightly. "Sorry."

"Is Leo okay?"

"He just got a little banged up, that's all." Because anything else was unthinkable.

My mind raced through the possibilities. Ligaments could be torn. The helmet-on-helmet impact made concussion likely. Then there were the bones. Two hundred and six in the human body, and the force could have easily snapped any of them. I worried most about the neck. With that could come internal bleeding, paralysis—death.

But that shouldn't happen to my son. He wasn't a starter, almost never played. He should be safe.

Then I saw Leo's foot move. Though only a twitch, I imagined him walking off the field, stiffly, maybe even limping or dragging an injured limb while supported on either side by teammates.

But that wasn't how Leo left the field. My son left on a stretcher, carried from the field to an ambulance waiting just on the other side of the gates.

I checked my phone. A text, from Sam's number but, I was now certain, not from Sam.

*Sorry about Leo.*

ONLY HOURS EARLIER, I had believed nothing I saw that day would disturb me more than that photo of my husband having sex with another woman. Then Leo was taken away on a stretcher. Seeing him like that rattled me in a way nothing had since Audrey was hospitalized as an infant.

I hadn't taken that number on the back of that photo seriously enough. With Sam already gone and my children safely with me, what more could be taken?

The answer, apparently, was everything.

Previously, I had considered that the numbers on the rock, the wrapper, and the photo might be a countdown of days. But maybe that wasn't it at all. The night Detective Rico had found the rock, there lived three people in my home that I loved beyond measure. Then Sam had disappeared, leaving only two. If something happened to Leo . . .

Though the diagnosis of a concussion didn't require a CT or MRI scan, the doctor was concerned enough about the hit Leo had taken to request tests. Once he was rolled away, Zoe left to see to Boo and Smooch. She asked if I wanted her to take Audrey—my daughter could certainly use the distraction—but I declined her offer. Until I found Sam, I wanted both of our children near me.

While I waited in the padded chair outside the imaging room with Audrey, I turned my attention back to the text I had received from whoever had Sam's phone.

*Sorry about Leo.*

I typed: *Who are you?*

*I'm Sam.*

*Who ARE you?*

*Why don't you believe me?*

*Because you aren't Sam.*

*Of course I am.*

*Stop.*

*If I weren't Sam, how would I know about the fight Leo and I had the night before I disappeared?*

This stopped me. What fight? I hadn't heard about any fight.

"Sam" typed over my silence: *I'm sure Leo didn't mean the things he said that night.*

Then the realization hit like a slap. *You've been eavesdropping on us.*

*You sleep on the left side of the bed. Your bathrobe is dark green, the same shade as your eyes. The same shade as my favorite bra.*

My blood froze, and I pulled Audrey closer to me. *You're watching us too.*

*Of course I'm watching. I'm your husband.*

I thought of my son, his battered head and body being scanned in the next room. *Did you hurt Leo?*

*How would I hurt Leo? I wasn't there.*

*What did you do?*

*Really, Cassie.*

Though I knew he wouldn't say anything to incriminate himself, I asked anyway: *What do you want?*

*I want you to be happy, Cassie.*

*I'm going to the police.*

*They didn't seem to believe you the last time.*

So he had listened to me, even there, in the police station. Unless he knew someone who had passed along this information? Both choices left me chilled.

*You're not my husband.*

*Not anymore.*

*Why are you doing this?*

*We all make choices. Like you did, that night on the trail.*

*Carver?*

*I told you I'm Sam.*

*Hannah?*

*You're being tedious.*

*Did you hurt my husband?*

*I'm fine, Cassie. Great, actually. I've found someone who doesn't work all the time.*

The words brought back an argument about my long hours at the clinic. More than a month before.

*A woman who's not holding on to that extra fifteen pounds six years after childbirth.*

I had voiced this insecurity a week earlier when Sam and I had been alone in our bedroom—though apparently not alone at all.

*I'm not sure if this new relationship will work out, so I hope you can leave us alone. I know how you can be when you're jealous.*

With these words, I could suddenly see Brooklyn, or the young woman in the photo, brutalized and left in some public space for the police to discover. With evidence on her that would lead back to me. Rico already had reason to be suspicious of me.

But I was more afraid for Sam. My hands trembled as I typed: *If you hurt Sam, I'll end you.*

The taunt came quickly, and I sensed the sick joy in it: *And how exactly will you do that? I mean, if I weren't Sam. Which I am.*

*I haven't decided yet. But I went to medical school. I'll come up with something creative.*

*I think I should go to the police.*

If he did, this conversation would cast as much doubt on me as it did him.

Then he typed: *Especially after what happened with Lester. I heard you actually poisoned him. Poor dog.*

A familiar anger flooded me, but this time, I didn't fight it. On my virtual keypad, I stabbed out a threat: *I've decided whatever I do to you will involve scalpels. Retractors and clamps too.*

*I know you're hurting, but at least you have the kids.* I pulled Audrey closer still, so she sat more in my chair than hers. *I hope to see them soon.*

*Is that a threat?*

I could see that "Sam" was typing, and each of the seconds spent waiting raked at my nerves. Finally, the text popped on the screen: *Why would I threaten my own children?*

# 23

As a teenager, I plowed my car into the neighbor's living room. On purpose. It wasn't without cause—I'd caught the creep staring in my bedroom window on several occasions—but I concede there were more practical steps I should have taken.

Another time, I throat-punched a bully who had stolen a smaller kid's backpack. Again, that probably shouldn't have been my first course of action. Especially since it was less about protecting that smaller kid than the fact that I hadn't punched anyone in months.

So I was angry, a lot and often with little provocation. But as an adult, I had realized most problems were better solved with diplomacy and intellect and empathy.

This was *not* one of those problems.

Thus far, I had done everything right: on the trail that night, it was clumsiness, not recklessness, that had sent me careening down that hill. I had called 911. Later, I had cooperated with the police and updated them at every step. I had even been civil to the woman who claimed to be screwing my husband. True, over the past couple of days, there had been moments I'd gotten angry. But I'd fought it.

I didn't fight it now. With the texts threatening my children and Leo in the next room getting another MRI, for his knee this time, I was well and truly pissed.

I spotted Zoe walking down the corridor and waved her over. She handed me my laptop bag. "How's Leo?"

"Mild concussion, and they're worried about his knee. Perla's on her way?"

"Right behind me." She returned my house key. "She found something at the house, but I'll let her show you."

When Perla Anderson arrived five minutes later, Zoe took Audrey to another set of chairs halfway down the corridor.

Years before, I had treated Perla's Rottweiler for hip dysplasia. It had been a while since I had seen her, but she was nevertheless who I'd thought of after the latest string of texts.

Perla wore her usual uniform: jeans, a messenger bag, and a novelty T-shirt, this one proclaiming: *I'm not lazy. Just buffering.* Last time she had been in my clinic, she had been finishing her master's in computer science. Like then, she smelled of clove cigarettes and the coffee she sipped from her travel mug.

She put down her bag and motioned to the one Zoe had just given me. "Is that it?" she asked.

I pulled out the laptop, logged in, and handed it to her. I did the same with my phone.

She balanced her coffee between her legs as she tapped at the keyboard, her nails jagged nubs.

"Zoe said you found something at our house?"

She paused in her typing to reach into her pocket, then opened her palm. There rested three circles, all white and about the size of a penny.

"You were right to think someone has been eavesdropping on you. I found these on your ceiling in the living room, kitchen, and master bedroom."

Perla took a sip of coffee, then reached into her other pocket. This time, she hesitated. "I found this too." She pressed a small, hard object in my hand. It was a USB wall charger, also white, the kind everyone in our family used to charge our cell phones.

I wrinkled my nose as I studied it, not understanding at first. I opened my mouth to ask why she had given it to me, but then I noticed it: a small hole that shouldn't have been there.

"A camera?" When she nodded, I shivered. "Where'd you find it?"

"Your bedroom."

In my head played all the camera could have witnessed. Sure, there was the sex, infrequent as it had become, but there were other moments when Sam and I had shared tenderness or insecurities that seemed even greater violations. All the moments we thought we were alone but someone else listened, and watched.

My stomach roiled. I might never go home again.

"You're sure that's all of them?"

"I swept for other devices, but that's it, at least as far as bugs." I didn't like the way she said that last part, or the way she scowled at the screen of my laptop.

"Is there a way to tell who's texting with Sam's phone?"

She shrugged. "It may not even be Sam's phone. With caller ID spoofing, it would be easy enough for the texts to appear to come from anywhere."

"Can they be traced?"

"It's possible, but it's not easy. Plus, you have other issues."

Perla tapped the screen, clicking through a series of social media posts, leaving me only a few seconds to read each.

*JL's team sucks almost as hard as his girl.*

*JL's so fat and stupid the only letters of the alphabet he knows are KFC.*

*JL's bitch opens her legs for everyone except him.*

One post had a photo of a drooling bulldog and a girl's name. I assumed the name belonged to "JL's" girlfriend.

Another showed a badly edited photo of a guy in a football jersey doing obscene things to a pig, with the caption: *The closest JL gets to the pigskin.*

"What's this?"

"I pulled those from Leo's social media."

Teenagers have lives and secrets and bad choices they hide from their parents. Of course they do. Still, it was with unshakable confidence that I said, "Leo wouldn't do this."

"I figured. Obviously, your security's been compromised."

My anger flared. I felt naked, exposed, almost as much as I had when Perla had shown me the camera. "Why would someone target a child?"

I corrected myself: *Children*. Leo, and the boy being taunted.

"People are assholes."

In this case, true enough. "So someone has our passwords."

"Which is why you should change them."

"But how could this happen?"

Perla chewed on a hangnail. "Someone could've physically accessed one of your phones, or your computer, or gotten in some other way. Phishing emails, for instance."

"I wouldn't have opened an email like that."

She smiled, in the same way I did when Audrey mentioned unicorns. "There are other ways to steal passwords too. Someone could've planted a keylogger, for instance. It could be integrated into your keyboard, and how're you going to catch that?" I knew she meant *I* wouldn't catch it, because I had no doubt Perla would. "Any software you have scanning for an intrusion would miss hardware. And you probably have other computers, right?"

"Sam has one he uses for work, and Leo has a laptop."

"Then there's a chance one of them has been compromised," she said. "Whoever's targeting you could also have gotten your passwords by looking over your shoulder while you're on your laptop at a coffee shop."

*Coffee shop.* I thought of Brooklyn, then Hannah. If Carver had been stalking Brooklyn, then it could've been him too. Really, it could have been anyone.

"Or say you find a USB drive you think contains patient files. Plug it in, and the malware does the rest."

I opened my mouth to say I wouldn't plug an unknown USB drive into my computer, but she stopped me. "Before you say that's not possible, remember this: a shared computer is only as safe as its least diligent user. The scary part is, most of this isn't advanced stuff. Anyone with access to a search engine could pull it off."

"So, anyone."

"Pretty much."

The door from Imaging swung open, and the radiology tech pushed Leo's wheelchair through it. Slumped in his seat, hands folded in his lap, my boy looked so much like a younger version of himself that my heart ached.

Perla took this as her cue to leave. Before she did, she downed the last of her coffee and stowed her travel mug in her messenger bag. When she pulled her hand from the bag, she held two plastic-wrapped packages.

"After searching your home, I figured you might need these," she said.

I took the packages from her. They contained two prepaid cell phones. When Perla tried to hand me my laptop, I pushed it away.

"I don't want that."

She stowed it in my bag and slung it with hers over her shoulder. "I'll check it out further and get it back to you."

I moved toward my son, but Perla touched my arm. Her eyes flashed with an intensity I suspected mirrored mine.

"Remember: sometimes people are assholes," she said. "If someone's messing with your kid, it's okay for you to be one too."

# 24

<hr>

Audrey rested in the chair beside Leo's hospital bed, curled into an impossibly small ball, head propped on my folded sweatshirt. With Audrey asleep, Zoe headed home, leaving me alone with Leo.

The MRI had shown Leo had torn his meniscus. No surgery was needed, but he would be off football for the season. While we waited for the doctor to release him, Leo shifted in his bed, restless and sullen. "Where's Dad?" he asked.

I could have stalled, or fallen back on the excuse I had given the kids earlier about Sam attending a teachers' conference. But there had been enough lies.

Instead, I told him I didn't know where his dad was. Then I took a breath and told Leo the parts I felt he could handle. But, really, what kid could be expected to handle any of it? I hardened the edge of my voice whenever I felt it wavering.

I ended with, "I'm sure he's okay," although I was not at all sure he was.

Even before I told Leo his dad was missing, every glance in his direction had wounded: his face was a younger version of Sam's, the flesh surrounding his swollen eye shifting in color over the past few hours from pomegranate to plum. But the signs of physical suffering were shadows of the pain Leo displayed now. At fifteen, he usually showed signs of the man he would one day become, but in that moment, he was 100 percent kid. I read the question in his expression as clearly as if he had shouted it: *Why?*

I rested my hand over his, letting it linger a moment longer than he normally would have allowed, before pulling it back. "I've filed a report with the police, so they'll be looking for him."

When Leo's eyes widened at my mention of police, I backtracked, reciting the line given to me earlier by Officer Torres: "Don't worry. Odds are your dad chose to leave and that he'll be back."

Was it any better for Leo to think his dad's absence was voluntary? Judging by my son's face, not by much. I got it. Torres's words hadn't given me much comfort either.

Audrey adjusted in the chair but remained asleep. At least one of my children was at peace.

I turned back to Leo to find he too was staring in the direction of his sister and to the window beyond. Who knew which of the two drew his attention more.

"Does she know?" Leo asked. In profile, he looked even more like his father.

I shook my head.

"I don't think he'd leave us forever," I said. "When you were a baby, if he ran out to the car, the mailbox, the backyard, wherever—he took you with him." I allowed myself a brief smile at the memory of an infant Leo swaddled to Sam's chest, chubby appendages jutting like overfilled balloons from his sling. "He loves you, and he would never leave you. Maybe he just needed to do something alone, something important."

"What's more important than us?"

"Nothing." It was the truest answer. "But maybe there's something he needs to do before coming back to us."

Leo didn't ask what that might be, and I didn't know how I would have replied if he had. The question he asked, though, was worse.

"Do you think something . . . *bad* . . . happened to him?"

I lied as easily as I had ever done anything. "Of course not."

Leo's face relaxed, and I let him have his moment. Then I steeled myself and asked, "Have you seen your dad around school the past couple of weeks?"

My son's jaw tensed, and his eyes darted away. "I don't know."

I tried to keep my voice soft, reassuring. "You don't know, or you don't want to tell me?"

"I don't always see Dad."

He was lying, but I decided not to push. I knew Sam hadn't been at school the past couple of weeks, and judging by the way Leo squirmed in his bed, he did too.

The second question was more difficult. "Do you know a girl named Hannah?"

Leo smirked at that. It was Sam's smirk, reaching all the way to his eyes. "Come on, Mom."

"Come on what?"

"There are, like, a couple of thousand kids at my school, and half the girls are named Hannah. I know ten at least."

"Any of them students of your dad's?"

I had picked my words carefully, but it didn't matter. Any hope I'd had that the rumors hadn't reached Leo disappeared with his smirk.

"Is that her name?" he asked, his voice suddenly small and a little angry.

I didn't want to assume we were talking about the same thing, so I asked, "Whose name?"

"No one's." It seemed my son had the same idea.

The sigh that slipped out rattled my chest. I was so freaking exhausted. "I know it's hard, Leo, but you've got to tell me."

"It's nothing, Mom. Kids say stupid sh—stuff all the time."

I rose from my chair and sat on the edge of his hospital bed. This close, I felt the heat radiating off him. Sam and I used to joke that our son was part terrier because he always ran a little hot.

*Used to.* Without realizing it, I had settled into thinking of my marriage as belonging to the past. That wasn't acceptable. None of this was.

I realized suddenly how hard it must be for Leo, attending the school where his father taught. In the best of times, there would be the expectation of good grades and even better behavior. And in times like this, when rumors suggested his dad was sleeping with a student . . .

I took Leo's hand and squeezed. I could have encouraged him to share details of the rumors he had obviously heard, but did I really need to know more? Did I need to know the color of her hair, or if they had been spotted together outside class, or what acts my husband had allegedly asked her to perform, especially if the price for knowing was my son's pain? He couldn't give me a name, and anything else he could give me would just hurt us both.

"It's okay, Leo," I said. "You don't have to tell me."

Relief flooded his face. Then I handed him his new phone and relief shifted to confusion.

"What's this?" he asked. "Where's my phone?"

"We need to use these until we find Dad." I forced aside the doubt that it could end any other way.

"But how will Dad call us?" The hope in his voice shattered my heart.

"He'll find a way," I said. "You can't call him, though, okay? Actually, don't call anyone for a while."

He scowled. "Why not?"

I hesitated, but I couldn't keep this from him. Not if I wanted him to be safe, which was what I wanted above all else. So I told him that someone had stolen his dad's phone. I didn't mention the texts. I told him about the audio surveillance of our home, skipping over mention of the camera found in the master bedroom. Then I described the social media posts Perla had discovered.

"JL?" He grabbed his new phone, then realized it wasn't his old one. He set it down in frustration. "What did he look like?"

I described him, Leo nodding more with each descriptor before finally saying, "I'm pretty sure that's the guy who hit me."

"Do you know him?"

He scrunched his nose in distaste. "I've seen him around, but I don't really know him. He's an idiot."

"How so?"

"I don't know. He just is."

"I'm going to need more than that."

Leo sighed. "After he hit me, he said something."

"Like what?"

"I don't know. I was out."

It was my turn to sigh. "Then how do you know he said something?"

"A couple of the guys said he was talking shit." He winced. "Sorry."

Swearing was pretty far down the list of stuff I currently gave a shit about.

"Trash talk?"

"Nah. It was personal stuff, like about his girlfriend."

I guessed it was related to the posts, but still I asked, "What about his girlfriend?"

"I don't know. I was unconscious, remember?"

I *did* remember. I would always remember.

Though it turned my stomach, I had to ask, "You didn't post those, right?"

"Of course not." Though he had to understand my need to ask, the question offended him. With his answer, I knew the fabricated posts had been meant to provoke. They were likely the reason my son was laid up with a concussion and injured knee.

Leo's eyes suddenly glittered, urgency sharpening his pitch. "Dad wasn't at the game?"

"I haven't seen him since yesterday."

"You're sure, right? You would've seen him if he was there, right?"

I remembered the crowd, not so large that I hadn't scanned it thoroughly at least twice. It had been dusk when I had arrived, but it hadn't been so dark that I couldn't see clearly. Still, I considered the question carefully.

"I probably would've seen him." I was no longer certain enough of anything to speak in absolutes.

When he answered, Leo's voice held equal parts excitement and confusion. "If Dad wasn't there, then why did I see his car?"

THOUGH IT HAD BEEN only a day since Sam had disappeared, the world today bore little resemblance to the one of twenty-four hours before.

Now, even the mechanics of breathing required thought. So it took a moment to process my son's statement.

"You saw your dad's car?"

"It was definitely his car," Leo said. "It had that stupid bumper sticker."

*Teach children how to think, not what to think.*

"How many people have that bumper sticker?" My son spoke with a certainty that unnerved me, especially given that Sam wasn't the last person seen driving his Camry.

"Does he know we're here?" Leo asked. "If he was at the game, then he might've seen what happened on the field. You should call him, tell him I'm okay."

His voice rang with so much hope that I had to turn away. I couldn't make that call, and a second later, Leo realized this too.

"Oh. Right."

Thinking of Sam made me glance down at my phone. I had missed a call, which didn't make sense. No one had this number.

Before I could check my voicemail, the doctor walked in. At the intrusion, Audrey stirred in the chair, her eyes blinking open beneath her bangs.

"Can we go home now?" she asked, her words slurred with sleep. Then: "Where's Daddy?"

The doctor focused on the first question, saying that everything was fine and that we could go home, though I knew we couldn't. She gave discharge instructions, which weren't complicated but which I memorized with a zeal born from a desire to control one small part of our lives.

As soon as she was gone, I checked my voicemail. It was Perla. Of course.

Her message was brief: "Some woman has been calling your old phone. She seems pretty desperate to talk to you, but she didn't give her name. Just a number."

She recited it quickly before hanging up.

Reluctant to call back from my new phone, I figured I would get the kids to the car and then look for a pay phone. I figured it would take only a few minutes before I could return the mystery woman's call.

I was wrong.

On the way to the car, I texted Zoe my new number and told her we were on our way to the house. Then I scooped up a sleepy Audrey. We walked in silence away from the hospital and toward our car. What else we were walking toward, I couldn't guess. I needed a plan, one that kept my children safe. One that brought Sam home.

Audrey's arms were slack around my neck, her body drooping with fatigue. As she started to slip, I hoisted her higher, and her head thudded onto my shoulder.

I found comfort in the weight of her and her warm breath in my ear. The task felt familiar. Normal.

I suddenly tightened my grip to keep Audrey from slipping again, my heart seizing. There, in the hospital lot, two rows removed from where our own car was parked, sat a blue Toyota Camry. Just like Sam's.

Leo saw the car the second I did. Though its appearance left me frozen, it had the opposite effect on Leo. Too late, I realized I had neglected to tell Leo about Carver Sweet taking Sam's Camry from our driveway.

Leo ran toward the car, his recent injuries making his gait awkward but not slowing him.

*No, Leo.* My mind screamed, but I remained silent. The words would have been wasted. There was no stopping my son.

My own legs began pumping an instant after Leo's, Audrey bouncing against my chest as I ran.

Even with his injured knee, Leo covered the distance quickly. He checked the back of the Camry first. I knew what he was looking for: the bumper sticker.

Next, he peered into the back driver's-side window. But his urgency had faded. I had already scanned the license plate. I knew.

He turned when I caught up with him, fresh heartbreak straining his face. "It's not Dad's."

"I'm sorry, Leo," I said. And then, reluctantly: "But it's probably a good thing it isn't his."

I started to explain to my son why I was relieved the car wasn't Sam's, but my words stuck in my throat.

Because I noticed three things, almost simultaneously.

First, a dark stain on the back seat where someone had installed a car seat. Stolen, I guessed, to cover the blood.

I knew the car seat was stolen because the second thing I noticed was that the car was definitely Sam's. Someone had disguised it by swapping the plates, scratching off the sticker, and installing the car seat over the bloodstain. But there was no disguising the small dent where Leo's bike had fallen against the driver's-side door, or the smudge of white paint on the bumper from when we had repainted the fence.

Unfortunately, I noticed the car seat and the dent and the smudge before I noticed the most important detail: the reflection. In the glass, I caught sight of the shadow of the man who had been driving my husband's car.

The man responsible for putting a bloodstain on Sam's back seat.

# 25

Carver Sweet stood on the balcony less than twenty feet away, cast in the yellow glow of the parking lot lights. From Audrey's hospitalization as an infant, I knew the balcony opened off a lobby that offered vending machines, a TV, and tables of magazines meant to distract the families of surgical patients. Six years ago, I had been more inclined toward restless pacing than thumbing through copies of *Entertainment Weekly*.

Scanning a cluster of cars to the right, at first, Carver didn't see us.

I handed Leo my purse and set Audrey on her feet. Then I nudged them both toward our rental car. "Lock the doors. Call the police. Now."

Leo hesitated, the concussion and late hour adding to his confusion. "Who is that guy, Mom?" Then he saw my face, and his own went pale. "You can't—"

I cut him off, my words a determined rush. "I'm not letting that bastard out of my sight this time until the police come." I pointed to where Carver stood. "Besides, he can't hurt me from there. Go."

"But what if—"

"If he moves, I'll get in the car and run his ass over." I repeated more firmly this time: "Go."

Carver turned his head in our direction, and Leo ran, pulling Audrey with him. Behind me, I heard the car door open, then slam shut, but I kept my eyes on the man on the balcony.

Upon noticing me, Carver cocked his head and went still, observ-

ing me in the way I had often seen in cats with birds. Since he lacked
the power of flight, he couldn't reach me quickly, but even from that
distance I could see his mind puzzling over his options.

"You again." He sounded almost amused, though irritation flared
there too.

My own voice held no amusement and something much stronger
than irritation. "What did you do to my husband?"

He laughed so softly I barely heard it. "You must've seen the blood
in the back seat." He stepped to the edge of the balcony and peered
down. Gauging how far of a drop it would be to the sidewalk below?
"Remember what I told you two nights ago. I warned you that your
life was already fucked up, but you didn't know it then. I guess now
you do."

"Where's Sam?" I asked. "Why're you doing this?"

He continued as if I hadn't spoken. "Heard that boy of yours took a
nasty hit tonight."

At the mention of Leo, my breath quickened. There was a tremor
in my voice when I spoke. "You won't get close enough to hurt my son
again."

He continued to survey the ground. "I'm pretty close right now."

"Are you? Why don't you jump down here so you don't have to
shout?"

*And so you can break your leg, or, better, your head?*

Just as Carver considered his odds, I considered mine. How long
before the police arrived? How many security officers were on duty?
And were they even equipped to handle a man like Carver?

He weighed my request to jump as if it had been a serious one. "I
think I'd make it, but while I won't need my mobility for very much
longer, I do need it now," he said. "You know who can take a fall—
that friend of yours, Brooklyn. I came here looking for her, but she's
already been released."

"She isn't a friend, but I'm glad I was there that night."

He chuckled, but his eyes closed to slits. "I was less pleased," he
said. "When I was in prison, inmates had an almost sacred belief in
coincidence. You know, 'Sure, it was my backpack, but that wasn't my

heroin.' Or, 'Yeah, I was with my girlfriend that night, but it was some other guy who slit her throat.' But, you see, Cassie Larkin, I don't believe in coincidence. So how do you know Brooklyn?"

I remained silent, listening for sirens, passersby, or the calls of my children.

"Your *friend* isn't here, and she isn't at her apartment. Do you know where she might be?"

I said nothing, but my face betrayed me. "You *do* know." His expression darkened. "I'm going to need the address."

"And I'm going to need you to screw yourself."

Carver's stare was nearly a physical force. The weight of it pressed against me. "Why are you helping her?" he asked. "You've risked quite a lot for someone you say isn't your friend."

"I don't need a relationship with someone to help them."

"That's a curious thing to say. If you did just stumble on the scene that night, poor you, but there's little to be done about it now." He leaned against the railing. "Like I said, I'll need that address."

"I think I was clear in my answer to that. Remember—it involved screwing yourself?"

A car passed but it wasn't the patrol car I waited for. Carver shifted, his face cast in full light now. Somehow, the half-shadow had made it less monstrous, partially obscuring the intensity of his purpose. Obscuring that ropy scar along his jaw. He seemed to grow aware of how long we had been standing there and the risk that stillness brought him.

"You seem to have forgotten your first question," he said.

Though he hadn't answered it, I hadn't forgotten. I had asked what he had done to Sam.

Staring up at him, my vision constricted, and I felt as if my entire body were being squeezed, the pressure threatening my ability to remain standing. If Carver had pursued at that moment, I wasn't certain I would've been able to flee. Like in my van two days before, the threat of Carver immobilized me, and with the same suddenness it had that night.

Then it subsided, though the shakiness and erratic heartbeat remained.

"I found your husband's photo in your wallet, so imagine how surprised I was to find him with her," Carver said. "She left him behind, of course, and so I took him. He was breathing then. I don't know about now. I placed him on a pile of feed sacks and watched as he rolled, facedown, on the burlap."

I didn't know if what Carver said was true, but I recoiled at the thought of it—that Sam might be miles away from the life we had shared for nearly two decades, cold and alone and injured. Or worse.

*Please, God, don't let it be worse.*

As much as I had ever loved Sam, I now hated Carver with the same intensity.

"I can tell you where your husband is, if you tell me where Brooklyn is."

I had no allegiance to Sam's lover. I had already saved her once, and that was more than anyone could expect of me. Besides, I could call to warn her before Carver made it out of the parking lot.

But what if she was asleep, or she was out and her friend was home instead? I had no doubt Carver would torture anyone to get the information he wanted.

Knowing this, I almost gave Carver the information anyway.

Instead, I invented an address. But my hesitation gave me away. He studied me for a moment, then shook his head, the gesture mimicking regret. "I don't believe you," he said. "You were supposed to let her die. Eventually, you'll realize how much that decision cost you."

Carver tensed, and I recognized the coiled energy. Recognized it, and readied for it. As if connected by a wire, we acted at the same moment. He sprang, landing not on the concrete but on the grass, while I took off in a sprint.

Had he cracked his skull? Shattered a tibia?

Then I heard him. Footsteps behind me keeping pace, even if one footfall landed with less certainty. A sprain, I guessed. Not nearly as good as a shattered tibia.

Even wounded, each of Carver's longer strides matched two of mine. I might make it to my car ahead of him, but would I get inside before Carver wrapped his enormous hands around my throat?

As I ran, I told myself it was the wind I heard and not Carver's breathing. He couldn't be close enough for me to hear his breathing.

I cut sharply to the right, toward my car. Leo, bless him, had already started it.

Though adrenaline propelled me, Carver's rage provided a superior fuel.

My legs pulsed as I focused all my energy, all my breath, all my everything on reaching my car. With Carver only feet behind me, it seemed too great a distance to cover.

Then, suddenly, the car inched closer. Closer. It took me a few seconds to realize the car was moving. Slowly. Twenty feet from us, then ten. Then my son stepped on the gas—he hadn't yet gotten the hang of acceleration—and Carver bounced off the hood. He landed on the asphalt, and I got a glimpse of Leo's face, and I realized I was wrong: Leo understood acceleration just fine.

I jumped in the car as Leo scooted to the passenger seat. I intended to hit my pursuer a second time. But Carver got to his feet quickly, injured but still fueled by his rage. Then he ran, disappearing just as the police cruiser arrived.

The darkness absorbed Carver as if it recognized he belonged to it.

# 26

I had spent so much time with the police lately, I wondered if I should whip up some friendship bracelets. The officers didn't find Carver, or if they did, they didn't share the news with me. Sam's Camry had also disappeared from the lot. I wasn't surprised. Carver seemed unusually adept at evading the authorities.

When talking to the police, I didn't mention how Leo had plowed down my would-be assailant, and the officer didn't notice the small dent Carver had left on the hood.

Detective Rico wasn't there, and for that, I was grateful. I wouldn't have been able to lie to him so easily.

After the kids and I were in the car, I turned to face them.

"We should probably talk about what just happened," I said.

Audrey wriggled out of her booster, leaning over the console that separated the front seats. "You mean about how Leo hit that man with the car?"

"That's part of it, sure."

While I had been talking to Carver, and then the police, Audrey and Leo had waited in the car. Still, I wondered, *How much had they heard?*

"You didn't tell the police I hit that guy," Leo said. It was rare that I had my son's full attention, but I had it now.

"That's right."

"Why not?"

I had reasons. Several, in fact. Earlier, the person texting me, who might have been Carver, had mentioned a fight between Leo and Sam. Then Perla had shown me "evidence" of Leo's cyberbullying. That was after the alleged target of that bullying had attacked my son. I didn't like where this was headed. Didn't like it at all.

"I'd rather the police focus their attention on me."

Audrey inched farther onto the console so that half of her body now rested on it. She leaned against me. I drew resolve from the warm weight of her. "Does not telling them count as a lie?"

"It does."

"Did that guy do something to Dad?" Leo asked.

Audrey's eyes snapped fully open, her eyebrows buried in her bangs. "What do you mean? Daddy's at a conference for teachers."

I took a breath, then another. Then I told my daughter that I had kept the truth from her. As I talked, I studied Audrey's face, confused but expectant, then Leo's, lips drawn tight in anger. No matter what I said, and even if Carver was arrested and Sam found, my children's lives had permanently changed. The bedrock beneath them had shifted, split. Especially Audrey's. Sam had given her part of his liver, and on his shoulders, she could touch the sky. Yet he had disappeared. Worse, he had gone missing while with her. I might be able to repair that fissure, but I would never be able to erase it. Its jagged edges would remind Audrey and Leo, forever, that their parents were fallible. Vulnerable. And that was the best case. The worst case . . .

"I didn't want you to be afraid."

Audrey scrunched her face. "But that's a lie too."

"It is. I'm sorry."

"Daddy lied, too, on Halloween. He said he'd be right back."

Leo cut in, impatient. "You didn't answer, Mom. Did that jerk hurt Dad?" Leo's face may have been a younger version of Sam's, but the edge in his voice he had inherited from me.

I wanted to reassure him and his sister that their father was fine, but I couldn't. I searched for words that wouldn't sting but were more honest.

"I think that man knows where your dad is."

"Then the police should find him and ask him," Audrey said.

I kissed my daughter on the top of her head. "That's what they're trying to do."

My voice was steady, so my children bought it. They believed. But I didn't. I knew no one would fight as hard to find Sam or protect my kids as I would. As Perla had said earlier, sometimes you had to be an asshole. After the day I'd had, I would have no problem following that advice.

ON OUR WAY BACK to Zoe's house, the heater in the rental car decided to malfunction. It hissed a stream of tepid air, which I directed toward the windshield. The defrost cleared stripes not quite wide enough to see through. I connected the stripes by wiping away the condensation with the sleeve of my sweatshirt. I was damned tired of things breaking.

Audrey asked a couple more questions and then fell into silence. Leo was quiet, too, staring out the window, connected only to the earbuds he had fished from the glove box. I sneaked a glance at the back of my son's head, a wall that discouraged questions and kept me from his thoughts.

When I pulled the car up to the curb in front of Zoe's townhome, Audrey ran ahead to knock. By the time Leo and I reached her door, it was already ajar, my daughter wrapped around Zoe's waist. Boo bounced around their ankles.

"I tried calling you," she said, and it triggered a memory. The phone call I had meant to return before running into Carver.

I swore under my breath, then excused myself, leaving the kids with Zoe, and got back in the car. I found a pay phone outside a convenience store a few blocks away. The handset was sticky and smelled like fermented berries.

The woman who answered was warm in her greeting. "I'm glad you finally called, Cassie." As if I should recognize her voice, which I didn't.

Fortunately, she picked up on my bewilderment. "It's Helen, from Lake Park Drive?"

The neighborhood where Sam disappeared. "I remember." *Now.*
"You saw Sam and Audrey on Halloween."

"She's such a lovely girl, and your husband—so handsome."

"Thank you." I tried not to sound as if I was rushing her, even as my
pulse quickened. Fortunately, she got quickly to the point.

"Remember the Gardners' house?"

After Brooklyn's story, I would never forget it. "Abandoned two-
story, rotting jack-o'-lantern on the porch?"

"That's the one," she confirmed. "This evening, I was talking to a
neighbor, and he mentioned he saw Sam go into the Gardners' house
on Halloween."

She paused, and I reflected that pauses were rarely followed by good
news. No one hesitated before telling you that you had won the lot-
tery. Good news was breathless and eager. Bad news came slower.

Finally, she said, "He wasn't alone." Another pause. "There was a
woman. This neighbor said she and Sam seemed—"

"Friendly?" I suggested.

"Intimate."

I gripped the sticky handset until my knuckles lost color. I would
probably lose skin when I tried to pry my hand free.

"Did your neighbor mention anything about this woman's appearance?"

"Not much. He described her as attractive, a brunette, but otherwise unremarkable."

Helen's vague description bothered me. Brooklyn? Or the young
woman in the photo? Both were brunettes. Something else was there,
too, but it was like trying to catch smoke with a pool skimmer.

"My neighbor couldn't be sure, but he thinks Sam might have been
back at the house earlier tonight."

My heart raced, the go-to speed these days. Stupid stress hormones.
"Is Sam there now?"

"I'm sorry, honey, he isn't. But if you want to take a look, I could
meet you outside with a key. I used to water their plants, and I don't
think they've changed the locks yet."

I asked her to call Detective Rico and tell him what she saw, then thanked her for the information.

Helen assured me there wasn't need for my gratitude. "It's what I would do if it were Bob," she said. "In the meantime, I'll call this detective, after I see if my neighbor can give me a better description of that woman."

# 27

—

I beat Detective Rico to the abandoned house. On the doorstep, I closed my gloved fingers around the key Helen had given me, its metal edges digging into my palm. I wondered if I would need it. Sam and Brooklyn had managed entry, and they hadn't had a key.

I tried the door. The handle moved freely in my hand. I slipped the key into my pocket and moved into the house.

I pulled a small flashlight from my sweatshirt pocket, but for the moment, it was as unnecessary as the key had been. Outside, clouds shrouded the moon, but a streetlight in front of the home cut through curtainless windows, illuminating my path. I kept the flashlight in my hand but didn't bother switching it on.

The house was large but uncluttered by furniture, making the search go more quickly than I had expected. I finished checking the downstairs and attached garage in a few minutes.

I started up the staircase, each step hesitant. Though I had no reason to doubt the integrity of the steps, I still expected them to shift beneath my feet.

Halfway up, at the landing, the staircase angled to the left, thwarting the streetlight's glow. I paused on the steps and turned on my flashlight. I swept the beam up the stairs, toward the doors of the second-story bedrooms. One door was open, but the beam died at the room's threshold. The other doors were closed.

I took a moment to survey my surroundings. Nails trailed the staircase walls like drunken ants, marching up in an uneven line but going nowhere. Dozens of family photos had hung there once, the memories lingering in the outlines where the frames had protected the paint from the sun. Would the walls in my own home soon look like this?

I kept the flashlight's beam at waist height as I climbed the last few stairs. I walked through the open door first. A bathroom. The shower curtain had been removed. I checked the drawers. Empty.

Next, I checked the bedrooms that, judging by the pastel zoo animals in one and glow-in-the-dark stars in the other, had probably belonged to the children. In the room with the stars, a garbage bag sat propped in the corner. I dumped its contents on the floor. I unwadded each ball of paper, looked inside a child's discarded sneaker, shook the broken action figures, even sniffed the discarded tube of acne cream. When I was done, I scooped the debris back into the bag. It didn't feel right to leave a mess.

I saved the master bedroom for last, and my heart thudded as I approached its closed door. I held my breath as I pushed it open.

Unlike the other rooms, this bedroom was furnished, barely. A single pair of plaid curtains hung in the window that faced the street. A king-size bed remained, although it had been stripped of its linens. I stood there, frozen, staring at that bed. I tried not to think of a reason it alone would remain in the otherwise empty house.

I turned away from the bed toward the walk-in closet. Even the poles had been removed, their holders unscrewed from the walls.

I opened the door to the master bathroom. Sadness lived in the other parts of the home—the picture nails, the discarded toys, a single forgotten mug in the kitchen—but in the master bathroom, there were glimpses of rage. One hole in the wall was the size of a fist, another one the shape of a boot. Someone had also thrown a hammer at the shower's glass door, shattering it. The hammer remained in the puddle of shards.

In the rest of the house, the parents may have hidden their fury over the foreclosure from their children, but here, in their sanctuary, it had been unleashed.

I touched the hammer-cracked tile of the shower walls with my fingertips. Dry. But I wasn't really checking for moisture—I was avoiding that big bed in the master bedroom.

I returned to the bedroom and moved closer to the bed. The mattress sagged in the middle, and the right side bore a body-shaped stain a shade between yellow and brown. There were no pillows, no sheets. The box springs remained, but there was no headboard.

The bed was the only piece of furniture in the room, and the only item visible except for the single pair of curtains that hung on the street-facing window. The window that looked out onto the side yard was uncovered, its glass cracked.

Both windows were fully open, and neither had a screen. With no breeze, the curtains hung limp, but the cold seeped around their edges. I was glad for my sweatshirt. Lately, I had been prone to feel any chill more acutely.

I dropped to my knees and focused my flashlight under the bed. I steadied myself before looking beneath.

I identified small foam bits in the corner as earplugs, so I left them. Other than small tumbleweeds of dust and hair, the only other items I could see were a sock, a plastic hanger, and a ball of wadded-up paper.

I stretched my arm and, with a moderate amount of effort, managed to fish all three items from beneath the bed. I surveyed my "evidence": the child's sock had a hole in the toe, the hanger was cracked, and the paper ended up being a department store receipt for pants from the year before.

Nothing that would prove Sam had been here. But hadn't that been what I had wanted—to cast doubt that my husband had been on this bed with another woman?

I closed my eyes and pictured Sam's face. The dense brows that knitted together when he was thinking. His smirk. The calluses that were the only hard part of him. When frustrated or angry, Sam wasn't the type to yell. Instead, he would fix things. After one recent argument, Sam had sanded and refinished our dining room set.

Though less than a minute had been lost in concentration, I suddenly felt vulnerable, my back tingling as if I were being watched. I bolted upright, hitting my head on the edge of the metal frame that held the box springs. I rubbed the back of my head.

No one watched me. At least as far as I could tell.

My hands were icy as I slid them under the corner of the mattress. I meant to heave it to the side, but I had forgotten how heavy king-size mattresses could be. I ended up shimmying it sideways in an awkward series of stops and starts, until gravity aided me by pulling it the rest of the way to the floor.

My breath came in heavy bursts, though not because of exertion.

A small plastic wedge of yellow and red sat at the corner of the box springs.

Sam *had* been here.

I picked up the zombie teeth he had modeled Halloween morning. The last time I had seen him.

I stared at the piece of plastic resting on my upturned palm. It was smeared with reddish-brown paint.

But of course it wasn't paint. It was blood.

# 28

---

I knew I should call Rico to make sure he was on his way, but I was frozen, transfixed by the bloody teeth I held.

I supposed I was being dramatic. It wasn't as if the small chunk of plastic dripped blood. Only a smudge barely recognizable as blood. Still, it was my husband's blood, and I fought the urge to wipe my palm on my jeans, or throw the teeth on the mattress where he may have lain only hours earlier. With someone else.

I tried to make that last part matter to me, and later it might, but all I saw was the blood. There was now no outcome I could imagine that ended in anything other than tragedy.

The longer I stared at the rust-colored blot on my palm, the more my hand shook, until the plastic teeth bounced off and landed on the floor.

Though my hand was empty, I kept my arm, bent at the elbow, extended, my fingers frozen.

Using my left hand, I pulled my phone from my pocket and fumbled to dial Rico with my thumb.

I hung up when I heard the car. I moved to the window and looked between the crack where the curtains met. No need to make that call after all—the police were already there.

The police cruiser arrived first, then the tech who took my gloves as evidence.

I had wanted to run out the back door, or at least dispose of the gloves, but those were the choices of a guilty person. I was merely desperate. As I talked with Detective Ray Rico, I hoped that desperation didn't show.

Rico's jacket was pressed, but his white shirt had wrinkled since the last time I'd seen him. He wore no tie. When he saw me noticing, he smirked.

"Long day," he said. "Heard you had a run-in with Carver at the hospital."

"Surprised I didn't see you there."

"I thought I could catch a twenty-minute nap at the station." He motioned toward his wrinkled shirt. "It's hard to keep up with you."

Despite his slightly disheveled appearance, Rico's eyes remained sharp, and his questions came quickly.

"You entered through the front door?"

"Yes."

"And you borrowed a key from a neighbor?"

"From Helen."

"I thought you said the door was unlocked."

"I borrowed the key but ended up not needing it."

I uncrossed my arms. I had read somewhere that crossed arms made a person seem guilty, and I couldn't risk that. Especially since I had walked out to meet the police with my husband's blood on my hand.

"Tonight's the first time you were in possession of that key?"

That seemed an odd question, but I answered it quickly. "Yes."

"And you don't have any other keys to the property?"

As I shook my head, it hit me: Rico might be able to arrest me for trespassing. Was that why he was so interested in how I had entered the house?

"Explain again what brought you here."

There was no malice in his voice, but his gaze remained pinned to mine. Though we had met only days earlier, the creases below his eyes seemed to have grown thicker, the circles darker.

"Another neighbor"—I paused to fill in the name but realized I'd never been given one—"he told Helen he'd seen Sam going into this house on Halloween, and again earlier this evening. She called me."

"What's this neighbor's name?"

"I don't know."

"What's Helen's last name?"

I didn't know that either, so I pointed across the street to Helen's house. "She lives there, in the yellow one-story."

While Rico jotted something in his notes, I slipped my hand in my pocket to retrieve my phone, intending to show proof of Helen's call. Then I remembered that Perla had my old phone—the one Helen had called—and my return call had been placed at a pay phone.

Fortunately, I'd memorized her number. I gave that to Rico, as well as Perla's contact information.

He made note of both, then said, "Tell me exactly what Helen told you."

As I recounted the brief conversation, I again wondered why the neighbor's description of the woman bothered me. *Attractive, brunette, and unremarkable*, he'd said. As Sam's wife, of course I was bothered by mention of the "attractive" woman he may have been sleeping with. But it was more than that. A doubt burrowed into my brain, too deep for me to grab.

Rico stopped taking notes. "Why didn't you call the police? After running into Carver Sweet at the hospital, I would think you'd have called."

"Helen called."

But my spine prickled, and I knew before Rico said it. "We didn't get a call from anyone named Helen. We did, however, get a call from someone reporting an intruder at this address. Do you own a gun, Cassie?"

His voice was soft, and this was the first time he hadn't addressed me as Dr. Larkin, but I took no comfort in his casual approach. When I was eleven, I had tried to escape the neighbor's dog through a hole at the bottom of our fence. But I had misjudged the size of the hole and got stuck. While the neighbor's dog had mercilessly licked my exposed ankle, the broken planks had pressed against my back, their jagged teeth forcing me against the dirt. Each attempt to wriggle free made the vise tighter, until I could draw only shallow breaths.

I felt the same now.

"I don't own a gun," I said, with a rough voice I barely recognized.

"The caller reported that the intruder had a gun. After what your family's been through, I understand why you'd carry one." His eyes aimed for sympathy, and they came close. But I'd heard somewhere that detectives usually knew the answers to the questions they asked. If true, did Rico have "proof" I had a weapon?

"Will officers find a gun inside the house, Cassie?"

Would they? I had thoroughly searched the house, but I wasn't sure. "If they find a gun, it isn't mine."

I tried to read Rico's eyes, but they gave away nothing. "The other thing is, the key you gave us doesn't fit this lock."

*It didn't?* Then: *Of course it didn't.* Uncertain how to respond, I said nothing.

"You've never been here before, right?"

"I've been in the neighborhood when I was looking for Sam, but I've never been inside this house."

"You mean, before tonight."

"Of course." I realized I'd crossed my arms again. I uncrossed them.

"Where are your kids, Cassie?"

I felt the crease between my eyebrows deepen. Not a question I had been expecting. "With a friend."

"Both of them?"

"Of course. Why would you ask that?"

"I heard Leo was hurt pretty badly playing football."

"He has a mild concussion and a torn meniscus," I confirmed.

"He can walk, though? And drive?"

Had Rico learned that Leo had run over Carver? My eyes darted to my rental car for signs an evidence technician was examining the hood, but the car sat untouched under a streetlight.

Rico noticed. "Need to leave?"

My heart hammered. "Leo's injured, but he can walk. As far as driving, he's only fifteen."

"But he has his permit?"

"What are you asking, Detective?"

"Just making sure I've got the details right. Before you came here, you dropped Leo at his friend's house?"

"My friend, not his," I clarified. "Why are you asking about Leo?"

My question hung in the air, unanswered. "Does this friend of yours have a car?"

"Of course she does."

"Leo would have access?"

"What does any of this have to do with finding Sam?"

The full weight of Rico's attention fell on me. Sympathy remained in his expression, but it battled with something else—suspicion? "I have a nephew, just graduated college. He was in an auto accident when he was in high school. You know how it can be—inexperienced driver, bad weather. Weather wasn't so bad tonight.

"I tell you this because since my nephew's accident, I've become pretty good at reading scenes."

My heart sank. "Has Sam been in an accident?"

"I wouldn't know," he said. "Not yet." This time, there was no mistaking the suspicion. But, given the nature of his questions, I had a terrible feeling it wasn't directed at me.

"The kid who hurt your boy? I heard the play was dirty, and I can understand why that might make someone angry. Does Leo have a temper?"

I was suddenly terrified of saying the wrong thing. "No more than any teenager. Why?"

"That kid crashed about an hour ago, hit a tree, but there's also a dent on the opposite side of his car. I'm guessing when the investigation is done, we'll find that someone ran him off the road. Like I said, I'm pretty good at reading accident scenes."

"Are you insinuating Leo's involved?"

"I'm just trying to get to the truth, and he and the boy *did* have history."

The way he said it left no room for doubt: Rico knew about the cyberbullying. I wondered what else he knew. "What were Leo and Sam fighting about the night before your husband disappeared?"

The texts. There had been two. The first had alluded to the fight. And then the second one: *I'm sure Leo didn't mean the things he said that night.*

I realized then that Rico knew everything. Not everything as in the truth, because if he did, Sam would be home. This would be over. No, what Rico knew was all the "evidence" manufactured by the person targeting my family.

Anger had been my go-to emotion for years, but I had no room for it now. Fear and confusion forced it out.

"I don't know anything about a fight," I said. "I wasn't home that night, remember?"

"You didn't hear about it afterward?"

"We had more important things to discuss." The night air was cold but too still and held an expectant edge. "You know about the social media posts."

It wasn't a question, and he supplied no answer. His broad face betrayed no emotion, his body as motionless as the air.

"They were faked, but most moms would say the same," I said.

I could've expanded with examples of Leo's kindness, or argued how the posts displayed a cruelty I'd never witnessed in him. It wouldn't have swayed Rico, but it would've bought me a few minutes before my next confession. Because I knew I'd have to give the detective all the information if he was going to find Sam.

My cheeks burned, and I had to swallow twice before getting the words out.

"There was a photo too," I said. "I'm not sure if you know about that, but I'm guessing you will. Someone will want you to know."

I paused to steady my breathing.

"The number one was written on the back—three days, three numbers. I suppose I should've told you about it, but I didn't want it to sway you in the wrong direction, and, if I'm being honest, I didn't feel much like sharing a photo of my husband having sex with another woman. But I can get you that photo in the morning."

Sam's reputation. Our marriage. What was the point in protecting any of it at the expense of my son's safety and Sam's life?

Rico waited to make sure I'd finished, then asked, "How'd you get the photo?"

"My daughter found it in her backpack."

"Where was the backpack?"

"In her cubby at school."

"When?"

"This afternoon."

Rico studied me through narrowed eyes. "Is there anything else you haven't told me?"

I sighed, so deeply it rattled my chest. "I'm sure there is, but I can't think of anything right now."

He rubbed his eyes, and I sensed his own confession coming. "I talked to the principal at the high school." He made a show of consulting his notebook. "Chuck Diggs. Principal Diggs said Sam might have been sleeping with his students."

"He wasn't."

"Sam's friend, Ozzy Delgado, said the same thing, that Sam would never touch a student."

"Because he wouldn't have."

"But Ozzy did say he was sleeping with someone. So a cheating husband disappears. Okay. The story tracks. Either Sam left because he wanted to pursue this adulterous, possibly illegal, relationship, or you found out about the affair and there was a fight. In this scenario, we don't know where your husband is—a hotel? a ditch?—but we have an idea what led to his disappearance. Which means we know where to look."

Rico let his words settle. I couldn't move. I wanted to leave, but I also needed to hear where he was going with this.

"See, at first, that's what I thought happened," he said. "Then your son gets injured in a football game, and the guy who hit him ends up in the hospital too. The storyline shifts. Leo has a temper. He fights with his dad—about the affair?—and then Sam disappears. Leo bullies this boy online, and then that boy nearly dies in an accident."

I couldn't help myself this time, "Do you really believe my son capable of that?"

He shrugged. "I don't much like anonymous tips. I prefer when the person making the accusations is willing to stand behind them. That said, I don't really know your son."

"Then let me tell you: he's not."

Rico tucked his notebook inside the pocket of his jacket. "I'm married. Twenty-six years, three kids, two still at home. I understand the impulse to protect your husband and kids," he said. "But I *am* going to need that photo as soon as possible. If I'm going to find Sam, I'm also going to need you to be straight with me. You can't hold stuff like this back, even if it shines an unfavorable light on your family."

The detective's tone sounded less sympathetic than it had earlier, and when he walked away, I got the unshakable feeling I had disappointed him.

# 29

---

After checking in with Zoe, I sat in the car and contemplated my next move. At first, the brisk air seared my lungs, but the interior quickly became swampy with my breath. I cracked the window, then wiped the condensation from the windshield with my sleeve.

Though Helen's house had been dark when I had gotten into the car, lights blazed there now.

Helen's description of Sam's lover continued to trouble me.

*Attractive, brunette, and unremarkable.*

It certainly sounded like Brooklyn, but I suddenly seized on the last of the descriptors—*unremarkable.*

Midbreath, the memory landed, just beyond reach. I forced myself into stillness, holding my exhalation, afraid the memory would be as easily chased away as a butterfly pausing for nectar.

Then it hit me, and I released my breath.

When I had asked Audrey to describe the woman she had seen with her dad on Halloween, Audrey had told me the woman had been wearing a costume. Gray wig. Painted face. Like a broken doll.

Hardly *unremarkable.*

Helen had lied. More than that, she had described Brooklyn as she normally was, not how she had appeared on Halloween. So Helen had seen more than she had admitted.

I got out of the car, taking the blazing lights as an invitation. Not that I required one.

With the side of my fist, I knocked on the door. Immediately, it opened—but instead of periwinkle hair and a creased brow, I was greeted by a middle-aged man wearing a knit cap, a thin robe, and a scowl.

"What do you want?" The man pulled his robe around him. At this hour, it likely offered inadequate protection against the chill.

"I'm looking for Helen."

The man's expression shifted from annoyance to confusion. "Who?" He tugged on the edge of his knit cap, his nose red from the cold.

I repeated myself, this time describing Helen. Seeing no reaction, I added details as if the man wouldn't know an elderly woman lived in his home unless I chose just the right word to describe her.

*Ah, yes, I wasn't sure, but since you mentioned her snub nose . . .*

The man in the knit cap and thin robe shook his head. "My wife and I have lived here for four years." His tone was apologetic, but he closed the door a fraction. For all he knew, I could be connected to the trouble across the street. Which, I guessed, I was.

It hit me then that I had first met Helen on the street, and, earlier that night, on the doorstep of the abandoned house. I had never actually seen Helen leaving or entering the house she claimed as hers.

"Maybe she's a neighbor?" I asked.

"Never seen anyone like that." His eyes drifted across the street. "So—do you know what's going on over there?"

I reached for my phone, for photos of Sam, before realizing I had nothing to show this man. Per Perla's instructions, I couldn't even give him my new number. "They're looking for a man who disappeared last night."

Before I could describe Sam, the man in the robe said, "Oh, it's about that teacher? Yeah, the police were asking around about him earlier." He dropped his voice to a whisper. "Honestly? My guess is that guy ditched his family."

The man's face grew weary, his tone wistful, as if such a thought had occurred to him too.

I felt suddenly dizzy. "Why would you say that?"

"Isn't that always how it happens? Either the guy left, or the wife killed him?"

He moved to shut the door, but I stretched my arm across the threshold. With my other arm, I gestured toward the house where Rico and his team still milled.

"Do you know who lived there?"

The man furrowed his brow, considering how helpful he should continue to be to the persistent stranger on his doorstep. He must have recognized my level of persistence and that giving me a name was the only way to be rid of me, because, finally, he answered.

The name he gave me was not Gardner.

WHILE TALKING TO THE man who wasn't Helen, I had missed a call from Zoe. When I called her back, she rushed through her first piece of news: Perla had texted Zoe asking that I stop by on the way home. *Nothing urgent*, she'd texted.

Zoe quickly moved on to her second announcement, delivered without pause for breath or breaks between the words. Still, I understood it clearly enough: she had found Hannah, or so she hoped. Zoe forwarded to my phone a photo from the yearbook and an address.

I checked the time. Though it was late, it was a Friday night. Hannah would likely be awake. That's if she was home.

First Hannah's house, then Perla's, I decided.

I started the car, rolling down both windows. The cold air served the dual purpose of defogging the windows and keeping me alert. On the way, I stopped at an ATM, then I headed across town to confront a teenage girl who had started rumors about sleeping with my husband.

A COUPLE OF BLOCKS from Hannah's house near a twenty-four-hour market, I spotted a teen couple on the sidewalk. The boy wore jeans and a sweatshirt, hood pulled over his head. The girl wore the same, though her jeans rested lower on her hips and her sweatshirt fit more snugly.

They were easy to spot, especially the girl. She reminded me of a colorful moth—maybe an elephant hawk-moth with its yellow wings and pink spots—as she flitted from streetlight to streetlight, laughing, weaving, casually flirting with the boy who walked beside her. She moved from one pool of light to the next, unconcerned about the darkness beyond and of the creatures in it that could grind her wings to dust.

*Yeah, I was in a foul mood.*

The girl was only a few years older than Leo. Legally an adult, but not by much. I recognized her from the yearbook photo. Hannah Zimmerman.

The boy moved in a straight line that Hannah bobbed around, touching first his right elbow, then popping up on his other side to brush her fingertips against his left shoulder. The boy was mesmerized by her, and her carelessness became his own.

They seemed on a course for the market, so I pulled in the lot and waited. The couple stopped in a puddle of light twenty or so feet from where I was parked. I got out of the car and leaned against the door, preparing to call out Hannah's name in my best nonthreatening mom voice.

Before I could, the young woman approached me. As she did, she pulled her boyfriend along by the hem of his sweatshirt.

Hannah turned up the wattage on her smile. Dark and pretty, Hannah was probably used to getting what she wanted. Right now, I apparently had something she wanted. I figured it was either drugs or beer, and the location made me guess the latter.

Hannah nudged her boyfriend forward. Hands thrust in his jean pockets, he flushed as he kicked at an invisible mark on the asphalt with his right sneaker. I had no doubt whose idea this was.

"We were wondering if, like, you know, maybe you could buy us some beer." The boy's face flushed, his words nearly lost in his mumbling.

The mom in me couldn't help it. "Do you think it's really a good idea to be approaching strangers in convenience store parking lots?" *Or, for that matter, drinking beer.*

The boy looked chastened—I got the feeling he wasn't as committed to this as his girlfriend—but Hannah looked irritated.

She switched off her full-wattage smile. "Who are you, my mother?"

*So . . . pretty, but not very original with the comebacks.*

I reminded myself that I wanted something from this girl. "Your name's Hannah, right?"

The girl draped a hand on her boyfriend's shoulder, nails sky blue and filed to points. She tried for flippant. "Buy us a twelve-pack and I might answer that."

I considered threatening to tell her parents, but that seemed a sure way to end what I hoped would be a productive conversation.

"Let me rephrase: Your name is Hannah Zimmerman, and you claim your art teacher pressured you to have sex with him."

I kept my tone as neutral as my mood allowed.

"Mr. Larkin? Yeah, that's what happened." Hannah seemed unconcerned that her boyfriend was within earshot. "I was, like, failing, and Mr. Larkin asked me to stay after class. He said if I gave him a hand job, he'd give me a B. And if I had sex with him, he'd give me an A."

I allowed myself a second of relief. That she had called him Mr. Larkin made me doubt the rest of her story. "Just like that?"

Her smile was predatory. "Totally. I guess his wife's a bitch or whatever." Even though I hadn't introduced myself, I had no doubt Hannah knew who I was. Who else would be here, in a convenience store parking lot on a Friday night, asking these questions?

"So, did you accept his offer?"

Hannah looked at the boy, while he stared at the pavement. "Mr. Larkin's hot for an old guy, so the hand job, sure. But, like, I have a boyfriend. I wouldn't have sex with him."

"And then Mr. Larkin gave you a B?"

"Actually, he gave me an A." Her smile edged toward a snarl. "I guess he really liked it."

She was eighteen years old, but she was also pretty much a kid, so I decided against punching her.

"How much?" I asked.

Her face scrunched in on itself—the pert nose, the perfect brows, the glossed lips—so she acquired that just-sucked-a-lemon look. "What?"

"Let's cut the crap. You didn't sleep with my husband."

"I told you, it was just—"

"No, it wasn't. Not even that. So you got something out of it, and my guess would be money. How much?"

She aimed to look offended, but the sneer ruined it. "I'd never do that."

Coming here, I had intended to make a play to Hannah's conscience: *Mr. Larkin could lose his job. You wouldn't want that, would you?* But I realized Hannah wasn't the kind of girl who had a conscience.

I reached into my purse and pulled out five twenty-dollar bills. "Was it more than that?"

I had her interest. "Hyperthetically, what if I had, like, been paid to make some shit up?"

Of course, she meant *hypothetically*. No wonder she was failing most of her classes. I pulled out two more twenties.

"Let's talk *hyperthetically*." I felt a little bad for mocking her, so I softened my tone. "You've already been paid by whoever hired you, so anything I give you would be like a bonus. I'll give you forty bucks for every *hyperthetical* detail I find useful."

I needed to stop doing that.

Hannah thought it over, but only for a few seconds. "Okay, maybe someone asked me to start the rumors, but I didn't mind. Like I said, Mr. Larkin's hot."

I remembered Brooklyn's story about Hannah in her bloodied ballet slippers, digging a grave for her dead dog. And I thought about how ill-tempered I had been at her age. That and a couple of deep breaths kept me from giving in to my anger. Not that it was easy.

Hannah's boyfriend continued to stare at the ground, his eyes focused on a small weed growing in a crack. He used the toes of his sneaker to grind it into the blacktop.

I turned my attention back to Hannah, handing her forty dollars. "Who asked you to start these rumors?"

She shrugged. "Some bald dude I met in the parking lot."

I kept my expression neutral even as the words settled against my eardrums like spikes: *Some bald dude.*

"He gave me a few hundred bucks," she said. "I told you two things, so is that worth eighty?"

I gave her forty. "Can you describe this man? I mean, other than being bald."

"He was a big guy. And old. Like forty or fifty."

I handed over two more twenties. I tried to calculate how much more information I could buy.

"Do you remember anything else about this man? His car? His clothes?"

"No."

"Did he have a scar?"

I held my breath as she considered the question. "I don't know. Maybe." When I didn't hand over any cash, she added, "Come on, I should get something for that."

I gave her another twenty. "Did he say anything about why he would want you to start the rumors?"

She shook her head. "He said something like, 'You wanna make three hundred dollars?' Then he told me to start telling my friends I'd had sex with Mr. Larkin. That was it. When I agreed, he told me he'd know if I didn't keep my end of the bargain." Hannah's face lost the sneer, and she wrapped her arms around herself. "He looked kinda creepy when he said that. Then he walked away, off campus. I never saw his car, and he never came back."

"When was this?"

She held out her hand, palm up. I gave her another twenty.

"I don't know. About a month ago?"

So long before that night on the trail.

Unnerved, I got back into my car. I expected Hannah and her boyfriend to try to rope another stranger into buying them alcohol, but the boy shook his head and started back in the direction from which they had come. The boy seemed to have some sense after all, even if he could've used better taste in the company he kept.

# 30

---

Perla lived in an apartment in Fountaingrove, once a Utopian community founded by vintner Thomas Lake Harris. At the time he lived, Harris was believed to be immortal and thus lay dead for months before his followers admitted he wasn't sleeping.

No immortals currently resided in Fountaingrove, although some of its wealthiest residents came close. A few years before, that's what the area was known for: its Utopian roots, its mini-mansions, and the expressway that divided it. But that was before a firestorm that burned more than 36,000 acres and left twenty-two people dead.

Among the houses that had survived the devastation were apartment and condominium complexes carved into the hillside, named to pay homage to the million-dollar views—views now marked by blackened manzanitas and the skeletons of homes being rebuilt.

I stopped at one such place now, Vista Bella, an upscale community of townhomes done in earth tones and stacked stone. I climbed the steps to the apartment number Zoe had given me. I rang the doorbell, then rapped softly on the door.

My knocks went unanswered. I called Perla several times, but my calls rolled to voicemail.

I weighed whether I should try the knob. Perla's lack of response worried me. It was likely locked anyway.

It wasn't. Just like the door at the abandoned house, this one opened in invitation. I pushed it open, just a little, and called her name. "Perla?"

I risked a single step over the threshold, into the living room, which was dark and crammed with furniture too large for the space.

"Perla?" I called again.

Still no response.

Though I felt like an intruder, concern drove me deeper into the apartment. I walked quickly through the other rooms—one bathroom, one bedroom, and the kitchen. On the kitchen counter rested a mug of coffee and half a muffin. I dipped my finger in the coffee, piercing the oily sheen to test the temperature. Cool. The meal could have been abandoned midway through, or Perla might not have felt like cleaning up after herself. When I had been single, my clothes remained in puddles on the floor until laundry day.

So all I had determined in my quick search of the apartment was that it was empty, but I really had no way to tell how long it had been that way.

Nothing seemed out of place, so I left Perla's apartment, locking the door behind me.


ON THE WAY TO ZOE'S, I stopped at home to check messages on the landline. There were two. The first was a sales call. The second was from my father: "I can't reach you on your cell, and I just wanted to give you a heads-up . . . I'll be there early tomorrow." He gave the name of his hotel and his room number.

*Stubborn man.* I allowed myself a brief smile.

For the second night in a row, when I got to her home, Zoe waited.

My friend offered me the use of her computer to check my email. Then she hugged me, with less than her usual enthusiasm, and said, "We'll talk in the morning."

I didn't like the way she said that.

I knew I needed sleep, too, but instead, I logged on to the computer. Most of the messages were work-related, and I was preparing to log off when one email stopped me.

*Linda? Who's Linda?*

In my exhaustion, I stared at the screen for a solid thirty seconds before remembering: Linda was the manager from the coffee shop I had visited earlier. As I had requested of the barista, she had emailed me a video link with a one-word subject line: *Thursday*.

The day Sam disappeared.

It looked like I owed Josh two hundred bucks.

My finger hovered over the video's play icon. My lungs seized, and my finger froze there, unable to tap play.

I inhaled deeply, but it did little to steady me. I couldn't bring myself to view the video because of what it represented: truth. Ozzy, Brooklyn, Helen, Carver, maybe even the police, they all had their agendas. But the coffee shop manager had sent this video because I had asked for it. She didn't care about Sam, or about me. We were strangers to her, and she to us. Unlike the photo left in Audrey's backpack, I had no doubt about this video's authenticity.

I tapped play.

The manager had sent only the clip that interested me, so the couple walked immediately into the frame. A petite brunette wearing a ponytail and yoga pants, followed by a tall man with dark close-cropped hair. I recognized the crooked grin even from a distance. I rested my fingertips on the screen, on his face, but felt cold glass instead of skin.

*Sam.*

In the video, Brooklyn took a seat at a small table on the patio, her back to the camera. Sam sat opposite her, his face fully exposed. He leaned into the table, his grin slipping, his expression suddenly serious. He reached forward to place his hand on top of hers.

I tried to convince myself it was a gesture of comfort even as his hand lingered.

Still, I forced myself to watch. I couldn't read lips, so I tried to read body language.

Brooklyn seemed to relax when Sam touched her, her erect back softening into a slouch as she, too, leaned forward. I wondered what other gestures they might have shared had there not been the table between them.

I was so fixated on the images that I didn't at first notice the time and date stamp in the corner. The coffee shop was a few minutes from the high school, and the couple had been recorded at 12:23 p.m.—on Sam's lunch break. They wouldn't have had time for a tryst and an espresso.

But did that make the subtle intimacies the couple exchanged better, or worse? It was one thing to meet for a hookup, but another entirely to meet because of a connection.

Then I remembered: Sam had been suspended by then. They would have had all the time they needed.

On the screen, Brooklyn reached across the table, touching Sam's face, and my own cheeks burned as if slapped. Sam brushed her hand away and, for a moment, I allowed myself to believe the gesture was driven by loyalty to our marriage. But then he smiled again, and his hand was back on hers.

The digital stamp read October 24. The video wasn't from the day Sam disappeared at all, but from a full week before. The video may have corroborated Brooklyn's story that she knew Sam, but otherwise, like Helen's house, it was a dead end.

When Sam and Brooklyn stood to leave, I moved my mouse to stop playback. Then I saw him: a man at the table behind theirs, obstructed until they moved offscreen. The man was in the corner of the frame, barely visible, except for a thin crescent of his hairless head.

# 31

Despite my certainty that I would never sleep again, exhaustion had overwhelmed me. I had fallen asleep on Zoe's couch, which was very comfortable for sitting but not so much for sleeping. As I shifted into a sitting position, removing the one-eyed Smooch from my chest, my stiff limbs protested and my neck cracked. In my twenties, I could unfurl from any position with the grace of the cat I had just displaced, but now I popped and snapped like a bowl of crisped-rice cereal.

I checked the time on my phone. 5:48 a.m. I needed to go to my father's hotel once the kids woke up, but I wasn't going anywhere without at least a gallon of coffee. I moved into the kitchen and sat on one of the stools that butted up against the countertop. Boo sat on the kitchen mat, tail wagging and nose wriggling.

I had watched the section of video that featured the bald man so many times the night before, my eyes still felt as if they had been bathed in saltwater. There were no better angles, and the more often I watched, the less certain I became it was Carver Sweet. I forwarded the clip to Detective Rico anyway. The Santa Rosa Police Department had better tech and clearer eyes than I did.

Zoe pushed an omelet in my direction and brought me a mug of coffee, a piece of wheat toast, and a small bowl of sliced apples.

"You're totally getting a raise," I said, alternating between bites of green-pepper-and-mushroom omelet and sips of coffee. I usually skipped breakfast, but since I hadn't eaten since the half of a sandwich from the coffee shop, I figured this was more like a really late dinner. "Have you heard back from Perla?"

"Not yet. But there's something I want to show you." When I arched an eyebrow, she added, "After you eat."

She arranged strips of bacon in the skillet. "Daryl texted last night. Lester's apparently doing well, and he insists he's bringing in lemon bars on Monday."

Lemon bars were Zoe's favorite. "Better than his brownies."

"I don't know about that. He asked if I wanted regular, or ones with a 'kick.'" Zoe flipped the bacon in the pan. Then she turned down the heat and faced me, arms crossed. "I've needed to talk to you, but I wanted to wait until you got some sleep," she said. "I love you, Cassie, but you need to stop."

So the omelet was a bribe. "Love you, too, Zoe, but I can't."

"That man could've killed you last night."

"I don't think I'm Rico's favorite person, but I don't think he'd harm me."

"You know that's not who I'm talking about. For whatever reason, Carver Sweet seems to hate you."

"Brooklyn says he loves me."

"You know what I'm saying. He seems intent on hurting you."

When I thought of all my family had been through, my cheeks flushed with repressed anger. "I won't give him the chance."

"Seems he had one last night."

"I'm still here, unscathed and eating breakfast. Great omelet by the way."

"You're not changing the subject."

"That's exactly what I'm doing. Coffee's delicious too. Do I detect cinnamon?"

"I'm worried about you."

Along with my father, Zoe was the second person in half a day to express that sentiment. They weren't wrong. I was a little worried about myself.

"Listen, Cassie, I know you want to find Sam, but you're being reckless, and stubborn."

"Thank you."

"Not a compliment."

"You said you had something to show me?"

She sighed and retrieved an envelope from a drawer. I pushed my plate away, no longer hungry. I knew what was in that envelope.

"I need to get that photo to Detective Rico," I said.

"I can get it to him, but first, you need to look at this." Zoe laid the picture on the counter, then pulled out a magnifier from the same drawer. "Two things. Look at the edge of the mattress." She held the magnifier over the far right of the image, where the mattress met the edge of the carpet. "It's just a little off. Not quite as straight as it should be."

Even under the magnifying glass, the mattress looked straight to me. As much as I wanted to believe the photo was fake, I wondered if Zoe was finding flaws where none existed.

She read the skepticism on my face. "The second thing is more obvious." She moved the magnifying glass so it hovered over where Sam's arm crossed his lover's body.

"See the woman's hips here?" I appreciated that Zoe used the word woman, not girl. She slid the magnifier upward, over the point where my husband's arm crossed the woman's midsection. "Now look at the spot right above her waist."

I could see it. Kind of. Something was off, but I couldn't name what it was. Zoe pointed. "The woman's waist doesn't quite blend with her hips." She traced a line, and though the difference was slight, I understood what Zoe was saying.

"Her top half's just a little smaller than her bottom half."

Zoe nodded. "As if someone wanted her frame to appear narrower. Younger." She dragged her fingertip to the edge of the mattress. "That's also why this part curves slightly."

For a moment, I got caught up in Zoe's excitement. The photo was doctored. But then I realized what she hadn't said.

"So the photo was manipulated to make the woman in it appear younger. But she wasn't inserted entirely? Like a photo of Sam wasn't combined with a photo of the woman?"

"Probably not," she admitted. She quickly added, "That doesn't mean there aren't other explanations."

"Such as?"

Zoe had spent a lot of time with the photo, and that she hesitated told me what she couldn't say aloud. Still, she tried. "It could be an old photo. From before you and Sam were together."

I looked at the photo as a wife, not an evidence technician, and traced a small scar above his hip. We had gone to Tahoe a couple of years before. Leo had given the sled a push while Audrey was still settling in, and the bad angle led Sam and Audrey into a rock. Sam wouldn't have gotten hurt if he hadn't wrapped himself so completely around our daughter.

"It isn't an old photo."

"Since the image has been manipulated, at least we know now it could be Brooklyn, right?" Zoe said, as if I might find comfort that Sam had cheated on me with only one woman.

I had little enthusiasm for her theory. "Hair color's right, I guess."

Leo shuffled into the kitchen, and Zoe and I both jumped.

"You're up early." I folded the photo and handed it back to Zoe, who slipped it back into the drawer.

"I smelled bacon." Leo grabbed a handful of the strips but stopped. He wrinkled his nose. "Is something burning?"

My eyes dropped to the pan, but the bacon sizzled half-cooked, and the fan above the stove would've eliminated any smoke there. In the air, I detected nothing but the scent of bacon and coffee.

Zoe turned off the burner anyway, and we both scanned the room. The air remained still, clear.

Suddenly, my fingers tingled, an icy finger trailing my backbone. Zoe started, "I don't—" but I interrupted.

"Wake your sister."

Because I smelled it. Smoke, subtle but acrid, the scent of smoldering wood corrupted by—something.

I turned to Zoe to ask her to call 911, but she already had the phone in her hand.

"Do you have a fire extinguisher?"

She pointed to the closet.

On legs that weren't entirely stable, I ran to the closet, grabbed the extinguisher, then leashed Boo.

"Where do you keep Smooch's crate?"

Zoe cradled the phone and pointed again, this time toward her bedroom.

As I crated Smooch, I identified the second scent. It was the smell of road trips and boat docks, benzenes and hydrocarbons, evil and intent. Gasoline.

Leo returned with a groggy Audrey at his side, moving with greater speed, no longer motivated solely by my urging.

"Fire Department's on its way," Zoe said. She grabbed her purse, keys, and the crate, while I lifted Boo, tucking him under the arm that didn't hold the extinguisher. A few quick strides and I was at the front door, placing my palm against it. Warm, not hot. Still, I gestured Zoe and the kids toward the back door. There, Zoe joined me in placing a hand against the wood. Cool to the touch.

"Got everything?" Leo and Zoe nodded, but Audrey peeled away from her brother and ran to me, wrapping herself around both my legs.

"Mommy?"

"We've got to leave, Peanut. Go with your brother."

But she buried her face in my stomach and her grasp tightened, her arms twin bands of tape holding me in place. This was it. This was her limit. Apparently, fire be damned, the only way she was leaving was in my arms.

I handed Leo the dog and scooped up Audrey, tilting my chin toward the door. Zoe nodded, twisted the knob, held her breath, and threw the door open.

Outside, the tang of gas was stronger. The flames weren't yet visible, but I knew they were there, waiting to trace the line of gasoline that led to a puddle on the back stoop.

I yelled for Leo to be careful not to step in it, the sudden vision of burning pajama legs speeding my heart and my step. Not real. But it easily could be. I pushed through it, forcing myself and my family forward.

We left a wide berth as we approached the front yard, and now we could hear it. A soft crackling, like the snap of small bones. Still no flames. A beast in hiding, but its breath growing thicker in the air.

When we turned the corner, we finally saw it: a small pile of what might've been rags had been set ablaze in front of the house, though the fire was spreading quickly beyond it. I caught the shimmer of gasoline, a pool on the front doorstep identical to the one in back. Then flames leapt into it. Dancing. Bloating. Consuming.

I placed Audrey on the ground and pulled the extinguisher's pin, aiming the nozzle toward the house, where fire licked the exterior wall, and squeezed, but the flames reached with gas-soaked tentacles in both directions. I swept the extinguisher from side to side. It was like trying to stanch the flow from an artery with a cotton ball.

A small crowd had gathered on the sidewalk, most in nightclothes but some already dressed. I ignored them, my finger tight on the trigger until the last of the spray dripped from the nozzle. A neighbor stepped in with a second extinguisher, another with a garden hose.

Together, we hobbled the fire. Firefighters were on their way. It was probably enough to keep the blaze from spreading. But I wasn't sure.

I dropped the now empty extinguisher and walked toward the charred lump that had been the fire's source. Closer now, I saw it was a pile of clothing. Most had been torched, but a scrap of denim remained recognizable.

Jeans, the same wash Sam had been wearing the night he had disappeared.

I knelt down. On the jeans, I smelled no gasoline, and they had been placed apart from the other items. There was no way for me to tell if the jeans really were Sam's, but the deliberate way they had been staged made me think they were.

At the least, they were a message. Shaking and reeking of smoke, I had a message of my own I was very eager to deliver.

# 32

---

I didn't wait for the firefighters, or the police. After extracting from Zoe an assurance that she and the animals would find someplace safe, someplace I didn't know about, I gathered the kids and headed to a hotel across town. Not to stay myself, but to meet a man I hadn't seen in six years.

On the way, I called Detective Rico. Dawn had just started to reach across the sky with fingers still more gray than blue, but Rico answered on the second ring.

"Hello?" If not for the moment he took to clear his throat, I wouldn't have guessed I had interrupted the detective's sleep.

"My friend Zoe's house was set on fire."

"Good morning, Cassie." He coughed, clearing more phlegm. "So it's a fire today, is it? Everyone okay?"

"We're fine." I gave him the address of Zoe's townhome. "After our conversation last night, I didn't want to be accused of keeping anything from you."

"No, we wouldn't want that." Any trace of sleep had slipped from his voice, that familiar edge back. In the background, I heard the squeak of coils decompressing as he stood from a bed or a couch.

"Of course there's no way to tell for certain, but I'm pretty sure Sam's jeans were left there for me to find. Near a pile of clothing used to start the fire."

"I don't suppose you're still at the scene?"

"Not right now, but you know how to reach me."

"You're currently number three in my contacts." I wasn't certain he was joking. "Just don't go changing it again."

The way things were going, I couldn't promise that. "Did you get that video I sent you from the coffee shop?"

"I did. You got that photo for me?"

"About that . . . I'm not going to be able to drop it off after all."

"Oh?"

"It's at Zoe's house."

Though the photo was evidence, and though I hoped the fire hadn't breached Zoe's threshold, part of me wanted the photo to burn.

"I think we need to talk in person."

"Probably, but it can't be now."

Somewhere in Rico's house, a child laughed. I was suddenly jealous, wanting that levity for my own children.

"Can you drop by the station at nine?" Rico phrased it as a request, but I could tell it wasn't one.

"I'll see you at nine." *If I can make it.*

He picked up on my hesitation. "I really need you to be there, Cassie." A pause, then, "And bring Leo."

I started to ask why he needed to talk to Leo, but Rico cut me off. "Gotta go." Suddenly distracted. "See you and your son at nine."

Intuition told me it wasn't his family that pulled him away. The detective's behavior reminded me of Sam's the morning he'd gotten that call from Brooklyn. I tried not to dwell on how that particular situation had turned out.


A BANK OF GRAY clouds crawled across the sky, and a frigid wind had started to blow. Despite the chill, I stood outside the door to my father's hotel room, unable to knock.

"I'm cold," Audrey said. Still in her pajamas, the jacket I'd grabbed for her was too thin for a November morning. She burrowed into Leo, using him as a windbreak.

On the way to the hotel, the kids had asked questions about the fire, but they had quickly realized I had no answers. Once at the hotel, I hadn't been sure whether to leave the kids in the car, unaccompanied and vulnerable, or bring them inside to meet a grandfather Leo barely knew, and Audrey didn't know at all.

After a minute's hesitation, I had decided the greater threat was to their physical rather than emotional well-being, so I had led them up the hotel stairs to the spot we now stood.

I finally rapped on the door, and it swung open immediately. I stared into the face of my father.

Red McConnell's hair had thinned in the past six years, and the crevices under his eyes had grown more pronounced. He moved forward as if to hug me, but something in my face pinned his arms to his sides. He nodded in greeting instead.

Audrey stepped forward. "You're my grandpa," she said. "The other one. Not Daddy's. His name was Frank, but he's dead."

"I'm sorry to hear that."

"We went to visit him on his farm when I was little. Grandpa Frank grew beans, but he also had chickens. Can I watch your TV?"

"Of course."

Audrey grabbed the remote off the bedside table and jumped up onto the bed, creating a nest for herself out of pillows. Leo dropped himself in a chair, earbuds in, eyes attached to his phone. They both gave the appearance of normal, though I noticed the signs: Audrey's voice, an octave higher than usual, and Leo's stare, glazed and distant. They hadn't cracked, but they were close.

"I tried calling your cell," Red said.

"I have a new number." I gave it to him, with instructions to call only in emergencies, and even then from a pay phone.

He raised his eyebrow at that, and I could tell he wanted to ask. I was grateful he didn't.

Red watched his grandkids, and I could guess what he was thinking: How much should he say in front of them? The silence between me and my father grew more awkward the longer we both pondered that question.

I spoke first. "You didn't have to come."

"You needed me. Where else would I be?"

I bit my tongue to keep from asking: *What about when Audrey needed you?*

He answered the unasked question anyway. "I know there have been times I could've done more, and I'm sorry for that. You smell like smoke."

"Long story." I planned on telling him—I'd come primarily to warn him and tell him he was safer at home—but I couldn't yet find the words. "Did Sue come?"

"I suppose she might have, if we hadn't broken up three years ago." Intended as a joke, the words instead served as a reminder of all the time lost. Even Red couldn't work up a smile.

"Seeing anyone new?"

"Not really."

Another pause in the conversation. Mentally, I prepared my best small talk—it's probably colder here than Arizona, right?—but before I could speak, Red said, "I didn't fly seven hundred and ninety-eight miles to talk about my failed relationships or the weather."

Parents were sometimes telepathic like that.

"Seven hundred and ninety-eight miles, huh?"

"I Googled it."

For the first time since entering the room—and maybe for hours before that—I smiled. "You would. You probably prepared a speech too."

"Wrote it on a napkin on the plane."

"Practiced it?"

"My seatmate pretended to be annoyed, but I think he really developed a secret crush on you."

"That must be some speech."

"I might've also shown him photos."

I thought again of the time we had lost. "I've changed a lot in the past six years."

"Not so much, and the photos were more recent than that." When I arched my eyebrow in query, Red said, "Sam emailed me photos of you and the kids at the beach last year."

Sam had been in contact with my father? Before I could ask him to elaborate, Red asked, "About Sam . . . do they know?" I strained not to look at Audrey and Leo.

"Some."

For most of my childhood, it had been just the two of us. While it felt good to fall back into the familiar rhythms, talk of Sam and his secret conversations with my father sobered me. It reminded me of how I had felt looking into an infant Audrey's jaundiced face after Red told me he wouldn't be tested because he hated needles and, besides, Sam or I would probably be a better match anyway.

"I'm still angry with you."

"I know. But that doesn't mean I can't be here for you now."

I glanced at Audrey in her nest of pillows. "She was really sick." She had nearly died. But I couldn't add that last part, especially in light of all that had happened in the past couple of days. It seemed dangerous to release that thought into the universe.

"If you had been that sick as a baby, I wouldn't have survived it," he said. "You've always been stronger than me."

I didn't feel particularly strong. I felt as if one misplaced footstep would drive me to my knees. "Apparently, since I don't mind needles."

He winced at the jab. "Fair."

"Sam really sent you pictures of me and the kids?"

"I think since his own parents are gone, he's more keenly aware of what I gave up and what our distance might cost you."

His phrasing surprised me. "What you gave up?"

Red moved closer but didn't touch me. "I can say I'm sorry or that I handled it badly, but we both know any apology wouldn't be enough. What I can do is help you now."

"I miss him," I said, my voice low. "I've heard some horrible stuff about him in the past couple of days, but I still miss him."

"Whatever you've heard isn't true. Sam is a better father than I'll ever be, and I've never seen a man more in love with his wife."

I looked for signs he meant what he said, because I wanted to believe in the Sam he described.

"So are you going to tell me why the kids are still in their pajamas and you smell like a campfire?"

I grabbed Red's hotel key card off the table and led him outside. Once the door was closed, I told him everything. I might have been angry at him but, other than Sam, there was no one I trusted more—which was why his betrayal six years before, and Sam's now, left me so unsteady.

After I finished, I said, "I need to find him."

"Like the police said, most married men leave voluntarily." He was quieter now, less on Sam's side. Understandable.

"So you believe he was having an affair?"

"Don't you?" Though he had been certain of Sam's fidelity before hearing my story, he had doubts now. "But that doesn't mean he won't come back. I know better than most that men can be idiots."

"Even if he was cheating, that doesn't mean he left voluntarily."

"In which case, the police are looking for him."

"I get the impression that they're looking less *for* him than *at* us as suspects."

"If they're searching for suspects, then that means they think there's been a crime. They're not going to ignore that."

"I know Sam better than they do." Did I? My father's doubt was contagious.

"I'm sure you do."

I couldn't be certain Red believed what he said, but the words nevertheless gave me comfort.

"If it had been Sam on the trail that night, he would've stepped in too," I said. "He would've gone in with a clearer head than I did, and he would've tried to talk it out even though the guy was nuts. But he wouldn't have hesitated."

"I know. Sam's a great guy." The admission came grudgingly. I knew firsthand it wasn't easy to forgive the person who had caused your child pain.

"That's not it." I knew I wasn't explaining it so Red could understand, so I searched for a memory of Sam that would illustrate my point. I had dozens to pick from, but I chose the day I had realized I loved him. "A few months after Sam and I met, we came across this man and his son at a gas station. The boy must've been about eight, and his father pushed him, complained the boy was moving too slowly. Then he punched the boy in the back.

"I was weighing options—get the gas station attendant, call 911, step in. Though it was only a few seconds before I made the decision to call 911, Sam was already on the ground. He'd been knocked out. He'd stepped in and the father, who outweighed Sam by at least thirty pounds and was obviously more accustomed to using his fists, hadn't much liked the interference."

Remembering Sam like that brought fresh pain.

"By then, the gas station attendant had come out, the police had been called. I'm not sure what happened to that man, but Sam ended up with a nasty bruise. The first thing he said afterward, 'Better me than the boy.'"

"You feel obligated to do right by Sam because he wouldn't hesitate to do right by you?"

"*Obligated* isn't the word I'd use. And there's more to it. When Audrey needed a liver, Sam didn't ask about the risks to him. Not once." I touched Red's arm for the first time. I needed him to hear what I was saying. "That's not a jab at you. That's just how it went down.

"Having lived through my teen years, you may think I can be reckless, and maybe I can be. But I think before I act. Sam doesn't. He believes good people should prevent bad things from happening. Always. A moral obligation, he calls it. In his mind, that's just the way things are."

Red nodded in understanding. "You think this *moral obligation* may have gotten him hurt."

"Yes."

"I admire Sam, but I live by a different code, and it has a single imperative: keep you and the kids safe."

"Like six years ago?"

Red's face went ashen, and I instantly regretted my words. When I had imagined myself a pastry chef in middle school, my father had eaten pies made with too much sugar, cookies made with too little, and cakes either charred at the edge or swampy in the middle. Often both. I never did get the hang of it. My father had swallowed every bite. This was a man I should've been able to forgive.

He grabbed my hand and squeezed it. "There's more to that story, more that I couldn't tell you then."

This surprised me. "Tell me now."

"Like I said, my main concern will always be keeping you safe, and distraction can be dangerous."

"Go ahead—distract me."

"It's not important, not now." He shook his head. "You and the kids can stay with me."

"We can't. And it *is* important. It's more of a distraction not knowing what the hell you're talking about."

"I know you're angry, but please—stay with me. Let me help."

"You used a credit card, right? Checked in under your own name?" When Red nodded, I continued, "It's not safe for us here, and isn't that what you want most—our safety?"

The words had more bite than I intended.

"We can find another hotel," he said.

"They'll still keep records."

"A seedy one where they don't ask questions. Or we could go camping somewhere. I bet there are a lot of places to camp around here."

As much as I wanted to lean on my father, I couldn't.

"You don't trust me," he said.

"I do. As much as I'm able." Trust had become a fragile commodity in the past couple of days.

He stepped closer, and I thought he might embrace me. But he only moved closer to whisper, as if his next words might be overheard by someone who intended my family harm. "Where are you going to go?"

I started to say I didn't know, but then the idea hit me. "I can't tell you that," I said instead. "But thanks for coming. After I find Sam, I'd like to catch up and hear more about why you didn't want to help save your granddaughter's life."

Red cringed, and I was immediately sorry. "Isn't it enough to know I had a good reason?"

"Maybe," I said. "If you'd offered that explanation six years ago."

I gave my father a halfhearted hug and then went back inside the hotel room to gather my children.

# 33

My father followed us to the car. After the kids climbed in, he told me to be careful. He started to say more, but the slamming of the car door interrupted him.

Leo had climbed out again, his voice shaky, his eyes wide as he asked, "Mom, why do you have a gun?"

That was an easy question to answer: I didn't.

I leaned into the car and saw the weapon resting on the passenger's seat. Next to it, a Post-it, though not a number this time. A word, written in all caps, in red ink: TODAY.

"Mom?"

My mouth went dry, more at the note than the weapon. "It's not mine."

My father, who had been watching our exit from several feet away, started toward us. The hairs on the back of my neck prickled, and I asked him to stop.

"Dad, get your stuff."

The edge of his mouth lifted at what I'd called him, but he climbed the stairs to his room without question.

Leo eyed the gun. The fingers on his right hand twitched, and I laid my hand on his arm. "Don't."

He took a step back. "I wasn't going to."

I arched an eyebrow but said nothing. I understood his impulse—to touch it, to confirm it was real, because how could it possibly be?

By the time Leo had noticed the weapon, Audrey had already climbed into the back seat. Now, curiosity drew her to her knees.

"Sit," I said, firmly. When she did, I turned to Leo. "Watch your sister."

Neck still prickling, I dropped to my knees beside the driver's-side door. Crawling, I swept my fingers along the metal, probing crevices and bumps alike. As I searched, Leo's stare burned the top of my head, and Audrey's voice came at me equally hot, "Mommy?"

She threw open the back door, and it was only reflex that kept it from smacking me in the jaw. I pushed the door closed.

"Just a sec, Peanut."

Near the back bumper, I found what I'd been looking for: a small rectangle of magnetized metal. As easily as I discovered it, I worried there were other GPS trackers better hidden.

Had Carver placed it there that first night, before I realized Sam was missing? Maybe later at the hospital, while I had been awaiting Leo's MRI results? Or perhaps it was Helen who had planted the tracker while I was distracted by the sight of my husband's blood. I thought of all the places I'd been, all the people I'd seen, and all I knew for certain was someone had tracked me to Zoe's to start that fire, then to the hotel to plant that gun.

Then another thought struck me: Had I been tracked for months? Had Carver's appearance near my home that first night been the random event I'd first believed it to be?

A strange number popped onto the caller ID of my phone. As I hit the connect button, I held my breath.

Zoe didn't spare time for a greeting. "I've been talking to the police. Cassie—" Her voice broke, and she hesitated. When I pressed the phone more tightly against my ear, I caught the edge of what might have been a sob. "Perla's dead."

I placed my palm on the hood to steady myself.

"She was killed."

That couldn't be right. She'd been helping me. I'd just seen her. Only the night before.

I thought of the first time I had met Perla. She had been only five years older than Leo was now. So young then. So young still.

Then I realized there was no *still*.

"They found her body in her apartment late last night."

Each detail was a gut punch. Then the significance of it hit me: my phone and my laptop had been in Perla's possession. Either could've been used to track her to her apartment.

Perla was dead. Zoe hadn't yet said how she'd been killed, but I saw the gun on my front seat and I knew. She had been shot to death, for no reason other than she had been helping me. Then the gun that had been used to kill her had been planted in my car. I felt sick. It was my fault Perla was dead, as surely as if the gun had been mine.

"Cassie, the police are asking why you left before the firefighters came. What time you got to my place. Whether Leo was with me while you were gone. Why would they be asking about Leo?"

I grabbed the gun from my car, removed the bullets—couldn't chance a curious kid finding the weapon before the police—then wiped it all with the hem of my sweatshirt.

"Who found her?" I asked. Had she been killed before I had visited? And if so, where had the body been?

"What?"

I needed to know. To be sure. "Who found Perla's—" I couldn't finish the sentence. Couldn't say the word *body*.

"The police found her. They got a tip."

Of course they had. Just like they had been tipped to my presence inside the abandoned house—an intruder with a gun, Rico had said—and just like they had probably been tipped to the gun in my car. How much time did I have? Not much, I guessed. I was suddenly certain the news of Perla's murder was the reason for Rico's earlier distraction.

"I also overheard one of the officers mention the key you gave them. It matched Perla's locks. And something about prints on a wrapper?"

Understanding seized me: I had been in Perla's home. I had locked her door as I left. I had given the police her key. And I had turned over a wrapper that likely had on it only my fingerprints, or the fingerprints of my son. I had never seen the rock with the number three that Rico had mentioned, but I was willing to wager that it had been as carefully manufactured as the rest of it. Had the rock come from my own backyard? Had the paint come from our garage?

Suddenly, I remembered the text I'd received while Leo had been hospitalized: *I know how you can be when you're jealous.* At the time, I had envisioned Brooklyn dead, with evidence planted on her body for the police to discover. Right idea, wrong person.

I tossed the gun, bullets, and tracker into a dumpster. "Whose phone are you using?"

"A neighbor's. I didn't think you'd want me using my own."

"Get someplace safe."

I gave her Leo's number—I'd used my own burner to call Rico, and it would be easily traced. I powered down my phone—useless now—and took out the battery. I considered tossing it in the dumpster, too, but it seemed too valuable a resource to discard so easily.

Searching for the tracker, talking to Zoe, disposing of the gun—it had taken only a couple of minutes. But each second seemed a step closer to something horrible.

I motioned for my dad to get in the car. I couldn't leave him behind after what had happened to Perla. We would have to abandon the car, but for now, we needed to get away from the hotel. Quickly.

I told my dad: "Leave your phone."

He dropped it, stomped it, and kicked it across the asphalt. It skittered to a stop near the dumpster.

I pulled out of the parking lot just as I noticed the red and blue of a police cruiser's light bar reflected on the hotel's stuccoed walls.

I WASN'T RUNNING FROM the police. Not with the kids in the car. But that didn't mean I had to make it easy for them. Though I planned on calling Rico—especially since I wouldn't be able to make our appointment—I needed time to think.

I kept my foot light on the gas pedal and my eyes straight ahead as I pulled out of the lot, passing two police cruisers on their way in. I couldn't be sure but, when I risked a sideways glance, I thought I saw one of the officers look in my direction. As soon as I hit the street, I turned left and pressed hard on the gas.

Okay, so maybe I *was* running from the police.

I ignored Audrey's questions and my father's panicked stare, my attention focused on two things: the road ahead of me and my rearview mirror.

I ended up at the convenience store pay phone I had used to call Helen the night before.

"Where are we going?" Audrey asked from the back seat.

I steadied my hands on the steering wheel as I pulled over. "I'm going to have Grandpa call a friend of mine," I said, though this wasn't entirely true.

I glanced in the rearview mirror at my daughter's face. Definitely close to cracking.

"Dad, I need to leave you here, with the kids." I kept my voice light. "I'll be back in a few minutes."

He didn't ask. He had seen the tracker. He knew.

"Let me go instead."

I smiled at him, even as I wished I could accept his offer. "No offense, Dad, but I'm faster than you are."

But I wondered if I would be fast enough. What would be a safe enough distance away to ditch the car? And once I had, how many minutes would it take to run back to my family?

If the police were out looking for me, it wouldn't matter. Even an Olympian couldn't outrun a police car.

"I could be three cities away before your friend comes," he said.

"I'm not letting you do that."

"It wouldn't—"

I interrupted. "You weren't there six years ago. Be here now."

It turned my stomach to say those words, but they ended all debate, as I had known they would. As Perla had said: *Sometimes people are assholes.*

Before I left, I gave my father instructions and a number I had long since memorized.

"He'll help," I said, feigning confidence.

*Unless he wasn't home.*

*Unless he was sleeping.*

*Unless he decided he didn't want to risk arrest helping someone he barely knew.*

As I drove away, searching for a good spot to abandon the car, I wondered if I was making a mistake trusting a man who earned his living by baking pot-laced edibles.

# 34

———

Daryl lived on a four-acre lot between Santa Rosa and Sebastopol. The home was small and in need of paint, but the pot garden beside it was well tended.

Lester lumbered up the gravel driveway to greet the car. Daryl's braking took the Lab by surprise, and he bounced off the driver's-side door like a pinball against a bumper. The cone around his neck kept his snout from being snubbed.

"Sorry, Doc," Daryl said sheepishly. "I could've sworn I left him in his crate."

"I'm glad he's doing better. And thanks again for picking us up."

"No problem, Doc."

Daryl pulled the car alongside the front deck, killing the engine, and Audrey immediately snapped off her seat belt. She bounded out of the car with as much exuberance as Lester had shown ramming into it, all trauma temporarily forgotten. I wondered how long that would last.

Leo made no move to exit the car, so when my father climbed out, I whispered, "Watch them, okay? I need to talk to Daryl."

He nodded but avoided my eyes. I couldn't tell if it was because he didn't want me to see the worry reflected there, or the hurt of what I'd said to him earlier.

Inside, Daryl's living room wasn't what I had expected. The floors were stained concrete, and an abstract print played off the gray tufted chair and a purple rug I suspected was wool. An open laptop sat on the simple ottoman that served as a table.

Daryl lowered himself onto the couch, which was covered in a geometric print and positioned next to a large seven-leafed plant. That last part I had expected. The marijuana scented the room with skunk.

"He's male, but he's beautiful, so I kept him," Daryl said.

It took me a moment to realize he was talking about the plant. I asked the obvious question, "Lester hasn't tried to eat it?"

Daryl chuckled. "Once or twice."

His frayed jeans and ripped shirt looked incongruous against the sofa. "Nice place," I said.

"I inherited the furniture from my sister when she died last year in a motorcycle accident," he said. "She always had better taste than I did, and, unfortunately, a more reckless nature."

This from the "pot entrepreneur." "I didn't realize you'd lost a sister. I'm sorry."

"I think she would've liked the floors. A customer told me my old carpet dishonored my sister's memory. Plus, it reeked of weed."

Daryl crossed his legs, resting one flip-flopped foot on the opposite knee. "So, Doc, why're you here?"

I had chosen Daryl because a pot dealer's home wouldn't be the obvious choice for my family's refuge. Maybe for good reason.

"My husband's missing, and a former patient who was helping me was shot to death." I watched Daryl's reaction to that second part. His face was stone, his eyes red, hooded orbs, so I told him the rest of it. I figured by letting us into his home, he'd earned the full story.

When I finished, Daryl uncrossed his legs and leaned forward. "Can I be straight up?" he asked.

"Can you be any other way?"

Daryl grinned. "Nah, not really," he said. "I've only met Sam the once, but he seems like a standup guy. Besides, you're hot. That doesn't offend you, does it? Because you're a doctor?"

"Depends on where you're going with it."

He nodded as if I had said something profound. "Anyway, so you're hot, you're smart, and you've saved Lester, even when I couldn't pay."

This was pretty much near always, but I didn't say so. Lester was worth saving. "Not that I don't love a compliment, or several of them in this case, but . . . ?"

"Why would he leave you?"

"For another woman."

"Nah, I don't buy that."

"You don't think he was having an affair?"

"Oh, no, he easily could've been, but even the woman who told you they'd hooked up didn't think he'd leave, right? Besides, like I said, you're hot."

"So you've established."

"And you've got kids and I'm guessing a decent paycheck." Daryl looked sheepish. "Sorry again for not being able to cover Lester's surgery, but since pot became legal, it's harder to make ends meet, you know? I would sell my sister's furniture, but it's all I have left of her."

"It's fine, Daryl."

"Anyway, I think you need to strip away all the bullshit and focus on what you know."

I wasn't sure what he meant, and my face must've shown that, because he added, "What do you know to be true?"

"What do you mean?"

"When you were telling your story, you told me Sam was having an affair, but you don't *know* that. You *think* that."

"Based on evidence."

"But you don't *know* that." He settled back on the couch. "There's this guy I know, Jace, has a turtle named Turtle."

"Clever."

"Yeah, he's stoned pretty much all the time," said the man sitting next to a potted marijuana plant. "Turtle has unusual markings, on account of when he was little, he got clipped by a weed-whacker."

I winced at that. "Poor Turtle."

"Yeah, just missed one of his legs. Curious little bastard always where he shouldn't be."

"Like Lester."

He did that profound nod again. "So Jace's buddy Joe meets Turtle and insists the reptile is a reincarnation of his dead dad, because the dad's initials are etched on Turtle's back. He offers Jace a thousand dollars for Turtle."

"I'm guessing Joe was high at the time?"

"He's never not. Anyway, Jace insists the markings aren't the dad's initials but a palm tree, and they fight for hours over who's right, and Joe leaves pissed off and vowing to take back his dead dad. Later that night, Jace notices Turtle's gone."

"Stolen?"

Daryl grinned. "See, that's what Jace thought. He goes to Joe's house, and Jace ends up heaving a huge rock through Joe's front window. Gets carted away."

"Arrested?"

"Carried out on a stretcher. It was a really big rock, and Jace threw out his back.

"So when Jace gets out of the hospital, Joe agrees to keep the cops out of it, says he won't even charge Jace for the broken window—if Jace gives him Turtle."

"So Joe didn't steal him after all."

"Nah. Turns out Turtle got stuck in one of the bathroom cabinets. Like I said, curious little bastard."

I got where Daryl was going with his story. "You're saying Jace just assumed Joe took Turtle and could've saved himself a lot of hassle if he'd instead spent a few more minutes searching his house."

"Exactly right." Daryl laced his fingers and rested his chin there. "So—what do you know?"

I thought about that. Really thought about it.

"I know Sam disappeared while out trick-or-treating with Audrey." He nodded.

"I know he was suspended from work because of rumors he was having an affair with a student."

He nodded, more vigorously this time. "What else?"

"He may have been having an affair."

Daryl stopped nodding. "Nah. I mean, yeah, maybe he was. But what you know is there's a photo, which someone messed with at least a little bit. You know that Sam's friend thinks he was having an affair, and this woman—" he paused, giving me room to fill in her name.

"Brooklyn."

"You know Brooklyn says she and Sam were hooking up. But the video's the only undoctored, unbiased evidence you have, and it just proves they were tight. They could just as easily have been friends. Sam could've been helping this troubled girl—"

"Hannah. But she admitted she lied."

He smiled at me, in that indulgent way he might if I were Audrey's age. "Because liars wouldn't trade more lies for cash."

"True enough."

"Anyway, maybe Sam was helping Hannah, he seems the kinda guy who would do that shit. So Brooklyn and Sam are friends who're both concerned about this girl, and Brooklyn exaggerates the relationship. If Hannah's lie was convincing enough to get Sam suspended, couldn't Brooklyn be lying too? See . . . you don't *know*. So focus on what you do."

I thought of all the "facts" I'd taken for granted. Not just the affair. Sam's blood on those plastic teeth. Sam's jeans being used to set the fire at Zoe's. Because of the texts and the surveillance equipment found in our home, I knew we were being watched, and whoever was watching could fake either of those details.

"Perla's dead. I know that. Helen lied about living in that house. And I know that Carver Sweet killed at least one person, a girl named Natalie, and tried to kill Brooklyn."

"We'll see." Daryl pulled his laptop toward him but hesitated before typing. He looked at me, his eyes alert despite the pale cranberry color. "By the way, that stuff on the trail—that's some badass shit."

"It was some stupid shit."

"Badass," he corrected. "But next time, you won't catch him off guard. Going off without a way to protect yourself, now that would be some stupid shit."

"I'm not carrying a gun I don't know how to use."

"I could teach you."

I pictured the revolver that had earlier been planted on my passenger's-side seat. "No gun."

"Pepper spray then."

"You have pepper spray?"

"Of course," he said, as if possession of pepper spray should be a given. "Tasers, too, if that's more your speed. More important, though, is information." He tapped the keyboard to take the laptop out of sleep mode. "First, this skank, who you saved and who repaid you by sleeping with your husband—"

"Not quite the way it went down, and I don't know that I'd characterize her as a skank."

"Of course, you wouldn't. Female empowerment and all that. But if you've screwed the husband of someone I care about, or lied about it, the best I'm gonna call you is a skank."

Daryl typed Brooklyn Breneman's name in the browser, but the results were unexceptional. Apparently, she belonged to a couple of professional organizations and had been quoted in a news story on rising water rates. There were a couple of photos, too, with Brooklyn in button-up blouses. No yoga pants this time.

Daryl faked a yawn. "Let's move on to Perla."

He didn't need more information than her first name. Perla's photo was prominently displayed on the newspaper's website. One of those "happier times" photos the news organizations grab off social media. Perla and her Rottweiler, somehow making the same goofy face, above a headline: SANTA ROSA WOMAN SHOT TO DEATH. The three paragraphs that accompanied the picture didn't expand much on the headline.

Blackness pricked at the edges of my vision, so I closed my eyes. "Sorry, Doc," Daryl said.

I could hear his fingers tapping the keyboard. When I opened my eyes, Perla's photo was gone. Just like Perla. I didn't know which was stronger: the roiling in my stomach, or the urge to punch someone in the face.

"How about Helen?" Daryl said. "Do you know her last name?"

I admitted I didn't, but I gave him the address where Helen had claimed to live. Thirty seconds later, the grin was back, and Daryl pointed at the screen. "See, Doc. Another thing you thought you knew but didn't really. Like I was saying."

He nudged the computer toward me, and I read the information three times before I could convince myself of its truth. The property records showed the owner's name: Helen Staley.

"I DON'T UNDERSTAND," I said. "Helen didn't lie about living there?"

"Seems you *do* understand." The grin slipped from Daryl's face. "In light of what happened to Perla, I worry about this mysterious Helen. Though I guess we still don't know for sure if she lived there, only that she's listed as the owner of record."

"Which means the man who answered the door lied," I said. "Even if he rented, or even if he bought the place from her, he would've recognized the name. So what was that man doing in Helen's house?"

Daryl continued typing, more urgently now. "There's no way to tell, at least not with the information we have."

I took out my new phone, the one originally intended for Leo, to call Rico, to tell him about Helen, but then I realized he had access to the same information I did. Much more information than I did, in fact. He had likely already knocked on Helen's door, though I doubted the man, whoever he was, had opened the door for Detective Rico.

When I returned my attention to the screen, Daryl was typing "Carver Sweet" into the search engine. The first couple of hits linked to the local newspaper again, but, thankfully, directly to stories about Carver. I didn't again have to see that photo of Perla and her dog.

Daryl clicked the link for the most recent article, which I skimmed over his shoulder.

*Anne Jackson, 52, was found dead in her Cloverdale home late Wednesday, the victim of an apparent poisoning. Her husband, Carver Sweet, 58, is being sought in connection with the killing.*

*Sweet also attacked a second woman later that night, police say. Sweet fled after a passerby called 911.*

*The victim, whose identity is being withheld, was released from the hospital Thursday morning.*

Midway through reading, Daryl leaned back into the couch. "I kinda feel bad about calling her a skank."

I reached across him and scrolled down the page. I continued scanning the details of Anne's killing and Brooklyn's assault and comments from Sweet's neighbors. The attacks were "disturbing," the Jackson-Sweet marriage either "troubled" or "loving," depending on who was describing it.

Near the end of the article came mention of Carver's previous conviction thirty-eight years earlier.

> *Sweet, 19 at the time, served 15 years at San Quentin State Prison for the 1980 murder of ex-girlfriend Natalie Robinson, 16. Robinson's body was found buried less than a mile from her Napa home. The girl's skull was fractured, and her ribs showed signs of earlier trauma, but the cause of death was listed as asphyxiation. Robinson was unconscious but alive at the time of her burial, according to police.*
>
> *According to testimony at the time from the girl's mother, Delphine "Dee" Robinson, Sweet was abusive throughout the relationship, leading Natalie Robinson to end the relationship about a month before she was killed.*
>
> *Delphine Robinson died earlier this year at age 75 of idiopathic pulmonary fibrosis, a progressive lung disease.*
>
> *Neighbors say Delphine kept to herself in the decades following her daughter's death.*
>
> *"She rarely left the house after that," said one neighbor, who declined to give his name. "Losing a child in such a horrific way—how do you ever get over something like that?"*

Daryl tapped the screen. "Oh, great, Carver did his time at San Quentin," he said with genuine enthusiasm.

Still reeling from what we'd just read, I asked, with considerably less enthusiasm, "Why's that great?"

"I know a guy. He can get information on anyone who's been in the system, but he's especially connected locally."

"He can get this information legally?"

Daryl wrinkled his nose and brows simultaneously, as if trying to understand the word.

"It doesn't matter," I said. Whatever it took to protect my family, I would do, even if it meant illegal Web searches and pepper spray.

After several minutes more of searching and emailing, Daryl scrawled an address on a Post-it. "Carver's former cellmate, a pedophile named Ernesto Marino, goes by Ernie. My guy couldn't find a home address, but either Ernie or his girlfriend gets takeout from here nearly every afternoon." He handed me the Post-it. "Seems he has a real weakness for bacon-stuffed waffles."

# 35

---

I gave Audrey the last immunosuppressant from the old bottle and left three pills from the recent refill with Daryl. Just in case.

After hugging Leo as tightly as he allowed me, I pressed a folded piece of paper into Audrey's hand.

"My new number," I explained. "Call me for any reason, even if it's just to tell me something silly Lester did."

"He *is* silly," she said, but she offered no smile.

I hesitated. "Do you want me to stay?"

"Are you going to find Daddy?"

"I'm going to try my hardest."

"I want you to find Daddy." Her eyes burned with a faith I hadn't earned, and I pulled her closer to avoid that look. Still, I meant it when I whispered in her ear, "I will. Promise."

Daryl offered me the use of his ten-year-old Honda for the sixty-mile drive to San Francisco.

I ENTERED THE DINER in the Mission District through a red door and asked the staff about Ernie. Daryl's intel was solid: Ernie was a regular—he usually ordered bacon-stuffed waffles with whipped cream, an extra side of syrup, and two maraschino cherries—and he never missed a weekend.

Though I wasn't hungry, especially after the waiter described Ernie's usual order, I rented my prime spot facing the door by asking for a grilled cheese sandwich.

Thirty minutes passed, then forty-five. The waitress eyed me as I nursed my tap water, and I sensed she was preparing to ask, for the second time, if there was anything amiss with my sandwich. The diner was packed and my space at the counter therefore precious. I forced myself to take a bite of my food, even less appealing now that the cheese had congealed.

Picking at my sandwich and distracted by the crowd, I didn't notice the blonde in the blue cardigan until she was at the door, red takeout bag clutched in her left hand.

I abandoned the grilled cheese and walked quickly to the register, slapping the check and a twenty on the counter.

"What did that woman order?" I asked.

The man behind the counter reached for my check to make change, but I shook my head. I pointed toward the spot the blonde had occupied only seconds before. "What was in the bag?"

"Bacon-stuffed waffles, whipped cream, side of syrup, two cherries."

*Damn it.*

I left my change and hurried out the door.

ONCE I SPOTTED THE woman in the blue cardigan, I worried she would hop into a car. She remained on foot.

Because she carried the takeout bag and wore wedges, the blonde was slow and easy to follow, but I stayed half a block back. I resisted the urge to rush the woman right there on the street. It wasn't her I needed.

As the crowd started to thin slightly, the blonde in the blue cardigan stopped so suddenly I thought she might topple off her shoes. The brief pause before she looked over her shoulder allowed me the second I needed to tuck myself into the entryway of a pawn shop.

Had the woman guessed she was being followed, or was this routine behavior? Living in a big city, picking up takeout for a former felon, might make her more cautious than most.

I twitched with impatience. Nearby windows offered reflection, but they were too smudged to be helpful. In them, the blonde was one piece of the shapeless crowd.

Five seconds. Ten. I couldn't be sure the blonde had moved on. She might still be on the street, looking behind her for the strange woman who had followed her out of the diner. But I couldn't take a chance on losing her. I stepped back into the throng.

The woman had disappeared.

Frustration bubbled up inside me, but I forced it down. She couldn't be more than a few seconds ahead. My faster stride would swallow any gap between us.

At the end of the block, I still didn't see her. I looked left, then right. Had she gone into one of the stores I had just passed? I didn't think so, not with a bag of glop-topped waffles growing soggier by the minute.

I covered another half a block before I saw her again. Even with the bag she carried and the wedges she wore, the woman had started walking more briskly.

I quickened my own pace. I kept to the edge of the crowd, near the storefronts that might provide me temporary refuge in case she looked over her shoulder again.

The blonde turned a corner, and I followed. She crossed the street, and I did the same.

A group of about a dozen tourists surged between us. The woman looked over her shoulder once more, but I easily slouched behind a tourist.

A few minutes later, the group broke off, and the boutiques, bakeries, and thrift stores became glass-walled apartments. The woman slowed, and I expected her to duck under one of the red awnings.

She continued walking, less hurried now, her steps labored but steady. In those shoes, her feet must've been throbbing.

When the blonde crossed the street again, I forced myself to drop back. The crowd had thinned further, and there were fewer places to hide.

She turned another corner. A couple of seconds behind, I almost missed her as she climbed the steps of a Victorian row house. She didn't knock but instead used a key. This was her home.

In one of the windows on the second story, I saw the woman hand the red bag to a man fitting Ernie's description. He wore a baseball cap that he kept tugging over his forehead. Nervous habit?

Beside him, a small boy pulled on a backpack before disappearing from view.

Seeing Ernie with that boy made me very angry.

A second later, the woman and the boy emerged from the Victorian's door.

They got in a car, and I waited until it had crawled down the street before climbing up the steps to have a talk with a convicted pedophile.

# 36

I knocked on the door. When Ernie responded, I stopped short, my practiced speech forgotten.

"Oh," I said. "You're hurt."

The bill of Ernie's baseball cap had caught the edge of the door, slipping nearly off his head. He yanked it down so it again shielded his forehead, but I had seen what he tried to cover: a wad of gauze held in place by medical tape. At the border of the gauze, his skin was inflamed, the same shade of angry pink as his cheeks. A wound, obviously infected.

I forced my eyes from his forehead. "Ernie, right?"

The man angled the brim of his hat over his forehead. He did a double take, but recovered quickly. "I ain't buying anything."

"I just need to talk to you for a couple of minutes."

His eyes went flat, and his tongue darted to catch a dribble of what looked like syrup at the corner of his lip. "I was eating."

Strange. He still hadn't asked for my name. "That's a nasty wound you've got."

He tugged the brim of his cap again, his eyes narrowing. "I think it might be infected."

"I'm a veterinarian. I can look at it." There was little I could do for Ernie here—he needed antibiotics—but I wanted him to trust me.

Ernie's face flushed deeper crimson. "I don't want no animal doctor messing with my head." He again tugged at his cap.

"You should see a doctor then."

Judging by the fraying sweat suit and bad haircut, Ernie looked like the kind of man who didn't have a lot of cash to spare for health care.

"If you don't mind me asking, what happened?"

"I got in a fight." He puffed up his chest, signaling he had gotten in a few punches too.

"Did you call the police?"

Any rapport I may have been building dried up like a salted slug. "Why would I call those assholes?"

I fought the urge to step back, instead straightening my spine. "The guy you fought with—was it Carver Sweet?"

Ernie's eyes became slits, and I saw recognition there. It had indeed been Carver who had messed him up. "You know Carver?"

"He's done some pretty horrible stuff to my family." I motioned at his forehead. "I'm guessing you can relate. When was he here?"

"Couple of days ago."

Carver couldn't know I would seek out Ernie, so why had he? "What did he want?"

Ernie shifted slightly, poised to scurry back inside and probably slam the door. I stepped forward and put my foot on the threshold so he couldn't.

"Look, I just want a few minutes of your time. I can see to that wound—in exchange for some information about Carver."

He dabbed at the sliver of gauze that peeked from beneath the bill of his cap. Whatever was festering there had to hurt. Finally, he said, "I suppose I can let you in. For a minute."

Ernie turned around and walked back inside. He still hadn't asked my name.


THE AIR IN THE living room smelled faintly of infection, syrup, and processed meat. The only furniture in the cramped space was a small sofa, a table barely bigger than a board game box, and an oak chair that had been pulled from the adjacent dining room.

The waffles sat in their to-go container on the table, but he pushed them to the side.

"First aid kit?" I asked. He directed me to the bathroom cabinet, and I returned a moment later. I sat at the other end of the sofa, the kit tucked in my lap.

"Why did Carver come here?"

Ernie removed his baseball cap and placed it on the table, exposing gauze and its border of inflamed skin. When I leaned forward, he recoiled.

"Gimme a minute," he said.

I leaned back. "Have you kept in touch with Carver since you were released?"

He shook his head, then winced. He touched his forehead again. "Haven't talked to him in years."

"Then why did he come here?"

Ernie's eyes darted from the window to the door before landing on my face. "He's crazy."

"Even crazy men have their reasons."

Sweat traced the stubble on Ernie's cheek. A fleck of waffle was stuck there. "He wanted to know about Dee."

That wasn't one of the names I'd been expecting to hear. "Natalie's mom?"

His eyes were slits. "You know about that?" When I nodded, Ernie continued, "So you probably know what happened to Natalie."

I flashed to the photos Brooklyn had shown me, trying to remember the girl's face but only able to conjure the broken girl buried alive.

"I know some of it."

"That was brutal, man. She nearly died giving birth."

"Natalie had a baby?"

Ernie shook his head. "Stillbirth. Carver's kid. Dee found Natalie when she was bleeding out, saved her, but it didn't matter. She ended up dead anyway."

Though I had no time to waste, it was a solid minute before I could speak again. "Do you know what happened?"

"The police think she was hit in the head, but it took a while to find the body. She'd been buried, and whoever did it didn't wait until she was dead. They think she broke her fingers trying to get out, but it's hard to say. Like I said, it took 'em a while."

Though I'd read as much in the newspaper article, it still took a couple of tries to get my next words out. "You said *whoever did it.* Does that mean you don't think it was Carver who killed her?"

Ernie twisted his hands and looked away. "It could've gone down that way."

"But you don't think it did."

"I don't know, man. I really don't." When Ernie returned his attention to me, his eyes blazed. "It could've been an accident, and he tried to cover it up, or he could've killed her. I think maybe he *did* kill her. But whatever happened, Dee was angry, she'd just lost her daughter, and either way, Carver was gonna pay."

Ernie grimaced, then sighed, as if the decision he had just made came at a cost. "My head really hurts, man. You think you can look at it now?"

I pulled a pair of latex gloves from the kit. "Why did Carver want to talk about Dee?"

"Is there aspirin or something in that kit?"

I paused to retrieve a foil pack of ibuprofen. He swallowed both capsules before answering. "He knew Dee and I used to be tight, and he thought she might be behind some recent shit he was going through."

"What kind of 'shit'?"

"He was having some problems with his wife. That's all he'd say."

I scooted forward and started removing the strips of medical tape that held the gauze in place. "Why would he think Dee had anything to do with that?"

"She set police on him about Natalie, so why wouldn't she mess with him again? That was his thinking anyway."

The tape removed, I began to gently peel the gauze away from the wound. "It would seem a long time for her to carry a grudge, especially since Carver already spent years in prison for something he might not have done."

"You didn't know Dee." He used his fist to wipe sweat from his cheek. "Like when Natalie was alive, Dee wanted her to be perfect. Entered her in pageants, like when she was three years old. Almost a baby. Spray tan, false eyelashes, all that shit. Even when she wasn't competing, Dee tracked her daughter's diet on a chart on the refrigerator. Once, when Natalie gained a couple of pounds, Dee had her eat nothing but celery for a week, and when she snuck some crackers, Dee locked her in this box." He paused. "Makes me think of how Natalie died. If Carver didn't kill her, then Dee did."

Ernie jittered, tapping his foot. I suspected he offered the story to distract me from what he wasn't telling me. Finally, he said, "Do you know about her other daughter?"

My hand froze. "Other daughter?"

"Megan. Carver was asking about her too."

"I wasn't aware Dee had another daughter."

"Most people weren't." Ernie drummed his foot against the floor. "Look, I'm always getting judged for my past. But I love kids." Bile rose in my throat, and it was a struggle to keep the repulsion from my face. "Dee, though—she enjoyed hurting Natalie and Megan. I told you about the box, right? Sometimes, she would leave Natalie in the box for days."

"Sounds like a good friend you had there."

Ernie's shoulders tensed, and for the first time since we had entered the room together, he seemed to forget his pain. I sat very still, a couch coil digging into my thigh, the smell of processed meat mixing with the rusty tang of the bloodied paper towels.

"We weren't friends."

I worked to keep my expression neutral. I knew how easily cornered animals could snap. I returned my attention to his injury, my hand shaking only a little.

"What happened to Megan?"

"I don't know."

"Did Dee kill her too?"

"I told you I don't know."

Ernie's tapping foot and darting eyes told me he was lying, but I let it go. For now, he needed to believe I was on his side. "How did you and Dee meet?"

"When Carver and me were cellmates, she hired me to keep an eye on him."

I pulled the last of the bandage from his forehead and tried to mask my shock. The wound seeped, the drainage thick and yellow. The skin around it was hot. I could help, but he definitely needed antibiotics I didn't have.

Yet it wasn't the infection that stopped me. I had expected an open gash, but this was a carving. This wound had purpose. Four letters: PERV.

"You didn't think to put antibiotic ointment on this?"

"It wasn't so bad before."

I dabbed the wound with an alcohol swab, then opened a packet of antibiotic ointment and applied it to his forehead. He looked like he might pass out, a greasy sheen coating his face.

"Were you in touch with Dee in the months before she died?"

"Not really. Can I have more of those pills?"

I handed over another packet of ibuprofen. This time, I held onto them for a second before releasing them. "You're lying."

"No," he said, but his voice lacked conviction. He didn't mind sharing other people's secrets, but he wasn't so eager to share his own. "I mean, I didn't talk to her that much—a lot of these stories I got secondhand—but every once in a while, she needed help with something . . . not illegal, really. But it's hard for a convicted felon to get a job, you know?"

"What kind of *jobs* did you do for Dee?"

His face darkened. "Just stuff."

I took a square of gauze and secured it to his forehead with medical tape. I might have pressed harder than was entirely necessary. He winced. "I've got some pain pills," I lied. "Veterinary grade, but they'll work just fine. If I'm feeling generous."

"What does it matter?"

"I might have some antibiotics in the car too."

"That's cold, man. Aren't you, like, legally required to give them to me?"

The tremor in his voice told me he wanted those pills, badly, but he wanted to keep his secrets more.

"I'm happy to help you if you answer my questions."

"I've answered them."

I pushed, "What kind of jobs did you do for Dee?"

Ernie crossed his arms across his chest, and his lips tightened.

I only had one move left, and it was risky. I leaned in and tried my best to appear one kick away from disabling him. It wasn't as hard as it should've been. "How old's the kid?"

"What?"

"The boy I saw in the window, putting on his backpack."

Ernie stilled and said nothing.

"He looks to be about eight or nine. Who is he, Ernie?"

He hesitated, suspicious. "My girlfriend's son."

San Francisco rents what they were, I knew a guy like Ernie couldn't afford that Victorian row house on his own. "This is her place, isn't it? The three of you living together?"

When Ernie spoke, his tone was defensive. "Yeah, so?"

"You're a convicted pedophile, Ernie. You're living with a child. Does your girlfriend know?"

He squirmed. "She wouldn't care."

I very much doubted that. "What about Family and Children's Services—would they care?" I held his gaze even as he tried to break it. "How about your parole officer? Two times in prison already, can you really risk a third strike?"

His face wavered between anger and fear. "What do you want?" The tremor had returned. I had him.

"Answer my questions, honestly, and I won't tell your girlfriend about your conviction, or the authorities about your living arrangements." It was a lie, because I had been planning to report both since the moment I saw that boy in the window.

Ernie sighed and glared at me. "Dee hired me last year."

"To do what?"

Ernie shifted on the couch, his fingertips massaging one temple, his face settling into a scowl. "You got those pain pills? It really hurts, man."

I knew I would have to pay for any additional information. I foraged through my purse and pulled out most of the cash I had left, which wasn't much after the diner and paying off Hannah.

Ernie shook his head. "Pills." He leaned forward, eyeing my purse. If he made a play for it, could I stop him? Of course, there was also the question of what he would do when he discovered I had nothing stronger than a breath mint.

I opened my purse, my attention falling on the pepper spray Daryl had insisted I take. One capsaicin-laced stream would sear his eyes, maybe splash onto the gauze covering his wound. That would sting. Then I noticed the lump in the zippered pocket.

I pulled out the bottle containing Audrey's medication and shook out two pills.

"These're strong, so it's better if you only take one now." They *were* strong, but the pills Audrey took so her body didn't reject her liver would do nothing for Ernie's pain.

He studied the pills, his brow wrinkling. "What are these?"

"They're like oxy for dogs," I lied.

"What about the antibiotics?"

"I'll get those from the car when we're done."

Ernie swallowed both pills. I had only a few minutes before he guessed they were fakes and before he realized I had no antibiotics in my car.

I pushed, "What did Dee hire you to do?"

"Can I have another pill, for later?"

I retrieved another tablet but kept it clasped in my hand.

"Dee wanted me to find someone."

I stretched out my hand and unclasped it, an offering. "Who?" He snatched the pill from my palm. He swallowed the pill immediately, as I had known he would. Soon, he would start wondering why he remained clearheaded. Well, as clearheaded as someone like Ernie could be.

There was something in the way Ernie looked at me now that reminded me of the recognition I had seen on his face when I met him.
Fear constricted my chest, crushing it like a cheap paper cup. "You
know who I am."

"I just met you, man."

"Yet you haven't asked my name."

"Why would I? Some hot chick wants to see my place, I let her in."

It didn't make sense, but still I asked, "Did Dee hire you to find *me*?"

Despite the pain that cast his face in shiny pallor, his gaze grew
wolfish. "Cassie Larkin, Terra Linda Drive. Husband Sam. Two kids. I
gave Dee that information just before she died."

Breathless, I stood, but Ernie grabbed my arm. His breathing grew
labored, his eyes glazed. "What about those antibiotics?"

I yanked my arm free, backed up out of his reach, and then, just
in case, reached into my purse and palmed the pepper spray. Then I
gestured toward his forehead. "You should probably seek medical attention. From someone other than an *animal doctor*."

His gaze dropped to the floor, and he reached for his baseball cap.
He pulled it so the brim again shielded his forehead.

"Another piece of advice: you should move, especially since Carver
knows where you live." I paused to let that settle. "If Carver comes
around again, it could put your girlfriend and her son in danger. And
I know the last thing you'd want is to have a child hurt because of
something you did."

I left Ernie slumped on the couch, even the feverish spots on his
cheeks turning ashen. I made it as far as the porch before the screaming started.


I IMMEDIATELY RECOGNIZED THE screaming for what it was: an
expression of intense pain, beyond what might be caused by an infected
cut. Inside, I found Ernie curled up on the floor, legs twitching as he
held his stomach with both hands.

He moaned. "I'm gonna be sick." I rolled him onto his left side, and
he just missed vomiting on my shoes.

I looked around the living area but saw no landline, and I didn't want to compromise my own cell phone.

"Do you have a phone?"

Ernie was past speaking, but he managed to jerk a shoulder in the direction of the kitchen. I found his phone on the counter next to the microwave. It was protected by a password, so I used the emergency option on the lock screen to call 911. I didn't give my name, only the information that a man had been poisoned and that I would leave the bottle containing the suspected toxin on the coffee table.

When I hung up, I checked Ernie's pulse. It was weak, but his breathing was steady. I left the phone within his reach.

"I've got to go, but the paramedics are on their way," I told him, before checking his pulse one final time.

I couldn't stay, not with PERV carved on his forehead and my daughter's name on the bottle that contained the poison. Because I had no doubt Ernie's sudden distress was caused by the pills I had given him. Pills I could just as easily have given my daughter, who weighed just under fifty pounds compared to Ernie's two hundred-plus. Though I didn't know who, I knew someone had poisoned my daughter's medication—just as, according to the newspaper article, Carver might have poisoned his wife.

There were no words to describe the depths of my rage.

I put the bottle on the table, my hand shaking, and peeled off the label as best I could. Just so there wasn't any misunderstanding, I used a pen and paper from my purse to write the word POISON in all caps, drawing an arrow, too, and tucked the edge of the note underneath the bottle.

Then I stepped over the seizing pedophile and ran all the way back to where Daryl's Honda was parked several blocks away.

# 37

---

The sky had been scoured of fog by the time I crossed the Golden Gate, and the sun made its red towers glow. To the right, the city's dense skyline scratched the horizon. To the left, sailboats skimmed the Pacific Ocean, gentle waves lapping at their hulls.

Despite the view, I felt none of the usual amazement. Instead, I felt fear that Sam would never be found. Fear that I had made a disastrous decision leaving my kids at Daryl's. Fear that I would be killed, and my kids would lose a second parent, and they might never even realize I was lost.

But that outcome was far better than my greatest fear—that something would happen to Audrey and Leo. That particular fear had been magnified a million times over upon seeing Ernie writhing on his living room floor.

I had called Red on my run back to the car. Between breaths, I had told him about the poisoned pills and had warned him not to let the kids eat anything or drink so much as a glass of water.

Everything was fine, he had assured me. The kids were fine. Daryl was fine. Heck, even Lester was fine. His repeated use of that word had done little to calm me.

I was right to be afraid. That became clear half an hour later when Leo called. Daryl's Honda had Bluetooth, but my phone wasn't connected to it. I answered anyway, punching the icon to put my son on speaker.

"Everything okay?" I asked.

Leo was supposed to say what my father had repeated thirty minutes earlier: *Everything's fine.*

Instead, he answered, "I don't think so."

And just like that, I turned to ice. I worried that Audrey had taken one of her poisoned pills.

"Explain."

"You know Audrey's been missing Dad." He aimed for nonchalance, as if he had matured past any such longing himself. I ached with the urge to hug my son.

"Is she okay?"

"Mom, chill. She's okay. It's just, I thought you'd want to know that she might've done something stupid."

"What did she do?"

"I don't know if it's even a big deal or not."

I turned on the heater. "What did Audrey do?"

"She tried to call Dad. On Daryl's phone." Leo's voice was tinny, a reminder of the distance between us.

"Put Red on the phone."

"I will. It's just . . . that's not all. A guy answered. It wasn't Dad, obviously, but he told Audrey he knew Dad and that Dad was trying to get a hold of you but couldn't because he didn't have your new phone number."

My phone felt suddenly hot in my hand. "Did she give it to him?"

"She's six."

That was Leo's way of saying of course she had.

"Get your grandfather."

When Red came on the line, I rushed through an instruction. "Check with Daryl. I think he has a truck he sometimes uses for—work."

After I heard Red asking, and Daryl confirming, I added, "Get in the truck and head south." I strained to think of a landmark between Daryl's house in Sebastopol and the stretch of Highway 101 I was currently traveling. "We'll meet at the dog park where Lester got attacked by bees. Daryl will know."

Thankfully, I didn't need to stress the urgency of the situation to my father or offer an explanation. He would likely ask for one later, but at that moment, he mumbled a quick "Okay" and disconnected.

So . . . the asshole who had Sam's phone also now had my number. I considered tossing my phone from the car but quickly dismissed the idea. For now, I needed it, and besides, I was a moving target. A very angry moving target.

I pulled off the highway in Rohnert Park. Then I called Detective Rico.

"YOU MISSED OUR MEETING."

I had remained steady when talking to my kids and father, but at the sound of Detective Rico's voice, I nearly lost it. Stupid, I know.

"How much have you heard?" I asked, my voice cracking.

"Pretend I don't know any of it."

I started with something he *did* know. "Perla's dead." My damn voice broke again. I swallowed and took a breath. "That's why you had to get off the phone this morning."

"Yes."

It was only one word, but I took comfort in his honesty. Lately, everything had been deceit, even the afternoon sun that reached through the windshield with frigid fingers.

"I didn't kill her and neither did my son."

I could feel Rico weighing my guilt. Was he stroking his tie as was his habit, and if so, what was on it? For some reason, I pictured cats wearing sunglasses.

I steadied myself and took a chance. "There was a gun in my car. At the hotel. I threw it in the dumpster."

"We found it."

"Does it have my fingerprints on it?" *Or Leo's.*

"I'm guessing you wiped it down when you found it, but people rarely get everything."

I focused on the middle of that sentence: *When you found it.* I hoped that meant he believed me, at least a little.

"What do you think of me, Detective?"

"Are you asking if I think you killed your husband or Perla?" He paused, and my phone buzzed. I ignored it as I awaited his judgment. Finally, he said, "I don't."

It may have been a reckless question, but still I asked, "Why?"

"The *evidence*, the anonymous tips . . . it feels . . ."

Had I imagined the odd intonation on the word *evidence*? "Manu-factured?" I offered.

"Vengeful," he said. "But I'm still following the evidence." No into-nation this time. "Plus, while that helpful neighbor Helen apparently left town, we found some curious deposits in her account."

First Hannah, now Helen. It seemed there was a long line of people willing to screw over my family for cash.

"Tell me the rest of it, Dr. Larkin."

His use of my title felt like a message: *We're both professionals. I'm here to protect and serve, but we aren't friends.*

I summarized my actions of the past few hours, starting with the poisoned pills and working back to most of what Ernie told me.

"He said Dee hired him to find you?"

"Yes." I chanced a quick look at my phone, at the text I'd missed a minute before, and my foot slipped from the gas pedal. The car coasted to a stop, aided by my bumper's contact with a tree, and I stopped breathing. I might've said goodbye to Rico, but I probably didn't, my world suddenly reduced to the five inches of my cell phone screen.

*Leo.*

# 38

---

There are few places darker than a parent's imagination. First, we worry our babies will not be born, but it is when they are finally living outside our bodies, outside our twenty-four-hour protection, that our imaginations turn especially twisted. We fear our children will suffocate in their cribs, disappear from the playground, or take drugs laced with fentanyl and die quietly in their best friend's bedroom.

While parents imagine such things happening, we don't expect them. With Audrey, I may have imagined SIDS, but I had been blindsided by her diagnosis of biliary atresia. It had been the same the night before when Leo had been knocked unconscious on the football field.

But just because parents don't expect such things doesn't mean we don't plan for them. Sam and I had talked about online predators and stranger danger, spiked drinks, and fast cars until our kids were able to recite our lectures verbatim. We even had a family password: *Xyz*. Quick to type, easy to remember, never used in casual conversation. Our deal was if our kids got in trouble, they could call or text those three letters, and we would be there. No recriminations. No questions. If Audrey needed an excuse to leave a slumber party, we would provide one. If Leo's ride home had been drinking, we would come get him. *Xyz*. Leo's eyes had rolled nearly from their sockets when we had talked about that one.

"Yeah, like you guys aren't gonna ground me for, like, forever, if I get drunk," he had said.

I wanted to smile at the memory, but I couldn't. All I could do was stare at the screen of my phone.

*Xyz.*

The first time either of my kids had used the code word. I called back but got no answer. Despite my promises when making the pact with my children all those years ago, when it mattered, I hadn't been there to protect them.


I HIT THE STREET, and then the highway, well above the posted limit. The ringing in my ears was as sharp and insistent as the wind.

I tried Leo again, and then Daryl, but both calls went unanswered. Next, I called Rico back and gave him Daryl's address.

I was nearly at Daryl's myself by then, approaching the turnoff to Highway 12, when the message came. I had propped my phone in the cup holder, the screen angled so I could see it. I slowed before risking a quick glance down to see if it was Leo.

An image, too small to see clearly, had popped onto my screen.

Before I could pull over, my phone chimed again. Despite the precious seconds it wasted, I maneuvered the car onto the shoulder and picked up my phone.

A second photo was displayed beneath the first, both sent from a number I recognized: Helen's. Just like with Sam's texts, though, I didn't know who had Helen's phone, or if her number had been spoofed.

The wind that whipped the trees outside seemed to cut through the windshield and into me. I turned up the heat to its maximum setting.

I scanned both photos in only a second, but the details burned with great clarity.

The first photo, the one that had at first been hard to see clearly, was taken in Daryl's living room. Daryl was asleep on the couch, a blue-striped blanket pulled up to his chin. Leo and Audrey were prone on the floor beside him, a throw pillow tucked behind each of their heads. Lying on their stomachs, their faces were tilted just enough to afford them breath, and Audrey's right arm and Leo's left were extended, their fingertips touching.

But of course, they weren't really sleeping. They were drugged. Posed.

I saw this immediately, in the stick-straight positioning of my children and, when I zoomed in for a closer look at Daryl's face, in the white orbs visible behind half-open lids. Spittle glistened on Daryl's cheek.

Red wasn't in the frame. Where was Red?

The second photo was of Sam. This one was a close-up. Face ashen and bruised, his eyes were shuttered, his mouth agape.

I didn't think he was drugged as Audrey and Leo had been, but I couldn't tell if he was alive or dead.

The bruise on his forehead drew my interest. It had to have been inflicted while he was alive, while his heart was still pumping. The injury was a couple of days old, judging by its color—purple, not the red of a fresh bruise nor the green of an older one.

Sam lay against what might have been burlap.

In the photo, Sam's lips still held a hint of pink, but I took little solace in that. Even if I found hints of life in the photo, I had no way to determine when it had been taken.

I found it impossible to maintain my clinical detachment. This wasn't one of my patients. This was Sam.

I read the message: *If no good deed goes unpunished, the consequences of the bad ones should be even worse, don't you agree? So it's time to make a choice.*

A string of texts followed.

*You can choose to save your children, or you can choose to save your husband.*

My heart shattered, each piece heavier than the whole.

*If you call the police again, all three will die.*

*If you try to negotiate, all three will die.*

*If you make any calls from this phone, all three will die.*

*If you try to signal anyone, all three will die.*

The text-in-progress bubbles appeared on the screen. Another photo was delivered, this one of me in my car. I didn't look around to see who had taken the photo. It had been taken from my own phone.

The bubbles appeared again, then another text: *Pick now.*

It became clear to me that it didn't matter if Sam was alive, because, depending on my choice, he might not be much longer.

Another text, a single number: *3.*

I couldn't choose, even though the choice was clear.

As a father, Sam had been puked on, lied to, yelled at. He had wounded his feet on misplaced toys and had weathered heartbreaks, sleepless nights, and illnesses, both terrifying and imagined. He had sacrificed time, money, and the entirety of his heart—he had never ceased loving Audrey and Leo with unfaltering abandon.

*2.*

No matter if he had been unfaithful, Sam was a man who would risk his life to save a stranger. So there was no question he would surrender his life to save his children. Without pause or regret.

*1.*

I had believed the greatest test in my life would be Audrey's illness as a baby. Then Sam had disappeared, and my children had been threatened, and I thought, no, that would be my greatest challenge. But now, with a single word, I would be sentencing my husband to death.

I made the only choice I could and typed: *Children.*

# 39

---

Once off the highway, there were no cars, only weeds that threatened to overtake the asphalt. Forgoing the main thoroughfare, I approached Daryl's from a private road. The property owner might decide to take issue with my trespass, but that was the least of my concerns.

When the road veered toward a white ranch house with red shutters, I turned right sharply. The cracked asphalt became concrete, which became gravel, which became dirt and dead grass. No longer on a true road, I carved my own way across the uneven field. I rattled at each bump, barking my knee on the steering wheel twice, but I drove as fast as I was able.

Daryl's house grew on the horizon, until I could clearly make out its features even in the approaching dusk. I looked for police cars, but none had yet arrived.

A short wire fence separated the two properties. I slowed, intending to abandon the borrowed car and scale the fence. Daryl's truck was parked just a short jog away on the opposite side, its door open, closer to the main road. I could reach it in minutes.

As it turned out, I didn't have minutes. An unfamiliar white sedan pulled out of the carport, which had earlier been occupied by the car I drove now. At first, the white sedan appeared to be heading toward the driveway, but it turned abruptly, approaching the road from the backside of the property.

If I had driven in from the front, off the main road, I would have missed the white sedan. Had I not driven ninety on the highway to get there, I would have arrived too late.

I braced myself and then stomped on the gas. I hit the wire fence with a jolt, again banging my knee, two of the three wire strands of the fence breaking on impact. I dragged the third strand behind me. The car screeched in protest as the metal became entangled in the wheel well.

The white sedan disappeared into a stand of trees, a mix of oak and pine, but not before I saw a figure slumped against the front passenger window.

*Leo.*

If Leo was in the front seat, Audrey was likely in the back seat, still unconscious.

Though I had chosen to save the kids, they were being taken anyway. I hadn't really expected the bastard who threatened my family to play fair, but I *had* hoped, and I choked on the absence of that now.

The wire wrapped itself around the drive shaft, too, and the car shuddered to a stop. Despite the pain in my knee—I could tell it had already started to swell—I sprinted the few feet separating me from Daryl's truck. I prayed the key would be in the ignition.

It wasn't, and I almost dropped to my knees. But then the glint of green metal caught my eye. A keychain in the gravel, cut in the shape of a marijuana leaf and attached to the key to Daryl's truck.

I acted on instinct, clear thought a luxury that further endangered my children.

I threw the truck in gear, pressing the accelerator so it surged toward the driveway. I hit the road a second later, just in time to see the white sedan vanish around a bend in the road.

I reached for my phone to call 911 and realized my fatal mistake. I had left it behind in the disabled car.

I followed the truck, beating the steering wheel with the palm of my hand.

*Faster. I needed to go faster.*

The truck swallowed half of the gap between the two vehicles, but then the white sedan accelerated. I glanced down at my speedometer and cringed. Eighty. The road was posted at half that.

A crash at eighty would kill my children.

I reduced my speed, praying the driver of the white sedan would too.

After a moment, the car slowed, although it still outpaced mine. With the difference in speed and a well-timed turn or two, the white sedan would be able to evade me in minutes.

I expected the other vehicle to turn toward the freeway, but then I realized what the other driver likely had—there were more police cruisers monitoring freeway traffic.

I got a glimpse of a baseball cap as the car turned left, and the curve of a male jaw that seemed familiar, though in the fading light and with the growing distance between the two cars, it was impossible to see more.

As I pursued, memories intruded.

Audrey in her hospital gown on the day she had been transplanted with part of Sam's liver. After, her newly pink skin had been perfect except for the scar.

Leo as a toddler, at Salmon Creek Beach, studying a tiny crab he held on his palm. His nose had wrinkled as he held it up for my inspection.

Audrey fidgeting at her preschool graduation, because she wasn't meant for stillness, or for quiet. She had been meant to dance, to twirl, to laugh.

Leo at his high school orientation, leaving me behind to join his friends. I hadn't minded. My greatest happiness had always been in witnessing my children's joy.

Likewise, my greatest sadness had always been in seeing their heartbreak. I wouldn't allow the possibility that I couldn't save my children.

I released the memories, though they weren't distractions. Instead, they provided focus.

My respiration and pulse slowed, the waning light intensifying as my eyes adjusted. My knee ceased to throb. I was no longer plagued by fear, or fatigue. The world had narrowed to the road ahead and the white sedan.

The car turned suddenly, back toward civilization, and I recognized where we were. Though I came from another direction, I drove this road nearly every day. Nearly a mile ahead was my clinic.

I wondered at the location. Certainly, the abductor wouldn't want to continue this pursuit on these more populated streets.

Suddenly, brake lights flashed, and the car slowed nearly to a stop. It drifted toward the shoulder, and the back door behind the driver jerked open. From the back seat, a figure tumbled onto the road. I fought the urge to slam on my brakes—I couldn't risk losing control of the truck. Instead, I pumped the pedal, turning away from the sudden obstacle on the asphalt.

*Audrey.*

Having dumped half of his cargo, the driver of the white sedan pulled back onto the road. He drove with less urgency now. Without saying a word, he had given me another choice: I could pursue him, or I could save Audrey.

The other driver's leisurely retreat telegraphed how certain he was of my decision.

I pulled my daughter from the road, my heart breaking as I watched the white sedan carrying my son disappear.

# 40

---

Audrey's arm had abraded where it had scraped against the road, angry slashes embedded with asphalt bits. Her bones appeared unbroken, and her head free of injury, but I worried nonetheless. The same immunosuppressant drugs that kept my daughter from rejecting her transplanted liver also made her more vulnerable to infection.

That was when I noticed the note, tucked in Audrey's pants pocket: *Talk to the police and Leo dies.*

The letters were hastily written, the scrawl just legible. Probably written while I had been in pursuit.

I transferred the note to my own pocket. I secured Audrey in the back seat, taking care not to brush the raw flesh, and headed for my clinic a few blocks away. With Leo's captor headed south and me headed north, each turn of the wheels closer to help for my daughter felt like a betrayal of my son. I drove a little faster than was safe.

*First, Audrey. Then Leo.*

Audrey awoke with a whimper, which, upon reaching full consciousness, became a wail.

"Mommy, my arm hurts."

I kept my speed steady but chanced a quick glance to see if Audrey appeared disoriented. Though infection was my greater fear, even without a bump on her head, I couldn't rule out concussion. "How's your head feeling?"

"It's my arm, not my head."

I pulled in front of the veterinary clinic and turned off the truck. "Can you walk, or do you want me to carry you?"

"I can walk, but my arm hurts." I scooped her up anyway, her body hot and impossibly small against my chest.

"I'm not a baby," she protested.

"You're a big girl," I agreed. "But your arm hurts, remember?"

"Oh, yeah." Fresh tears spilled. "It hurts, Mommy."

"I know."

At the door, I lowered Audrey to the ground.

"Damn it."

"Mommy!"

"Sorry."

The door was locked, and my keys were with my cell phone in the car I'd abandoned back at Daryl's.

Dusk was descending with alarming speed, a reminder that there weren't many hours left in the day. Desperate, I looked around. A thousand rocks surrounded me in the landscaping, but all were rounded, none bigger than a half-dollar. Useless.

Then on one of the pillars, I spotted a piece of stone that wasn't aligned with the others. I went to it, tested it, and my heart soared to find it loose. I worked the rock free. Though small, it had a sharp edge. It would do.

I positioned myself in front of the window closest to the door of my clinic, wrapped my hand in my sweatshirt, and swung the rock toward the window's edge, the weakest part of the glass. A second swing, and the glass shattered. I knocked the biggest shards clear of the frame before reaching inside to unlock the door.

Audrey stared at me, her eyes nearly as large as the moon.

Once inside, I switched on the lights and glanced at the clock on the wall. How many miles had Leo's abductor traveled in the past couple of minutes?

I forced my eyes away from the clock and my attention back to my daughter. I gave her an ibuprofen.

*First, Audrey. Then Leo.*

As if she could sense my thinking, Audrey asked, "Where's Leo?"

I lowered her to the ground in one of the exam rooms and moved quickly to gather what I needed.

"I'll get Leo as soon as we take care of that arm." Audrey, distracted by her own pain, didn't seem to notice the catch in my voice, but I hoped she did notice the resolve.

The epidermis on a patch of Audrey's forearm had been scraped away, but the dermis underneath remained intact, and there were no lacerations that would require stitches.

Still, though there wasn't much blood, the suddenly exposed nerve endings made Audrey flinch at every touch. With patients, I easily distanced myself, knowing any short-term pain I was causing was in pursuit of long-term healing. But this was Audrey.

Cradling my daughter's arm over the sink, I irrigated the wound with a syringe until it was free of dirt and the bits of asphalt. Every time she winced or cried out, her pain may as well have been mine. I gritted my teeth and applied an antiseptic wash to my daughter's forearm, careful not to damage the skin further.

"Almost done?" Audrey asked, biting her lip.

*My brave girl.* "Almost done," I confirmed. I slathered the wound with an antibiotic ointment and used adhesive tape to secure a dry dressing to Audrey's arm.

I looked up at the clock. The distance between me and Leo had grown another six minutes. In the heat of the chase, if I hadn't left my phone behind, I would've called 911. But that was before the note planted on my daughter: *Talk to the police and Leo dies.*

The text, too, had warned me against calling the police. Would the person who pushed Audrey from that car even know if I made that call? Was there surveillance here that Perla had missed? The texts I'd received the day before had mentioned my interaction with Officer Torres, and I'd assumed my phone had been compromised. But what if I'd blamed technology for what had been human treachery?

*Who could I trust with Leo's life?*

I returned my attention to my daughter. There wasn't time for questions, but I asked the one that mattered, "What happened?"

"I think I fell."

"No, not your arm. Back at Daryl's," I said. It hit me then: I had no idea what had happened to Daryl, or to my father. The last I had seen of Daryl, he had been unconscious in the texted picture. And my father . . .

"I played with Lester," Audrey said.

"When I saw you in that car, I couldn't see who was with you."

"Was it Daryl?"

"I don't know. Was it?"

Audrey thought about it. "I don't think so. He took a nap."

"Did you take a nap too?" When Audrey nodded, I asked, "Were you tired?"

Audrey shrugged. My mind raced through the options. A paralytic would incapacitate Daryl and the kids, but it would also prevent them from breathing. And how would the assailant get it anyway?

A sedative like flunitrazepam was easier to come by, but Audrey didn't seem to have any withdrawal symptoms. Headache. Disorientation. Seizures. She likely would have experienced some of this had she been given a dose large enough to knock her out.

Then there was the matter of time. If hidden in food or drink, a sedative could take hours to work to full effect.

An injection? It certainly would act more quickly, but again, there was the question of access.

It wasn't an easy thing to knock out three people simultaneously, or four if I counted my father, even if two of them were children.

"When I was in the car, the man mentioned ghosts."

My daughter's words caught me off guard. "What?"

"He was talking to someone, and he mentioned whining ghosts."

I knew Audrey was getting her words mixed up, probably because of the sedative, but I pushed. "He was talking to someone on the phone?"

"Uh-huh."

"Did he say a name?"

"Uh-uh."

"Do you remember anything else?"

"Just the ghosts. Mommy, where's Leo?"

My head swam with questions and with thoughts so dark that, for a moment, I could see nothing else. But I forced myself back into the moment and to the question I had asked myself moments earlier: *Who could I trust with Leo's life?*

I picked up the handset of the clinic's landline and dialed Detective Rico, but the call was interrupted by the jingle of the bell attached to the front door. Though the clinic was closed, someone had just entered the building.

# 41

---

I squeezed my daughter's shoulder with a hand gone suddenly clammy. "Stay behind me, okay?"

I grabbed a pair of bandage scissors and moved into the lobby, where I found Detective Rico standing near the pet food display. He was back to wearing a tie, this one covered in rubber ducks. He tried out a smile, but it strained his cheeks, adding tension to his face.

"I was just calling you," I said.

"Were you?" He gestured toward the scissors I held in my fist. "What are those for?"

"To stab someone in the neck, but apparently I won't be needing them." I slipped the scissors in my pocket. "Why're you here?"

"You weren't hard to find. Your name's on the door." He motioned toward the broken window. "Plus, there's the alarm you triggered."

I leaned against the wall to steady myself. "How are they?" I asked, my voice weary.

Rico stared at me, unblinking, eyes no longer hooded. "Your father and Daryl? They're okay."

So my father had been drugged too.

I hesitated, uncertain how much to tell him.

*Talk to the police and Leo dies.*

"What's going on here, Cassie?"

I wanted to trust him, needed to trust somebody, but I knew that a missing adult and an abducted child were two very different police matters. The moment I told Rico that Leo had been taken, the case would get loud, quickly: An Amber Alert would be issued; details about that white sedan carrying my son would be flashed across digital billboards and cell phone screens. The Feds would be called in, and all available law enforcement would be alerted to my son's disappearance. Rico would probably request the records of the number that had texted me, even if it was likely a fruitless search.

Then there was Audrey, who would become a witness. Would Rico be the one to interview her? A child psychologist? I didn't know.

But I *did* know that even if every law enforcement official between here and Canada mobilized, even if the whir of a thousand helicopter rotors lent the sky the appearance of Armageddon, and, hell, even if the goddess of luck herself materialized in my lobby with a satchel of rabbits' feet and four-leaf clovers and promises of good fortune, it wouldn't be enough. This was Leo. My son. He had been taken, and there was nothing I wouldn't do to get him back—and that included trusting Rico.

Aware that the note I had been given warned against it, I nevertheless took a breath and said, "Leo's been taken."

THOUGH DETECTIVE RICO DIDN'T MOVE, not at first, the pulse of the room quickened.

"I figured it was something like that," he said, his voice as weary as mine had been moments earlier. At my look of surprise, Rico's lids lowered again until only small wedges of his eyes were visible as he laid it out for me. "You got to Daryl's ahead of us. You were in his Honda, found disabled at the scene, and now you're driving his truck. I ran the plates. You wouldn't have walked away from Daryl and your dad, unconscious like that . . . unless someone took your children," he said, looking at my daughter, "and then pushed one of them out of the car."

In my mind, I saw it again: Audrey tumbling onto the road, discarded from the moving car like a fast-food wrapper or the butt of a cigarette. I assumed the driver would just as quickly dispose of my son if he no longer served a purpose.

"I guess this means Leo's no longer a suspect?" My voice cracked on the question.

"I had to consider all the angles." A hint of an apology. He tightened his rubber-duck tie and started in on the questions:

*What happened?*

*What did you see?*

*What direction was the white sedan headed?*

*Can you describe the driver?*

Then he excused himself to make some calls. I used the break to place my own call, to my father.

When Rico returned, I knew that in telling him, everything had changed. What little control I'd had I had just yielded to the Santa Rosa Police Department. I didn't know how I felt about that.

The detective's gaze dropped to my daughter, pinned to my side.

"Audrey, right?" He didn't lean down or soften his gaze when addressing her, as other adults might have done.

She tucked herself mostly behind my back, only her head and one shoulder visible to the detective. He motioned to her hidden arm. "With all that gauze, that must be a terrible injury."

"I fell," Audrey said. Exhaustion made the simple explanation sound like deceit, even to me.

"Oh?"

"I think I was pushed from a car."

Rico's jaw clenched, but he kept his tone neutral. "Who pushed you?"

I was as interested as the detective in my daughter's answer, but she just shrugged with her uninjured arm.

Rico's eyes narrowed, an expression I had come to recognize: he was preparing to ask a question I wouldn't like. I braced myself, but instead of asking his question, he looked down at Audrey. I knew what his silence implied.

"Why don't you draw a picture?"

I ushered my daughter to Zoe's desk, tucking her into a chair with a fistful of pens and a notepad.

With Audrey out of earshot, Rico continued, his voice quiet. "No chance Sam did this?"

It was a challenge to keep my own voice from rising. "Of course not."

"You sure?" When I remained silent, he said, "I once arrested a guy who tried to smother his toddler because his ex-wife got custody. She thought her husband was a bastard, but she never imagined he'd do anything like that."

"Sam's not a bastard."

"He might not be, but do you know what makes a good cop? A good cop doesn't assume. You see a guy pushing a car down the street, you don't assume he ran out of gas. Maybe he stole the car. You stop that guy pushing the car, and you ask him what's up. So I'm asking. Could this be a custody thing?"

I glanced at the exit. A thickening gloom had settled against the glass, the tall hedge outside the door blocking all light, erasing all that had existed beyond the clinic lobby. A cold wind breached the shattered window, but I fought back the shiver.

"If Sam were involved, he wouldn't have pushed Audrey from a moving car," I said.

"If your husband's working with someone, it might've been that person who pushed her, or maybe Sam figured one kid was better than none."

"Leo's fifteen. It's hard enough getting him to do his laundry. There's no way he'd go along with being yanked out of his life like that."

Rico shrugged. "Like I said, just asking the questions."

I glanced at the clock again. In a blink, the minute hand had jumped from one number to the next. Five more minutes gone.

"We'll need to talk to Audrey more, find out as much as we can about what happened."

"Of course."

"You available to go to the station now?"

Another request that wasn't one.

Studying Rico's face, I was reminded of the day Leo had started day care. I had been terrified. Sam had done hours of research finding our provider, and the woman had come with triple-checked reviews. Under her nurturing hand, Leo had developed a love of storybooks and lingonberry pancakes, and she had a saintly patience for his tantrums. But the truth of it was if we had been unable to meet her weekly fee, the relationship would have ended. She had cared for Leo, but no stranger, no matter how carefully picked, could be expected to love with the same abandon and sacrifice as a parent.

I suddenly doubted my decision to involve the detective. Even if he was the best in his department, even if he had citations and awards enough to fill a swimming pool, there were still rules he needed to follow. There were reports to file, and interdepartmental cooperation to arrange. Leo didn't have that kind of time. The last note had said "today," and there weren't that many hours left before today became tomorrow.

"Of course I'll come to the station," I lied.

He touched my arm briefly, and I met his gaze, the intensity of his compassion making my eyes water.

"I'm sorry," he said, a sigh rattling his chest. "I've been watching my salt for a week, but right now I'd *kill* for a bag of Doritos." He pulled a folded square of paper from his pocket, unfolded it, then showed it to me. "Do you recognize this guy?"

As I studied the photo, my heart thundered. The man was bald like Carver, but that was where the similarities ended. Carver was older, all angles and scars, while the man in the photo had a long face— softer in the cheeks, thinner in the lips.

It was the man who had answered Helen's door. Was it also the driver of the white sedan?

"I saw him at Helen's house. Who is he?"

"Damon Kripke."

I swallowed around the knot in my throat. "What's his connection?"

"Haven't worked out motive yet, but he's got a record more extensive than my collection of novelty ties, and some of the evidence is starting to point in his direction."

"What evidence?"

"Helen for one. Hannah Zimmerman too. Both of them ID'd Kripke as the guy who paid them. And there's the video you forwarded to me. It's hard to say, but he looks to be the guy who was following your husband and Brooklyn."

He paused, in that way that told me he was holding something back.

"What else?"

"I followed up on that name you mentioned—Megan. As far as I can tell, Delphine didn't have any other children."

I heard the hesitation in his statement. "But?"

"It's probably a coincidence, but the timeline's right." Rico spoke slowly, as if measuring each word. "In the late seventies, a three-month-old girl with that name was abducted from a grocery store in Fresno."

Before I could push for details, Audrey rushed over to show us what she had drawn. I thought it might be a cat.

"Cool elephant," Rico said, and she beamed.

"It's eating peanuts."

He noticed my look of surprise and shrugged. "My youngest is an artist too. Who do you think picks my ties?"

Audrey stood on her toes so she could see the paper Rico had shown me of Damon Kripke. She tugged on the sleeve of my sweatshirt and pointed. "That's him, Mommy," she said. "That's the guy who left the note about Daddy being a pedophile. Did I say that right?"

Rico's eyebrows knitted together. That was one part of the story I hadn't shared with him.

"You and your mom are going to come to the station with me. You okay with that?"

As Audrey nodded, I glanced away, guilt drawing my eyes to the window I'd broken to gain access to the clinic. Glass fragments glinted on the tile beneath the window. On another day, the shards would've sent me on an immediate search for a broom and dustpan, worried a patient might injure a paw. Now, the glass seemed no more a threat than the sand from which it had been made.

I was in no hurry to fix it, because what could a thief steal that I would miss? What I valued most had already been taken. "My dad and Audrey can ride with you, if that's okay. I'll follow in Daryl's truck."

"You sure you're fine to drive?"

My heart went from a careful plodding to a full-out sprint. "I'm not okay, but I'm capable of driving," I said.

I pushed open the door, leaving to greet my father before the detective recognized the deception on my face.

# 42

---

The patrol car carrying my father pulled alongside the curb in front of the clinic. My father climbed out, but instead of heading toward me as I expected, he lingered at the curb, his back to me, his hands in his pockets. Even after the patrol car drove away and my father turned, he avoided my eyes.

Maybe I had been wrong to call my father. I worried that whatever drug had knocked out my family had taken a greater toll on him than Audrey. Should he even be here? Finally, my father looked up.

"You okay?" I asked.

He gnawed on his bottom lip, which was pressed into a thin, bloodless line, and his eyes jerked away the moment they connected with mine. There was something there he didn't want me to see.

At first, I blamed the ashen cast of his skin and clouded eyes on the last of the sedative he'd been given at Daryl's. I took a step forward, my hand landing on his arm, but he moved away, rejecting my comfort.

"What happened at Daryl's?"

His chin dropped toward his chest, his gaze with it. "I don't remember much," he said. "Any word on Leo?"

Audrey came out the door then, and my father raised an eyebrow at her bandaged arm.

"You're my grandpa," she said.

"I am." He attempted a smile, but it faded before it reached his eyes.

I watched my father for several seconds before steering my daughter back toward the door.

"Let's get you back inside, okay? It's much too cold out here."

After settling Audrey back behind the reception desk, I returned to my father to find him pacing. He returned his hands to his pockets and inhaled deeply. The breath escaped but carried no revelation with it.

"I was hoping you could go with Audrey and Detective Rico to the station," I said.

"Happy to, but where will you be?"

"Right behind you."

"Let's not lie to each other anymore."

I hesitated, then said, voice low, "I need to find Leo. At the station, I'd be useless, and if something happened to him while I was off somewhere sipping coffee from a cardboard cup . . ." I paused, studying him. "Is that what this is?"

"This?"

I gestured in a circular motion near his face. "This. You won't meet my eyes, you look like crap. You shouldn't feel guilty about Leo—"

"Of course I should, and I do, but this isn't about that."

I'd heard once that you can feel a person's negative energy from several feet away. The waves coming off my father could've been felt on the next block.

"Whatever it is, tell me."

Our eyes locked, and, finally, he said, "I wish I'd been able to save Audrey's life. I understand why you were so angry. Why you still are."

At his words, I reached for the grudge I'd carried for six years like some parasitic twin. I had blamed it for Audrey's illness, even though she had long since recovered, and trotted it out whenever I needed an excuse for why the world sucked, or for my own parental shortcomings.

*Sure, Sam, I may have missed Leo's game or been late to Audrey's party, but my father wouldn't get tested and couldn't help Audrey, and isn't that so much worse?*

With my fresher grief, the past seemed more insignificant than it had before, and my reliance on old grudges petty and potentially dangerous for my son. I had failed my own children too many times, but this wouldn't be one of those.

"I'm sorry too," I said.

Red's eyes misted at my olive branch, which he accepted with a nod, but his mouth remained set in a grim line. It was clear the conversation wasn't over.

"The day you called to tell me Audrey was sick, my first impulse was to help." His voice cracked. "I've always wanted nothing more than to take care of you. From that first night."

Eyes overbright now, shoulders squared, Red squeezed my hand. His palm was slick, mine cold.

"There's something I need to tell you," he said.

RED TOLD HIS STORY in a rush.

He started doing work on Dee's house in 1980, the spring Natalie Robinson turned sixteen.

Long before it became a private residence, Dee's home in the Napa Valley had been a winery. Built late in the nineteenth century, it was one of hundreds of wineries operating in the state in 1920. Then Prohibition came, and the Depression, and everything changed.

The production of sacramental wines, exempt from the Eighteenth Amendment, saved some wineries, while others changed crops, but most shuttered. Only a few dozen managed to survive.

Over the ensuing decades, some of the abandoned sites, known as ghost wineries, found new life as restaurants, shops, or even, once again, wine-producing facilities.

More than Prohibition, a tiny sap-sucking pest had doomed the winery that would become Dee's house. To supplement income lost to the phylloxera, a creamery had been built, but bad business decisions had doomed that too.

So it became just a home for an eccentric woman and her two daughters.

Though renovations had made the main house livable, its stone walls had started to crumble, mold had crept into its cellar, and wood beams shed splinters the size of toothpicks.

Dee recruited Red to restore the house to its historic glory.

The day Red met Dee's daughter Natalie, he made note of the boxy sweater, worn despite the heat, and immediately guessed the teen was pregnant. He also learned, just as quickly, that such matters weren't discussed in Dee's house.

Outside the house, however, he heard rumors: Dee hadn't been able to bring pregnancies to term since Natalie's birth—scar tissue, one person said; emergency hysterectomy, claimed another. Yet earlier that year, Dee had suddenly shown up in town with a baby in tow.

The baby's name was Megan.

Red had never been much for kids, but Natalie's little sister was the most beautiful baby he had ever seen. Her eyes glowed with an intelligence she would no doubt grow into, and despite her scratched skin and too-thin arms, Megan was quick to smile. Usually. Sometimes Red saw hints of a developing anger.

Because of the rumors, Red risked asking if Megan was adopted. Dee snapped, *She's mine*, which ended that conversation.

At least with Dee. When Red asked the same question of Natalie a couple of days later, the teen told him how earlier that year, her mom had spotted an infant Megan in a Fresno grocery store. *Wouldn't it be nice to have another little girl?* Dee had asked. As if they had been car shopping and she had been deciding whether to upgrade to leather.

According to Natalie, Dee had stalked the baby through the store, pretending to study jars of olives and tubs of yogurt, but really watching the girl whose mother called her Megan and who was only loosely strapped into the shopping cart. When Megan's mom had knelt down to retrieve a can of stewed tomatoes, it had slipped from her hands and rolled away from her. Away from her baby. Three strides and Dee had snatched the baby from the cart. Five more and she had cleared the aisle, the infant silent in her arms even as her mom began screaming. The sound had drawn the lone security guard away from his post near the exit.

Natalie insisted on Red's silence, and he gave it to her. Too easily, in retrospect, especially since he had weeks before noticed bruises on Natalie's arm, and scratches even deeper than the ones on Megan.

He blamed cowardice. He knew what he would risk by taking Natalie and her sister from the house without Dee's consent. Such a move would get his photo on every newscast and in every newspaper: the creepy contractor who abducted two girls, one a beautiful, very pregnant teen.

But Red couldn't stop running the angles. To make it work, he wouldn't be able to go home. Not until the police could be convinced the children were someone else's victims and that he only meant to save them.

Maybe he could go to the police before he took the girls? Tell them about Megan, have them check their records for missing babies.

But what if the police didn't believe him or Natalie had lied about her sister's name? What if the parents were looking for a Sara or an Angela instead? There would be an investigation, and Red wasn't certain the children would survive that.

There was also the possibility that Natalie had lied.

Still, there was no explaining those bruises on Megan and Natalie. That wasn't to say Red didn't try. An accident. Sports injury. A self-inflicted cry for attention.

Twenty-four hours later, Red stopped making excuses and made a decision: he would take Natalie and Megan from the house and work through the details later.

That night, Red noticed the sweat tracing Natalie's hairline, the intensity with which she gripped the edge of the dining room table, the way she pulled the oversized sweater around her like a blanket, and he knew. Natalie was in labor.

Dee didn't, so Red faked a distraction in the kitchen—the clatter of dropped tiles, followed by a lie that he had ordered the wrong size cabinets. Even from the kitchen, he heard the squeak of the front door he had been meaning to fix.

While Dee didn't hear the squeak, the silence pricked her ears. Red marked the moment she felt Natalie's absence by the darkening of her expression.

Outside on the porch, Dee screamed for her daughter. Then, spotting her, yelled: *What have you done?* Her eyes blazed, twin strobes of crazy.

Beneath the magnolia tree, Red saw the girl too. Natalie was crawling, struggling to stand. When he had first started work on the place, the magnolia had been thick with pink blossoms the size of teacups, but that night the branches were flowerless. Natalie was pale as milk, her face slick. She'd miscarried, she said. But was there too much blood for that?

Red noticed Natalie no longer wore her sweater. Had it been used to wrap a newborn, then discarded along with the baby somewhere in the darkness?

Dee walked the perimeter of the house, calling out as she did. *Baby, baby, baby.* As if a newborn, especially a dead one, were capable of a response.

While Dee called and Natalie bled, Red scanned the bushes and acres beyond for signs of life. Seeing nothing, he panicked over how to get Natalie and Megan to his truck, and how to find the baby. If it was even alive. Dee demanded Red leave, and he could tell she meant it. She herded Natalie inside.

*I can help her,* he said to Dee.

Dee returned to the porch with a gun. *This is our business. Get out.*

Red stalled, trying to come up with a new plan since his old one had been blown to shit.

*I have to get my wallet and my keys,* he told her.

Just then, in the distance, Red heard what might have been a baby's strangled cry.

Dee cocked her head, and Red thought she heard it too. Then he realized she was only studying him. For a moment, Red was sure he was going to get shot in the gut, or lower.

But, reluctantly, Dee allowed him entrance into the house to retrieve the wallet that was already in his pocket, even as she kept the gun aimed at his groin.

Then Natalie screamed—theater or a true health emergency, Red couldn't be sure—and Dee shifted her full attention to her daughter.

No trace of empathy settled on Dee's face, only frigid resolve. She rested the gun on the ground next to where her daughter had fallen.

Red tried one last time, *I can take her to the hospital.* Dee refused his offer by placing her hand on the gun.

The realization came then, a blow to his gut: three children needed his help, but he could save only one. Megan, the now fifteen-month-old Dee had abducted earlier that year, who was inside asleep. Natalie, the teen likely beyond his help. Or the newborn whose cry he was now certain he could hear.

With Dee distracted, Red slipped into the house and grabbed Megan, despite her age still small enough to hold with one arm. He focused on her heartbeat, erratic but strong, and tried not to think of the two children he was forced by circumstance to leave behind.

After leaving Dee's that night, Red never again returned home, not even to pack a bag. His only stop on his way out of town was at a pay phone, which he used to call 911. Red told the dispatcher about Natalie. He intended to share all of Natalie's story—the abuse, Dee's instability, the baby he left behind. But his new daughter started crying and, afraid of being caught with a stolen toddler, Red replaced the handset in its cradle without saying more.

Spurred by his tip, the police searched for Natalie. They found her two weeks later, but by then, she was in a box in the ground, dead.

THOUGH I KNEW IT was a trick of shadow, Red's skin appeared to sag, and his voice was weary when he ended his story.

"What happened to Megan?" I asked. But of course I knew. *I* was Megan. Which meant, "You're not my father."

Red grabbed my hand as if to emphasize our connection but released it just as quickly.

"I love you, Cassie. I'll die knowing my purpose in life was to raise you," he said. "But, no, I'm not your father."

# 43

———

Red's gaze wandered down the street, not toward anything but rather away from judgment. I sidestepped back into his line of vision. I forced him to look at me.

"So Dee abducted me from that grocery store in Fresno, and then *you* abducted me from her." My breath came in short, angry bursts.

"What else could I have done?"

"What about my parents?"

"It was only your mother, and she died years ago."

"How do you know that?"

Silence.

"How many years ago?"

When he answered, his voice was thick, strained. "About twenty years ago."

*Twenty years.* I was already an adult by then. In college. Only a couple of years away from meeting Sam, and then having kids of my own. "I could've known her. My mom."

Red struggled to hold eye contact. "It took me years to find her, and by then—"

"You didn't want to lose me?" My voice broke as I considered what *I* had lost, not to mention the cost to my mom, whose only mistake was dropping that can of stewed tomatoes on the grocery store floor. "What happened to the baby you left behind? Natalie's child?"

Red cringed and looked away again. "Later, I heard the police found only Natalie's body. No baby."

"But how can that be?"

He shrugged. "Dee was rich, and she was good at keeping secrets."

*Not as good as the man who had raised me, apparently.* "You're sure the baby survived that night?"

Red hesitated. "I want to believe it did."

I'm not sure I wanted the same thing. What would it have been like for a child to grow up in that house?

Suddenly, the mention of that other child's pain reminded me of my son's, and I seized on another detail from Red's story. "Wait. Where was Dee's house?"

My father cocked his head. "Why?"

Audrey's comment. When I had been cleaning her wound. The one I had dismissed too quickly then, but which now quickened my pulse. "Audrey heard her abductor talking about whining ghosts."

Red inhaled sharply as he made the same connection I had. "Ghost winery."

"Still know the address?"

"I'll never forget that place." But he didn't offer the address, instead stepping into the streetlight's glare and grabbing my hand. His skin was cold and damp. "Don't go."

"He's got Leo."

"Let the police handle it. That detective, Rico. He seems like a smart guy."

"He is. But if I'd been taken, what would you do?"

He didn't hesitate. "Anything."

I gestured toward the inside of the clinic, where Audrey sat at the reception desk. "Take care of her."

"I haven't given you the address." His voice wavered.

"You will. You owe me."

He took a step back and shook his head, even as we both knew he would tell me. Then he recited an address in Napa.

"We'll need to talk about this."

I didn't need to ask what "this" was.

"We will."

His breathing hitched. "After you find Leo."

"And Sam."

Red looked away to spare me the doubt in his eyes.

"Tell Rico where I'm headed."

"But give you a head start?"

We might not have been linked biologically, but Red knew me, maybe better than anyone.

"Give me ten minutes."

Once alerted by Red, Detective Rico would have protocols to follow, calls to make, perimeters to set on the property. And I could drive pretty damned far in ten minutes. I wanted him there, but only after I arrived.

I watched Rico's car pull away from the clinic, with Red and Audrey inside, then I climbed into the truck. From the heating vent, a folded sheet of paper protruded.

As I reached for it, my hand shook. The note was scrawled with a heavy hand, the black ink spreading at the edges of the words. When I touched the paper, ink came off on my fingers. *I warned you about the police. Now I'll have to kill them both.*

On the back of the note was the same address Red had just given me.

HOW LONG HAD THE note been there? I decided it must've been planted after Rico arrived, but before the other police cruisers. Either way, a risky move. I worried at that, and at the invitation.

On the highway, I drove faster than was prudent, trying to outrace my thoughts. Growing up, I had always been the girl without a mom, but it hadn't mattered because I had my dad. Then I had started junior high, and more of my classmates began wearing bras and makeup, and boys began paying attention even if they were as intimidated as hell by the bras and makeup. So I had invented a mom—in the stories I told my classmates, she was a pilot who baked elaborate cakes and knew the words to every Aerosmith song. When a group of girls discovered my lie, my downfall had been swift and painful. For them too. I might have punched one of them in the nose.

But, again, I'd had my dad. I'd always had my dad. Until now. With one revelation, I had lost him, and a mom who might have been a pilot who baked cakes while listening to Aerosmith, but whose occupation and interests and favorite songs I would never know because I would never know *her*.

Worse, my husband was missing, and my son.

From the note: *Now I'll have to kill them both.*

No. That wouldn't happen. I had already lost enough.


I CUT THE TRAVEL time to Napa by half. As I approached the property, I slowed. Like I had done at Daryl's, I headed for an adjacent parcel rather than coming in straight on.

I wasn't stupid. I knew I had no leverage. But I had my life, and maybe I could bargain with that.

The electric motor at the gate looked like it had broken years before, the drive-up keypad dangling useless beside it. A gust propelled the metal box against the fence, away from it, back again, the hollow ping of the pendulum marking time.

I rattled the rusted chain and padlock that secured the gate. The low-tech alternative proved worthless as well, the lock springing with the movement. The mechanism hadn't been secured. With another shake, the lock tumbled onto the gravel.

Come on in, it seemed to say.

I drove without my headlights on, my windows down. I heard the crunch of my tires on the gravel and felt the chill of the wind scrubbing my cheeks.

The road narrowed. I pulled the truck as far off the road as I could, parking it between two oak trees. Then I killed the engine and got out.

I took a breath and walked toward the lights of the house nestled on the hill, leaving behind the walnut trees and the narrow gravel road, passing what may once have been a guest house. Now all that remained were two walls that tilted in the absence of a roof and sagging floorboards open to the sky.

Nearer the main house, beneath an oak tree, I stumbled, landing on my knees. When I reached out for balance, star thistle stabbed my palm.

In the dark, I found the obstacle that had snagged my shoe: a single bone jutted from the hard-packed dirt. I shivered. I was in the right place.

I didn't dwell on the bone and its implications. I focused my attention on the rows of wine grapes that marched up a nearby hill, leading to a house with all its lights blazing.

In the distance, a car's headlights bobbed. I tucked myself behind the trunk of the nearby oak and stood still, watching. I hoped the tree and shadows would be enough to hide me, but if the driver was searching for me, he would find me.

The car veered toward the main road, passing a hundred yards from where I stood. If the driver spotted me, he gave no sign.

Once clear of the headlights, I continued walking toward the house. As I moved, I remembered the bandage scissors I had earlier slipped in my pocket. I pulled them out now, pressing against the tip for reassurance.

The road ended. With only my tiny scissors for a weapon, I started climbing toward the house at the top of the hill.

# 44

I didn't make it to the house. When I turned the corner, another structure drew my interest. A cinder-block creamery with pine slats blinding its windows, the rotted planks of its roof slumped in resignation.

My attention shifted from the creamery to its neighbor, a storage shed. The shed held my interest longer. Old, abandoned. The hard-packed dirt around it held more polish than the building that sprang from it.

It was the kind of place that might hold piles of burlap sacks. Like the one in that texted image of an unconscious Sam.

With the moon pushing away the sun, the cornflower sky deepened to indigo. I kept to the darkness beneath the oaks. As I approached the shed, burrs breached the barrier of my jeans, sticking to my socks. I tried the door. Locked.

Frustrated but not surprised, I planted my feet, palmed my scissors, then threw my shoulder against the door. My body took most of the jolt. I slammed against it a second time. The frame crackled, split. A third strike and I was in, brushing aside cobwebs that laced the entrance.

My shoulder throbbed as I stood in the threshold, surveying the shed—apparently once used for the storage of empty feed sacks. Fading light seeped in through the four small windows high in the rafters, filtered through clouds of dust and spiderwebbing.

Carver's earlier words, from our meeting at the hospital, tortured me now: *I placed him on a pile of feed sacks and watched as he rolled, face-down, on the burlap.*

Thinking of Sam that way—unconscious on his stomach, arms splayed useless to his sides—brought a sudden and dagger-sharp clarity. I worked to draw breath. Images flipped through my head in quick succession: Sam's arm draped across his lover. Daryl drugged with my kids beside him. Sam battered atop burlap. The images blurred, until Sam's arm became indistinguishable from Daryl's, the fabric of Daryl's sofa melting into a pile of feed sacks—a horror show inside my brain that I studied with new intensity.

I had been so focused on the woman in the photo with Sam and the possible ways the image might have been manipulated. But now I saw what I had missed before—in the picture of Sam and the woman, there had been no tension in his shoulders or in his arms. He had been posed in profile, the bruised side of his face hidden against his *lover's* chest.

The sound of a man clearing his throat made me jump, and I rammed my already aching shoulder into an industrial vacuum, mounted to a beam overhead.

"Finally, your timing doesn't suck," he said.

I immediately recognized the voice. It was the same one that had threatened me and my children.

The scissors clenched in my fist, I moved toward the voice and found Carver in the corner, mostly hidden by a stack of boxes. In his current condition, Carver posed no threat: he squirmed against ropes that bound his ankles and wrists.

"Care to untie me?"

"Not particularly."

Through the windows near the rafters, the rising moon cut through spiderwebbed glass and cast pale bands across Carver's face. His lip was swollen, and the ropy scar along his jaw had been scraped raw. Bits of gravel pebbled one cheek.

In my search for Carver, I had pictured him a thousand ways, but I had never pictured him helpless. Still, I couldn't discount him as a suspect solely because of his bindings. Criminals turned on one another all the time. Look at Ernie, who had shared all he knew for a few fake painkillers.

It was also a mistake to think of Carver as helpless.

"Where's Leo?"

He grinned, smug despite his compromised condition. "Shouldn't a mom know where her kids are?"

"Do *you* know where *your* child is?"

"You know about that?"

My intake of breath was sudden and sharp. So what Red told me about the baby was true, and Carver knew about it. I hadn't expected that. "My father, Red, worked here as a contractor."

"I knew Red, or of him." His words careful. "Through Natalie."

"He was here the night Natalie gave birth. To your child."

"And he didn't try to save her?"

*Her.* So the baby had been a girl.

Even as this fact registered, anger flared that he would blame Red. "As the father, wasn't it your job to protect your child?" I immediately recognized my hypocrisy: an hour earlier, I had blamed Red for the same thing. And who was I to judge, when I had so completely failed my own son? "What happened to her?"

"Growing up here, I'm guessing terrible things." For a moment, Carver's eyes went soft, his face slack. "Did you know that whenever Natalie did something her mom didn't like, Dee would throw her in a box? And she *really* hated her daughter getting knocked up. Usually, Dee would let her out after a day or two, but that last time, she planted her in the ground and walked away."

The casual way he said this made me want to stab him in an eye with my scissors. Left eye or right, I didn't care.

"You knew about the abuse and did nothing?" I asked. Even if Dee killed Natalie, Carver deserved every year he had served at San Quentin.

Carver's chest inflated, his shoulders spread, and I was reminded again of the beast he had been on the trail. "I didn't know any of this back then. Until recently, I thought Natalie had miscarried, and it was Ernie who told me about the box. But Red—he was here that night. He could've prevented all this shit from happening."

My hands tightened around the scissors so that the tip gouged my palm. I was done talking to him about his child. I wanted to find mine. "Where's my son? And my husband?"

"Probably dead."

I jammed my scissors into his foot, and he screamed. "What the—?"

"What did you do to my son?"

"I'm not part of that. I'm only here because that asshole Damon drugged me." His face darkened. "You stabbed me in the foot."

"You're lucky it wasn't your carotid artery." Which it might have been if not for the information I still needed. "Why would Damon drug you?"

He grimaced and raised his foot, angling it toward the shaft of moonlight so he could study it.

I sighed, impatient. "I barely nicked your toe."

Carver lowered his foot to the ground. "You know the story: Guy meets girl. Guy realizes girl's trying to fuck up his life. Guy tries to kill girl." He paused and tried on a smirk, but it wouldn't hold. "Then girl gets her friend to stab guy in the neck with a needle and toss him in some crappy shed."

My skin turned cold, and I rubbed my arms for warmth. Not because of the way the psychopath tied up at my feet scowled at me, but because of how long it had taken me to make the connection. *What do you know?* Daryl had asked me. He would've been disappointed it had taken me so long to learn that lesson.

"So it's not just Damon," I said. "Brooklyn's involved in Leo's abduction too?"

"You still don't get it. She's not just *involved*. She's planned everything. Damon's just some guy she's manipulating, just like she manipulated me. You, too, and your husband. That night on the trail when you fucked everything up—nothing about that night was an accident."

"I know. You ran Brooklyn off the road."

"*She* ran *me* off the road. She knew where you'd be, and when. She had a tracker on your car, right?" He must've read my doubt, because he sneered. "*Of course* she had a tracker on your car. She had one on mine too." The grin was back, and it was polar. "But her timing was off. I don't think she planned how close I'd come to killing her."

Carver's expression shifted then, a mix of hostility and confusion. "But I still haven't figured out why—why would my own daughter want to kill me?"

I easily came up with reasons. *Because you let her mother die. Because you never looked for her. Because you're an asshole.*

"You mean like you tried to kill her?"

"That was before I knew she was my daughter, and after everything she did."

"And now that you know she's your daughter, you aren't still planning to kill her?"

Carver remained silent, but I read the answer in his face.

I considered him and the ropes that bound him. If he set after Damon and Brooklyn, he would serve as one hell of a distraction.

He noticed me studying the ropes and nearly growled, "Untie me." My eyes dropped to his hands. They were clenched, as they had been the night we met.

"Because you asked so nicely, or because you tried to kill me?"

"I wasn't trying to kill you. I just wanted you to let Brooklyn die." When Carver saw I was making no attempt to free him, he leaned back against the wall. "Back at the hospital, I lied."

"I'm not surprised. About what?"

"I never brought Sam here."

I studied his face, but I no longer trusted myself to recognize deception. "I don't understand."

Carver licked at the cut on his lip as he squirmed against his bindings. "When Brooklyn and Damon ambushed Sam, I heard the tail end of their conversation. Damon mentioned dumping Sam here."

"But the blood on the back seat."

"Damon and I had a disagreement."

"Sam's keys?"

"He dropped them when those two ambushed him, and I took them. I needed a car." Carver's tongue darted across his laceration again, the same way a snake would flick its tongue to taste the air. "Do you know how my wife died?"

"She was poisoned."

He lifted his shoulders and squirmed against the ropes that bound his wrists. "That was Brooklyn. She poisoned my wife's tea and watched as I served her. Up until that point, we both thought Brooklyn was a friend. Invited her into our home. First, she posted some stuff online that got me fired. Then she emptied our bank account. Killed our cat and posed it on our bed as if it were sleeping. Then—Anne."

His entire body convulsed at the memory. "Each day, I'd find a note with a number. *3. 2. 1.* That last day, on the bottom of the box of tea, Brooklyn had written a single word in Sharpie: *Today.*"

At that, I felt as if I had been hollowed out with a dull knife and then scraped raw. Part of me had wanted to believe the threat was idle, that Sam and Leo would be allowed to live.

"And then—" Carver's voice caught in his throat. He cleared it and started again, "And then, Brooklyn knelt down and told my wife it was my idea, that I'd wanted Anne dead. I don't care if she's my daughter. For making that lie my wife's last memory, I *am* going to kill her."

Then Carver slipped the rope from his wrists, and I realized how foolish I had been.

# 45

Carver grabbed me and wrapped his arm around my neck. I strug-gled, but he was twice my size. He laughed darkly at the scissors still in my hand, put them in his own back pocket, beyond my reach, then dragged me from the shed.

He attempted to calm me. "Even if you stabbed me in the foot, I'm not going to kill you," he said. "Unless you keep struggling."

I clamped down on his arm with my teeth. He flinched, but he didn't release me, instead squeezing harder. The impression my teeth had made reddened with his effort. His arm spasmed on my throat and I felt his grip loosen slightly, a change in pressure that would have been imperceptible if it hadn't been my own neck he was choking. I'm not even sure Carver realized he was holding back. When the stars pricked my eyes, I released all the tension in my body. Though instinct screamed to fight, I let him lay my limp body, almost gingerly, on the ground.

I LET CARVER GO and opened my eyes only when I could no longer hear his footsteps. Even then, I lay there for another minute. In the past hour, I had learned so many things—about my father, about Carver, about the woman who had targeted my family—but I hadn't found answers for the only questions that mattered: *Where was Sam? Where was our son?* I wouldn't, couldn't, accept Carver's theory that they were dead.

My breath quickened when I finally stood. I patted my pocket for my phone but remembered it was gone. When I turned, intending to search for anything I might use as a weapon, I froze.

Carver was walking back toward me, and he wasn't alone. Damon walked behind him, shorter than Carver, but wider. Damon's head reflected the moon, the same light illuminating purpled lumps on his face and his swollen lip. Before Damon had taken down Carver with that needle to the neck, it looked like Carver had gotten some punches in.

At first, I thought I had gotten it wrong, that Carver had been working with Damon all along. Then I saw the gun Damon held in his right hand.

Even with the bruising, I recognized Damon as the man who had answered Helen's door and likely the man who had shielded most of his face with a baseball cap when he pushed Audrey from that white sedan.

Though Damon's gun wasn't trained on me, it would take only a fraction of a second for that to change. I stood as still as I was able.

"You're early, Cassie," he said. "We weren't quite ready for you."

I tried to read in the bumpy patchwork of his face how deep his commitment was to Brooklyn's cause. "Why are you doing this?"

Damon's eyes darted between my face and Carver's, and the hand that held the gun jerked. I recognized the desperation in his expression: he was bracing himself to carry out whatever horrible demand had been made of him.

"I'm doing this because I'm her friend, and she asked me to."

Damon's arm went rigid, the gun's barrel arcing so it pointed at Carver's chest. Carver's face settled into cast concrete, and his eyes stilled. All cockiness gone.

"She wanted more time with you, Carver. But with Cassie here now, it's too risky to leave you both alive."

I shook my head and Carver opened his mouth to speak, as if our objections had any power over bullets, but Damon stepped forward and lifted the barrel another couple of inches, now aligned with Carver's temple. He fired, point-blank, three times. Carver's mouth went slack, death consuming whatever he had been about to say.

Damon gestured with his gun toward the house. "Let's get this over with."

INSIDE THE HOUSE, a stone fireplace stretched two stories to a redwood-beamed ceiling, a chandelier of oil-rubbed bronze and a string of exposed bulbs hanging there. The two wings of the second story were connected by a catwalk that looked out over the living room, all in white linen and crimson leather.

I noticed all of this, but only until I noticed my son, propped and unconscious on the sofa, Brooklyn behind him with a revolver. Once I saw Leo, I noticed nothing else. Brooklyn lifted her gun to aim it at Leo's head.

I could have charged had the weapon been pointed at me. A few quick strides and I could've been there. I would've taken a bullet, probably more than one since the man behind me had a gun, too, but I doubted Brooklyn would have acted with enough speed to also shoot Leo. But with the gun locked on my son's head, I dared not move. All it would take was a quiver of Brooklyn's finger and the blast that followed would end me as certainly as if the weapon had been pointed in my direction.

Bruises still mottled Brooklyn's face, a mirror image of Damon's injuries. Made sense. They'd been caused by the same man. But in our earlier meeting, she had exaggerated the injuries to her arm. She was having no problem holding her gun.

Brooklyn squinted, her head tilted as she studied me. The corner of her lip curled, not quite a smile but close, and then, her eyes still on me, she asked Damon, "You took care of Sam, right?"

I caught my breath. *No.* I forced all my will into that denial, as if it could become a tangible thing capable of holding me up.

"Yeah, I took care of Sam."

I flashed to Carver's rage that night on the trail. Then, he had been an animal, beyond reason or thought. Brooklyn had deconstructed Carver's life, piece by piece, until all that remained was a husk empty of all but that limbic center of his brain that shouted, *Avenge.*

The thought hit me with such force, I nearly stumbled, *I will save Leo and then kill everyone else in this room.*

I shook off the thought. That's not who I was. I wasn't a killer. I saved lives, I didn't take them. I tried on the reassurance but realized it no longer fit, like a hand-me-down coat I wore despite the way its weight tugged on my shoulders or its wool scratched my skin.

"Have to say I'm surprised you got here so quickly. The speed you had to be driving, you're lucky you didn't get pulled over." Brooklyn smiled, but there was a hint of impatience there. "Ten minutes earlier, we wouldn't even have had time to kill your husband."

My muscles tightened as I scanned the room for weapons. For options. On the coffee table, I noticed a pack of gum, a wrapper beside it. The strip of foiled paper had been neatly folded into the shape of a heart. It brought me back to that last morning with Sam and the origami dog I had at first believed was from him. It suddenly occurred to me that Brooklyn had taken more care with that wrapper than she had with my husband.

"Don't forget, Sam's death is on you. Earlier tonight, I gave you a choice, and you chose the kids. Still, Cassie, you *did* call the police, and that decision has to have consequences, too, right? So who dies here: you, or your son?"

As easy a decision as I could ever make. "I'd gladly trade my life for my son's." The obvious question hung between us: *What prevented Brooklyn from killing us both?*

The night I'd met Brooklyn, for the first time in years, I had thought of the attack on a college classmate, and how I'd failed her. She had survived that night, but she hadn't survived the aftermath. A few years after Dirk pushed her from that balcony, she'd walked into the ocean and drowned. She hadn't intended to kill herself. After the attack, despite physical therapy, her body had been too weak to fight the current.

I suddenly remembered the dead girl's name. Stephanie. That night on the trail, I had thought by saving Brooklyn, I could atone for not doing more to help Stephanie. I thought I could make up for those fights I'd picked in high school and the hell I'd put my dad through. For not being there for Sam. But the truth was I should have let Brooklyn die. I should have saved Stephanie, but I should have let Carver have Brooklyn.

Brooklyn turned to Damon. "Make sure the kid's secure, then get rid of Sam's body."

Damon did as he was told. I heard a car start. I tried not to imagine Sam's body in its trunk.

It was just me and Brooklyn now, but too much distance stretched between us for me to grab the gun.

I let Brooklyn usher me out the door, leaving Leo alone in the house. Giving me time to think. Figure a way out of this. Brooklyn walked me back the way I had arrived on the property. The moon caught the drops of dew on the grass so the blades looked like chips of ice.

She sped up, forcing me forward, and I recognized her purpose. We were headed for the valley oak at the edge of the property.

I had noticed the tree upon entering, but I had been too distracted to fully grasp its size. The oak must have been several hundred years old, its trunk broad and its limbs reaching a hundred feet into the air. As we drew closer, the limbs filtered much of the moonlight.

The earth changed here, too, grass becoming weeds. I recognized some of them: the three-petaled tarweed with its sticky leaves, the hairless stems of what I suspected was nutsedge. But most of what grew here had been too trampled to identify, ground into a tangle of leaves, stalk, and stem.

Within the spears of light beneath the valley oak, there was only dirt.

On my death walk, I noticed it all. I gulped the air, crisp and sweet, filling my lungs to the point of pain. I teetered on the edge of hyper-ventilating. But I could not allow myself that weakness. I looked for an opportunity. I saw none.

At least every step I took with her was a step away from my son. With Brooklyn occupied with me, and Damon disposing of Sam's body, if Leo regained consciousness, maybe . . .

Brooklyn continued to herd me, and though she didn't speak, I heard her breath. Fast. Excited. Reveling in a moment she had probably spent a long time imagining.

The dark sky, the oak, and this woman all brought me back to that first night on the trail. I tortured myself with every choice I had made, that night and since. In hindsight, I would do so much differently, but I didn't think I could have stopped this. I was no more in control than the zebra herded into ambush by a pair of hunting lions.

I hated being that zebra. What could I do now that would save me, and save Leo? But she had me, at least for the moment, and she walked with the confidence of someone who knew it. Even if I managed to overpower her, it had never been my mortality that terrified me. Even if I escaped, it would be pointless if I couldn't make it back to the house to save my son, or allow him the time to save himself.

"You won't hurt him?" I asked, the question catching in my throat.

"No," she said.

We both recognized the lie.

In her excitement, Brooklyn had allowed the gap between us to narrow. I slowed to bring her even closer.

Then in the shadows beyond the oak, a nightmare took form. On the ground, a hole. It was impossible to misconstrue its purpose—the rough rectangle stretched as long as a human body. My body.

Though I hadn't measured it, I instinctively knew the dimensions were just about perfect. Labor hadn't been wasted to construct a grave larger than I needed.

We stopped beside the hole and she stepped in front of me so that we faced one another. Comfortable with her leverage, she nevertheless put nearly ten feet between us, and between her and the edge of the grave. So, unfortunately, she wouldn't fall in and save me the trouble of breaking her neck.

"This is where we gardened," she said. "Dee and me." She kicked a clod of dirt in the direction of the grave. "You know why we're here, right? I'd hate for you not to know."

I thought of what Red had told me about the night he had taken me from this place.

"You're angry because I escaped this place and you didn't."

Her face tensed, her voice angry. "You didn't *escape*," she said. "You didn't make a decision and walk away. You were *chosen*."

As a toddler, I had no role in what happened back then, but such arguments wouldn't serve me now. My captor was beyond appeasing.

"She made me bury my dog here," Brooklyn said.

"That story you told me about Hannah's abuse. That wasn't her story. It was yours."

The photos of Natalie she had shown me too: those had been hers, not Carver's. She had witnessed my repulsion at seeing Natalie's broken body even as she planned the same fate for me.

She glanced at the mound of dirt beside the hole, and her eyes glazed. For a couple of heartbeats, she disappeared into the past, and my foot slid forward. But before I could take another step, her eyes slid back to me.

"Dee was never very good at keeping her pets alive," Brooklyn said. "Did you know they found Jerusalem crickets in Natalie's grave? In the newspapers, they mentioned how she broke her fingers trying to escape, but they never mentioned the bites. Hundreds of them, according to Dee. She used to joke that when the police pulled Natalie from the ground, it looked like she had a bad case of chicken pox.

"But even if Dee killed her, Carver deserved prison for abandoning her like that. He deserved worse."

I heard something then. The scratching of a small animal. I thought of all the creatures that lived here, creatures my corpse would soon feed, and my stomach turned.

"I think it's time," she said. "We haven't dug Leo's grave yet, so I'll have to get Damon on that."

*Yet?* My mind stumbled on that word.

I had hoped to disable her and, barring that, I had expected a bullet. I had hoped that with me dead, she would have no reason to kill Leo. Too late, I realized a quick death had never been her plan, for me or my son. Pinned beneath the earth, I would die as Natalie had died, but only after she killed Leo.

From behind, two hands shoved me, hard, on my back. I tumbled face-first into the perfectly sized grave.

# 46

I wasn't alone in the box. I felt them, even as I heard their scuttling against the wood.

I probed the edges of the box, pushing against the lid even though I knew it wouldn't open. There were a few small holes, but they were plugged with dirt, and the earth piled on the box would hold the lid in place as certainly as concrete. I took inventory of my pockets, but apparently I had left my coffin-opener in my other pants. I wished for the scissors Carver had stolen from me. Then again, they had done him no good either.

I felt them again—the bugs. Hard little shells grazed my calf as several of them breached my pant leg.

I closed my mouth and screwed my eyes shut. There was nothing I could do to safeguard my thrumming ears.

The scouting party reached my knees. How many? Five? Six? I pressed my thighs together. I thought of Natalie being buried in a grave like this one, her skin covered in bite marks. My chest grew tight, my skin slick. I struggled to breathe, and this reminded me that my nose was exposed too.

Another bug, separated from the group, probed my neck.

I cringed as the insect's antennae tickled my earlobe. In the dark, I imagined beady eyes set in alien heads, mandibles nibbling, gnawing, scraping.

But the bugs weren't the real threat here. I tried to calculate how much time I had before I suffocated, but math wasn't my best subject, even with a clear head. And my head was far from clear.

Though math wasn't my thing, science was. I knew enough of that to realize even as I breathed my limited oxygen, I expelled carbon dioxide, the buildup of which would soon make the air around me unfit to breathe. My respiration and heart rate would become depressed, leading to intoxication, unconsciousness, and, finally, death. How long did I have? I guessed twenty minutes. Maybe less.

I suppressed the urge to scream. No one would hear, and it would deplete precious air.

I shifted, startling the bug closest to my head. It bit my earlobe, drawing blood. Had it started the same way with Natalie?

In that tight space, I had little leverage, but I summoned all I had to throw myself against the box's edges. Beneath my legs, I found patches of wood that had gone soft, but located as they were on the coffin's floor, they were of no use to me.

My thrashing made the insects angrier. They hissed, and fresh bites bloomed on my legs.

I tried to be grateful for the bugs and that stupid box. If Brooklyn hadn't been intent on her very specific torture, she likely would've buried me directly in the ground. In that case, I would've already suffocated.

My head ached from the carbon dioxide. Soon, I would get sleepy—was that starting already? My eyelids felt heavier than they had a moment before—and then I'd no longer be capable of making decisions. Next—death. For me and for Leo.

My lungs cramped. It was pitch black, a night more complete than the one several feet above my head.

In my grave, the bugs weren't my only company. The bite of memories was just as sharp.

Red letting go of the back of my bike, releasing me into the wind. It had been like flying, and knowing he was there, I hadn't fallen.

Sam in his hospital gown, reassuring me that he and Audrey would be okay. Though I had always been good with my fists, Sam was the strong one. *Had been* the strong one. Tears did me no good, but they spilled anyway.

The kids. Just that.

Then: a woman yelling at me to shut the hell up, followed by a sting-ing slap that had cut the inside of my cheek.

*Where had that come from?*

I banged my fists on the wood above me until they throbbed. Then I dropped my arms, a gesture that felt like cowardice.

I deserved this. I deserved all of it.

Out there, surrounded by limitless air and a thousand distractions, I could pretend I was blameless. But I wasn't. I had saved the woman who had killed my husband and abducted my son. I may have been pushed into this grave, but I had allowed myself to be led to its border. The worst of it: I had doubted Sam.

A bug bit my arm, breaking skin.

I had been stupid. Reckless. Cocky in my fury. But while I accepted my blame in this, Sam had paid the greater cost. Soon, Leo would, too, unless I stopped wallowing and got out of this box. When the bug bit again, I brought my elbow down on its carapace, crushing it.

I had taken my death for granted, and then, worse, Leo's. My head pounded, but I was no longer resigned to what had moments earlier seemed inevitable.

I would not die in this box like Natalie had, fingers fractured and skin broken by hundreds of insect bites.

I pushed my legs as far apart as they would go, creating a valley of my thighs. Not daring to hesitate, I brought them together quickly. Some of the insects were stunned, but others bit. I didn't care if I emerged bear-ing the marks of *thousands* of bites, I wasn't leaving my son to Brooklyn.

In the darkness, my fingertips took stock of my coffin. It was con-structed of old plywood. I let my hands wander along the parts of the box I could reach, searching for more soft spots. Then I worked one of my feet free of its shoe and poked at the bottom of the box with my toe, moving on to probe against the seams.

The box had been well constructed, but it was only as strong as the materials used to craft it. On my second inspection of the lid, I found a soft patch. Water damage. The wood had long since dried, but it re-mained weaker in that spot.

I beat against the lid with my knees and heard a crack. Somewhere. A few more thwacks and dust rained on my stomach. I shimmied upward a few inches, moving my knees as close to the middle as I could. I hoped this would be the spot left weakest by the heavy earth above it. Again, I rammed my knees against the lid. The wood creaked, threatening to split.

I paused, aware that breaking the box would create another problem. I tried to remember how deep the hole had been before it had been filled with dirt. Once I breached the wood, earth would pour on top of me. But how much dirt? I was pretty sure it had been a shallow grave, but I couldn't be sure it still wasn't enough to smother me.

But I had no other options. I resumed my pounding. Finally, a section of the board cracked, and I pushed it with my knee. I fought the impulse to force it completely free. Again, I was reminded how easily I could be suffocated by an avalanche of dirt, or at least immobilized by the heavy earth upon my body.

With one knee acting as a fulcrum, I used my legs and hands to push the dirt toward the box's edge. I worked quickly, with purpose, packing the corners with dirt, seeing moonlight now, my knees throbbing and my fingers raw with the scraping. I shimmied toward the opening, contorting in the cramped space, muscles pulling in directions they weren't meant to. Shoveling more dirt away, my fingers found the hole I'd made with my knees. I held my breath, screwed shut my eyes and mouth, clods of dirt hitting my face as I reached through the hole. Fighting against the earth's weight, I pulled myself through the opening. Coughing. Spitting dirt. But free.

One insect made the journey with me, its mandibles locked on my neck. I brushed it off, then squashed it into the earth with my palm.

No longer entombed, I stood up and heard the same scratching I had before being pushed into the hole, though it was fainter now. I imagined the bodies of those buried here digging with hands of bone, intent on returning me to my rightful place among them.

With as much power as I had left in my burning legs, I ran toward the lights of the house, which seemed impossibly far away.

# 47

―――――

I entered through the kitchen. It was dark, but all the lights blazed in the living room. Damon's voice carried. "Carver was a piece of crap—that woman, too, for what she took from you—but I'm not hurting a kid."

"You're an idiot."

By Brooklyn's sharp intake of breath, I guessed Damon had grabbed her. "Yeah, I think I am."

I risked a step forward, able to see into the living room now. Leo sat on the couch, where he had been the first time I had entered this house. His hands were secured behind him with duct tape, a strip of it also covering his mouth, but his feet were free.

Brooklyn touched Damon's arm, but her tone was harsh. "His parents are dead anyway. What's he got to go home to?"

He pushed her away, wiping his palm on his shirt. "You're a monster. You're . . ." He couldn't finish the sentence, his face pale, his voice shaky.

"I'm not a monster. I'm a monster's granddaughter." Her voice was ice, though I wasn't sure he recognized the threat.

Taking advantage of their distraction, I chanced another step. Still in the shadows, able to see them but not yet in their line of sight. I noticed Leo's eye had been blackened since I had last seen him, and my mood darkened with it. I hoped that meant he would be ready to fight if it came to it. I caught a glimpse of myself in the mirror—face streaked with dirt, eyes feverish.

"He's a witness, but okay. Whatever. We don't have to kill him. Is that what you want to hear?"

"That *is* what I want to hear, but I don't believe you."

Damon turned away from her and walked toward the door. "You don't want to do that," she warned, but he kept walking.

When Damon crossed the threshold, Brooklyn followed, and I moved quickly, stepping from the shadows into full light. Their argument carried from the front porch, a tangle of accusations and insults, and I was near the couch when I heard it—a crack that split into a boom, the same deathly echo I had heard when Carver was shot in the head.

She must have shot Damon.

"Why'd you do that?" she said.

I froze, believing for a moment Brooklyn meant the question for me, separated as we were by only a screen door and less than ten feet.

Then she shouted the question a second time, "Why'd you do that?" Directed at Damon, not me.

I grabbed Leo from the couch by his elbow and turned toward the kitchen to leave the way I had entered, but the screen slapped in its frame, and Brooklyn was again there. She held the gun in a relaxed grip at her side, but its barrel rose when she saw me.

She took a shot. We were closer to the hallway than the kitchen, so the gunfire forced us in that direction. With his hands tied behind his back, Leo's gait was awkward, but quick. We retreated farther into the house, turning instantly into the hallway, moving as fast as our legs and the limited space allowed. I yanked Leo by the elbow to telegraph turns but that was our only communication. We both understood the need for silence.

The house was large but not endless, and in the second hallway, I started testing doors. The first was locked, and the next two opened onto rooms that were unsuitable—one a bathroom with a small window, the second a walk-in linen closet with no window at all. But the third door swung open into a bedroom.

I pulled the door closed behind us and locked it. I resisted the urge to press my ear to the door. I couldn't hear Brooklyn, but I knew she was out there, trying doors as we had, quiet now, the time for taunts gone.

I opened the window and pushed out the screen. I untied Leo's wrists and yanked the tape from his mouth, then signaled for him to go first, but he was already pulling himself up. He bounded through the empty frame and dropped to the ground below in one fluid movement. My exit was less graceful, but with my son's help, I managed to land without my knees buckling.

The knob rattled in the room we had just exited. Then it stopped. The locked door provided only the slightest of obstacles, and given unlimited time, Brooklyn would find us. She knew this property's hiding spots better than we did, and she only needed to get close enough to aim her weapon.

My legs itched to sprint, but we couldn't run blindly, so I shot a glance to the left—a garden shed a short jog away and a detached garage just beyond that. I discounted both. Too obvious. Too far.

I thought of the cars parked on the other side of the house, but they were useless without keys.

I pointed Leo toward the deck on our right, off what was probably the master bedroom, and in a few strides, we were there, even as I heard a door slam.

I scanned the deck, praying for a crawl space, a nook, a hole in which to hide, even as my heart seized at the thought of again being wedged between earth and wood. But the deck was built better than my coffin had been.

The wind picked up, and my hair whipped into my eyes. I squinted to see.

We had to run, an all-out sprint, and even as I decided this, Leo glanced toward the field, and I knew he recognized this as the best option too.

I heard footfalls, and I whispered, with urgency, "Go," pointing Leo away from the sound.

Then my son was gone, but I stayed—making the same choice I had earlier, my life for my son's—and Brooklyn was there, holding her gun and looking very unhappy to see me.


BROOKLYN FIRED, MISSING AS I jerked right. When she shot again, the bullet tore into my left shoulder. Before she could take a third shot, I barreled into her. I grabbed her, my arms rigid, now close enough to smell the lavender and sweat that clung to her skin, then buried my teeth in her neck.

Brooklyn howled and lost her grip on the gun. It tumbled, but pressed together as we were, it became wedged between us. She clawed at my injured shoulder, but the pain wasn't nearly as heavy as my rage. I took a step back, and the weapon clattered to the ground.

Brooklyn and I locked eyes, and we both lunged for the gun. She hadn't had to dig herself from the earth and she still had two good shoulders, but I had my fury. A second later, I also had the gun.

"Dee kept your picture on the wall even after you were taken. Did you know that? She spent thousands on detectives, trying to find you. You weren't even hers. *I* was hers, by blood, and I was here. But it's you she wanted, *Megan*."

Buying time or eliciting sympathy, I didn't know, but I had neither to give. The anger wouldn't allow it, at least not for her. My compassion I saved for those she had hurt. Killed.

I pulled the trigger.

Nothing happened.

Out of bullets.

Shock dawned in Brooklyn's eyes, then something else. I'd seen that look often enough in patients, so I knew what her next move would be.

She turned from me and ran.

# 48

Brooklyn stumbled through the field, and I pursued. She might have spent her childhood hiding, but I wouldn't let her hide now. Though oaks, pines, and cypresses lined the property, she wouldn't have time to reach their shelter. I half expected her to stop at the shed where I'd found Carver—where she had kept my husband before killing him—but she lurched past without slowing.

There was only one other place she could be headed. The old creamery. The paint had flaked off the long-abandoned building, exposing the galvanized metal beneath. Plywood blinded most of the windows, though a couple of cracked panes remained.

Brooklyn raced through the open door only a few seconds before I did.

Creatures dead and hidden fouled the air inside the creamery. I heard their live brethren scuttling inside the pipes nested on the walls. My lungs seared, dust coating my throat. The moon slanted in through cracks in the ceiling and the walls, everything washed in an eerie white light.

Brooklyn rounded a piece of machinery that looked like it had once been used for bottling, several rollers on its conveyor belt missing. Her footfalls became slow, sloppy, and I pulled within inches.

We faced each other, and I could read her determination to kill me in the grim set of her mouth, the flare of her nose.

My own hands balled into fists. My medical training had taught me to save lives, but it had also given me insight into how to end them. Still, it was one thing to know where to strike for maximum injury, but it was another to reach those vulnerable spots.

Brooklyn knew the fragile parts too. She lunged, so fast I didn't see it coming, and slammed her fist into my temple. My vision clouded and I rocked on my heels, but I remained upright. I struck back, aiming for kidneys.

She stepped back, toward the machinery, planting her feet wide, shoulders rising to protect her neck. Then she came at me again, and though I saw it coming, the punch landed on the right side of my face. My eyes widened and I shook my head, straining to focus.

To conserve energy, I waited, studying her shoulders, watching her hands. When she took another swing, her shoulders fell away from her neck, leaving it exposed. I drove my fist into the side of her neck, toward her carotid artery, and she shuddered. She tilted slightly, wobbly now, and I hit her again, this time in the base of her throat. She crashed against the conveyer belt, and it was only the support of the machinery that kept her off the floor.

She straightened and grabbed her neck, gasping. I swung for her kidneys again, my aim truer this time. Her body went slack, and she crashed onto the ground, her head landing hard.

She wiped away the blood that seeped from a cut on her forehead. "You can fight, I'll give you that," she said, her words slurred. "Which kinda surprises me, since you've never had to fight for anything your whole fuckin' life."

With that, she got up. How the hell was she still able to stand?

I swung again, but it lacked power and aim. Brooklyn charged, her head tensed, her shoulders squared to take the impact, but I twisted, throwing my elbow toward her throat. Missed. Stumbling but somehow still on my feet. Staring into the face of the woman who had killed my husband, I surrendered to rage. I didn't intend to stop Brooklyn. I wanted to destroy her, until she was nothing more than a sack of snapped tendons and broken bones.

Her eyes burned, her intensity matching mine, but I had the reach. When she swung, it fell short, leaving her exposed. I exhaled—one small, sharp breath—focusing all of my energy into my fist. I snapped my elbow. The blow landed with a crunch.

As she stumbled backward, she grabbed the machinery for balance.

I took a step, but her next question stopped me. "Did you know there was a second grave?"

She smiled then, a mirthless smirk as cool as the air but not nearly as cold as her eyes. A recent memory returned—at the grave, I remembered a scratching I thought came from animals.

"Close to yours in fact, though on the other side of the tree," she said. "Even if Sam wasn't dead earlier, he certainly is now."

My heart shattered into a thousand jagged pieces. The skittering I'd heard. The scratching I'd ignored. Had it been Sam?

New grief settled in my chest so it became a chore to breathe. But I wasn't done. I felt a simmering, quiet rage still there.

Brooklyn had meant to distract with her revelation, and it worked. For a second, I couldn't move, torn between pursuing Brooklyn and running to my husband's grave. By leaving Sam behind, I was as much a killer as Brooklyn.

In that moment, I wanted to choose Sam, I should've chosen Sam, but adrenaline and anger wouldn't allow that. I stumbled forward, and Brooklyn's arm shot out, a rusty knife nicking my right side. So she hadn't been holding on to the machinery for balance. She had been looking for a weapon she had stashed. Growing up as she had, it made sense she had weapons hidden here.

Pain surged, and with it, anger. I blocked Brooklyn when she came at me again. My toe rammed a piece of metal that jutted from the ground, but it was just another ache I was beyond feeling. I grabbed the hem of her T-shirt, balling it in my fist and pulling her toward me.

Brooklyn thrashed, fabric tearing, but I held on, trading shirt for arm, twisting until she dropped the knife. Something popped. Shoulder or elbow? Didn't matter. It was hers, not mine. We fell sideways, my shoulder ramming a stack of rotting crates.

But Brooklyn took a harder hit, her head bouncing off the metal edge of the machinery. She lay there, as she had that night on the trail. I had saved her then. She tried to sit up, and my hand twitched. Even now, I wanted to offer it to her. But I couldn't. She might come for me, for my family. I had to make sure. The gun might've failed me, but years of youthful brawling wouldn't. When Brooklyn started moving again, I kicked her, my side throbbing in unison with my shoulder, until she stopped.

I SHOUTED FOR LEO as I stumbled from the creamery, but I was really just shouting into the wind. Leo might have made it to the road, or he might be hidden somewhere that muffled my shouts. I could only hope he would hear me and follow to the centuries-old valley oak at the property's perimeter, because I wasn't certain I had enough strength to dig Sam up by myself.

My hair whipped my face as I returned to the gardening shed near the house, found a shovel, then set out across the property as fast as I was able. When I pulled to a stop beneath the old oak, I welcomed the wind's chill but not its force, which flicked leaves and the occasional acorn from the branches overhead.

As I ran, I had prayed to find the second grave empty, mounds of dirt beside it, Sam waiting at its edge. But when I reached the grave, it remained undisturbed.

Beneath the tree, I started digging. Even with the meager shovelfuls of earth I managed, my arms burned. I listened for sirens, prayed for them, but I didn't slow, even as my heart rattled inside my chest.

A hand pressed against my back, and I jumped, reminded of the last time I had been touched in the same way at this place. My throat clenched, and I brushed away imaginary dirt.

This time, it wasn't a man pushing me into my grave. It was Leo. My beautiful boy.

I had been so focused on my task, I hadn't heard his approach. His face was slicked with sweat as if he had been running.

"The police?" I asked, and he nodded.

I handed him the shovel and fell to my knees.

Though he didn't know for certain why he was digging, Leo worked with an intensity I could no longer match. Even on my knees, I felt wobbly, but I scraped dirt from the grave as best I could. I noticed my fingers were raw, but they didn't hurt. Other parts of me were numb, too, including my head, and I fought the urge to vomit.

Sam's grave was even shallower than mine had been, and Leo quickly expanded the hole I had made, exposing the wood.

I pointed at the box, too weak to stand, let alone strike the wood myself. Leo understood. He brought the shovel down on the make-shift coffin's lid, the wood splintering more with each whack.

I bowed my head over the rim of the hole to listen, sweat dripping into my eyes, but I heard nothing. Blackness bled into the edges of my vision, followed by flashes of light. Blue and red light. I thought I heard sirens, too, but the wind whistled loudly against my ears.

Was Sam alive? Or were we too late?

There were men and women surrounding us now, in uniform mostly but some, like Detective Ray Rico, wearing suits. I'd been so focused I had not seen them arrive.

Earlier that night, Red had told me how Natalie had nearly perished beneath a tree the night she'd given birth, saved only to die later in that grave. Now, they were all dead. Natalie. Dee. Carver. Probably Brooklyn. With so much blood soaked into this land, how could any-thing but tragedy come to those born here?

Detective Rico loomed beside me, his brown suit streaked with dirt a shade lighter as he helped Leo and a uniformed officer pry at the lid. Strange to see Rico disheveled like that. No tie, either. Stranger to see the concern on his face.

Then together, they grabbed the lid and pulled. We could see him now—Sam.

I noticed Sam's left hand. His ring finger. That was the part of him that moved first. Then I saw the stretcher, and the paramedics who brought it, before finally succumbing to the void.

# 49

Later, Detective Ray Rico told me why Brooklyn did what she did.

While searching for Sam, I'd heard horrible stories of Dee's abuse, but others came out afterward. Most involved dark places and objects that could break skin, but the emotional abuse was just as scarring.

Almost all of the stories involved the boxes she made for Natalie and, later, Brooklyn. Over years of abuse, the plywood became stained with blood and urine, the inside of the lids marked with the scratches made by two desperate girls. Natalie was buried in her box, and Brooklyn tried to bury me in hers.

Usually, the girls would remain confined for three days. I got it now. The notes: *3. 2. 1.* A countdown, but also payback. We endured three days as horrible as the ones Brooklyn had suffered. She wanted us to lose everything, as she had.

Three was also the number of girls at the house that night, but I'm not sure if that played into it. Maybe that was just coincidence.

Brooklyn didn't find freedom until Dee's death in August. For someone whose liberty was so hard-earned, Brooklyn threw it away easily enough. She survived, but she's in prison now. I'm still not sure how I feel about that. Damon survived, too, and I've heard they still communicate. Can't say I'm surprised.

According to Rico, after Dee's death, Brooklyn found the photos of Natalie she had shown me. She also found the notes Ernie had given Dee before her death—notes that led Brooklyn to us: me, the woman who had been saved at her expense; and Carver, the man Brooklyn believed should've saved *her*.

For whatever reason, in Dee's things, there was no mention of Red. Maybe Dee didn't know he took me. Likely she thought Carver had, since he had been at the house that night too. Either way, I'm grateful for that omission. After all, despite everything, he's still my dad.

# 50

———

The day Sam came home, Audrey insisted on being in charge of the decorations, which is how the entryway wall had come to be filled with half-empty balloons. Who knew there were so many shades of pink?

Leo had been put in charge of the tape dispenser. Each time Audrey made him redo the design, he complained, as older brothers were supposed to, but his complaints lacked conviction. The balloon heart grew more crooked with each attempt. Sam would love it.

"This one needs more tape." Audrey pointed to a sagging balloon already secured with three strips.

"Yeah, 'cause that's gonna help," Leo said, but he pulled off a fresh piece.

My cake hadn't turned out any better—I blamed my bum shoulder—but it was handmade and it was chocolate, so even if it sloped, Sam would love that too.

The evil that had entered our lives hadn't made it over this threshold, and I would continue to force it back with pink balloons and chocolate cake and this. All of this.

"Done?" I asked, my voice cracking. "Because we've got a cranky patient waiting in the car."

"Are you crying?" Leo asked. He turned to Audrey. "Mom's actually crying over some stupid balloons."

"Of course she is," Audrey said. "She's Mom." As if that explained everything. I supposed, in the wake of what had happened, it did. But in this house, I only let the happy tears fall.

Audrey stood back, looked at the wall, and nodded once. "Done," she said.

At the car, I helped Sam from the passenger seat. He made the prerequisite joke about sponge baths meant to distract me from the way he winced when he got to his feet.

*Only happy tears*, I reminded myself.

I continued to feel guilt over being so easily manipulated into doubting Sam. In the video of him at the coffee shop, placing his hand on Brooklyn's, I hadn't seen the tears she had manufactured to invite the gesture. But I should have known. I should have seen through all of it.

He assured me it was fine, really, as often as I needed to hear it.

*Still a better person than me.*

Sam leaned into me, against my uninjured shoulder, as we crossed into the house. In the past, I might have pretended not to notice, but now, I accepted his weight. We both recognized it wasn't a sign of weakness. Rather, we were stronger together.

No more saying *I love you, but* . . . These days, we knew enough to stop after the first three words.

"Red coming?" Sam asked. I could tell he was surprised when I said yes. Red had saved me, a toddler he once described as showing signs of a developing anger. Fair enough. The invitation didn't mean I had forgiven him, not yet, but it meant I was trying.

Boo bounded at Sam's feet, nearly tripping him.

"Daryl said he'd stop by too."

Audrey shrieked. "Does that mean Lester's coming?"

I smiled and nodded. "And Lester." If he made it through the morning without an accident. I gave those odds at sixty-forty. "And Zoe."

"Do we have to wait to have cake?" Audrey asked.

Leo chimed in with, "Mom made it. We're probably extending our lives by waiting."

Originally, I had intended a smaller celebration—just the four of us—but Sam had insisted he could handle something larger. I had yielded for the same reason he had insisted: love was supposed to win.

We wouldn't allow someone's vendetta to change how we lived our lives.

"I think we should eat the cake now," Sam said.

"Okay, but it's your stomach," Leo warned.

We didn't bother with plates. I moved the cake to the kitchen counter, and Sam handed out forks. Audrey sat on a stool while the rest of us stood, with me close enough to Sam to feel his leg against me. I suspected I would need the reassurance of touch often in the weeks to come, but it was okay, because Sam seemed to need it too. He pressed his leg into mine, then covered my hand with his.

While we waited for our guests, we finished half the cake. Though a little dry and sloped, it was still the best food I had ever eaten. Despite Leo's grumbling, Audrey said she wanted that exact cake for her seventh birthday, which led to making plans for that.

Making plans. Something just a short time earlier I hadn't thought possible. Almost as impossible as the laughter that seemed to come so easily to the kids, and, once or twice, unexpectedly, to me too. I leaned into Sam, his warmth, and the cake, but most of all the laughter, serving as sentry against the darkness that was there, always there, but no longer strong enough to intrude. Not unless I chose to let it.

# ACKNOWLEDGMENTS

FIRST, I MUST thank all the readers who aren't related to me and yet nevertheless made it all the way to the acknowledgments page. I will always be in awe of that.

My deepest gratitude goes to my agent, Peter Steinberg, of Foundry Literary + Media, whom I've called amazing so many times he's probably grown sick of it. But without my *amazing* agent and his early belief in this novel, there would be no acknowledgments to write. Also, a huge thank-you to the entire Foundry team, with special recognition to Mike Nardullo and Richie Kern. I'm honored to be part of the Foundry family.

Thank you to my brilliant editor, David Highfill, for his encouragement and for always being right in the nicest way possible, and to everyone else at William Morrow. Also, thanks to Jennifer Doyle and the team at Headline. So many smart and talented people worked to bring this book to life. I'm indebted to all of them.

I'm also lucky to have had many wonderful friends and colleagues supporting this journey. There are far too many to list here, but some deserve special recognition. Judy Coffey, Diane Hernandez, and David Ebright for the gift of time. Denise Barredo, Karen Jacobsen, and Jason Turner for their boundless support. Bruce Baird for being there at the beginning, the last minute, and whenever I needed him in between. And Holly Clarke for being awesome in all things.

I'm also grateful to Retired Lieutenant Tom Swearingen of the

Santa Rosa Police Department for being so generous with his time and expertise. Chalk up any mistakes to my artistic license.

A special thank-you goes to Patty Hayes and Lisa Ostroski for answering all those bizarre texts about how best to kill someone. And you never once called the police to report my preoccupation. This story would have suffered without your insight and your patience.

I would also like to give a shout-out to Chuck Sambuchino, who found the flaws in those very first fifty pages, and Becky Jenkins, because even promises made in childhood are important.

Without many of these people, there would be no book, but without my mom, Norma, and my dad, Ron, there would be no author. So, yeah, thanks for that and for being my earliest and most ardent fans.

I would also like to express my appreciation for my stepfather, Rob Hodges, my extended family of Middendorfs and Harringtons, and the entire Chavez family. I could not have married into a more welcoming or kick-ass family. I'm blessed to love and be loved by so many.

Finally, thank you to my husband, Alex, and our children, Jacob and Maya, for suffering through all those spontaneous (and often longwinded) readings of random passages, for making me laugh, and for being the best people I know. You inspire me daily. This novel, and everything else, is for you.